This page is intentionally left blank.

George Caudill

DEVIL'S BACKBONE: THE INVISIBLE WALLS OF SEVEN MILE

Kaiser & Tilly Publishing

Devil's Backbone

The Invisible Walls of Seven Mile

GEORGE CAUDILL

Published by: Kaiser & Tilly Publishing

Text Design by: Brandon Leith

Cover Design by: Brandon Leith

ISBN-13: 979-8-9857307-2-2

Dedicated to my wife, Lisa, and my stepson, Brandon, for helping me overcome my struggles with dyslexia and for all their hard work and sacrifice in turning this dream into reality.

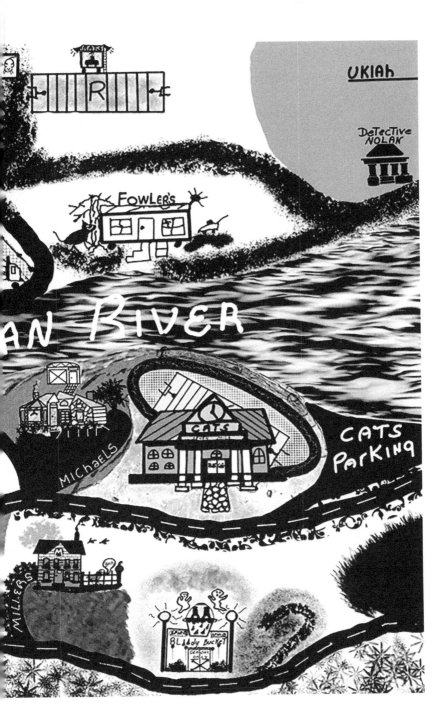

Prologue

A forty-something scar-faced man sporting a long beard, his hair tied in a ponytail, and wearing a fishing hat, floats the middle of a quiet river on a homemade raft he guides with a staff oar.

NATE:

Hello, I'm Nate. On my right lies a town. It's a poor town called Seven Mile. The people there call themselves River Rats. And on my left, another town. Not such a poor town, called, Seven Mile. The people there call themselves Blue Cats, as in blue channel catfish.

The towns of Seven Mile rest exactly seven miles south from Ukiah, California.

NATE (CONT'D):

The Russian River flowing under this raft divides Seven Mile from Seven Mile. The only way to get from Seven Mile to Seven Mile is the Seven Mile Bridge. Only once a year do vehicles drive over the lonely bridge. Crossing the abandoned bridge brings death to those who dare try.

What divided the once tranquil town of Seven Mile many years ago?

It was a game. A game invented around the year 1869 by a man named Walter Camp.

Does anybody care to guess?

Walter Camp created the game we call, Football!

A backyard game of football shattered two generations of a once peaceful, loving town called Seven Mile. The first generation drank the curse of Seven Mile. The second generation paid a devil of a price.

We welcome you to Devil's Backbone: The Invisible Walls of Seven Mile.

CHAPTER ONE

Devil Comes to Town

On a hot July evening in 1965, Ken Turner enters the door of his small-town home after a hard day's work.

U.S. Dynamite, the leading manufacturer of dynamite and other explosives for west coast mining companies, employs Ken and the majority of the Seven Mile population.

Farrah, Ken's wife, greets him with her usual warm welcome.

Ken washes and heads to the dinner table where Farrah, son Joseph, ten, and twin boys, Jack and Jerry, seven, anxiously wait to gobble their dinner.

Farrah has deliberately placed a flyer on Ken's plate - an invitation for a fun-filled church service this coming Saturday at Russian River Cove. Ken doesn't ignore the flyer, but doesn't show any interest in going to church either.

Farrah is excited about the new church opening in Ukiah. The pleasant gentleman who brought her the flyer told her it will be an enjoyable day for the entire family. A day full of song and rejoicing!

Noticing Ken's disinterest, Farrah pleads with him.

FARRAH TURNER:

Oh, come on, Ken. You told me nothing's on the calendar for the tenth. We can take the kids! Imagine the fun. Besides, God knows this town needs a new spirit.

Ken gives Joseph a wink.

KEN TURNER:

Can I take my fishing pole? Maybe I can hook a big one from the pulpit. Sounds like a great time to me.

YOUNG JERRY TURNER:

What's a pulpit, Daddy?

KEN:

Well, Jerry, it's a stage where a man stands shouting lies to a bunch of gullible folks - like your mother. Then he tells a funny joke to get your money.

Farrah slaps Ken's arm, sharing in his amusement.

FARRAH:

Oh, Ken! Pay your daddy no mind, Jerry. He's only joking.

The friendly man told me all of Seven Mile committed to his invitation. I told him he can expect us too. Please?

Farrah places her hand on Ken's privates, squeezing gently. He jolts, slurping his spaghetti strands, trying not to choke.

KEN:

Why not! But they better not go square dancing with rattlesnakes or slaughter any innocent chickens. *chuckles*

YOUNG JERRY:

Oh yucky ducky, Daddy!

Saturday comes quickly.

The Turners arrive at Russian River Cove to find many locals along with roughly one hundred and fifty members of Ukiah's church congregation. The congregation eagerly invites the families of Seven Mile to all of their upcoming services.

The ladies flaunt stylish dresses, and the men look debonair sporting coats and ties. The adults smile and shake hands, greeting and making new friends, while the children practice skipping stones on the calm water in the cove. An inspiring spirit fills the air.

Three sweet ladies from the church cheerfully serve an icy refreshment from a large, galvanized trough, encouraging everyone to come and drink. No one in attendance can pass up this enticing beverage.

Joe and his two brothers develop a thirst from skipping stones and line up for the drink. After a patient delay, the boys step to the trough. They can hardly wait as they watch the kind lady dip the cool, red refreshment into a clear plastic cup. They grab their drinks and move to the side so the others in the long line can indulge.

Joe detects small particles floating in his drink. He holds the cup close, swirling the drink and examining the debris.

YOUNG JOE TURNER:

I'm not drinking this crap!

4

YOUNG JACK TURNER:

Me either! There's shit in it! Yuck!

YOUNG JERRY:

Watch this!

Jerry gulps his drink, then grabs Jack's and shoots it. Showing off, he goes for Joe's too. Joe quickly dumps his drink on the ground.

YOUNG JOE:

That's enough!

Jerry sticks his tongue out.

YOUNG JERRY:

I'm tellin' Mom you were cussin'!

The church organizers have staged a flatbed semi-trailer decorated with flowers perfectly in front of the cove. The congregation's chairs are arranged with a slight bend and staggered, making it possible for everyone to view the cove's soothing backdrop and the soon to appear Speaker, who recently moved from Indiana to the

Redwood Valley area. A wooden altar sits proudly in front of the trailer - a flawless arrangement for an impressive church service.

The church's choir takes the platform opening with the appropriate, "Shall We Gather at the River?". All in attendance join hands, singing the popular hymn.

The crowd, fully immersed in their singing, suddenly veer their attention to a sleek Rolls Royce making a turn at the end of the Seven Mile bridge. An extraordinary vehicle never seen in these parts of California before.

The Rolls travels slowly as not to disturb the dust resting on the dirt road leading to the gathering. The driver parks in front of the crowd for all to see.

Three large men exit the vehicle. They gaze into the crowd. After a brief pause, a well-framed, attractive man with dark, slicked-back hair, wearing designer sunglasses and a tailored suit, removes himself from the fancy sedan.

Chirping Towhee birds from the surrounding woods fill the silent void as the three large men escort The Speaker onto the platform.

The Speaker wastes no time taking the microphone.

THE SPEAKER:

Beautiful people, please be seated.

The Speaker preaches with a soft, peaceful tone, but as he continues, his voice explodes with more power than an atomic blast. He glides forcefully from one end of the platform to the other, displaying tremendous energy, full of charismatic charisma.

THE SPEAKER:

I'm a prophet! A god! All who believe in me will obtain wealth and will be healed of any kind of sickness!

The Speaker's confidence and persuasion bring acts of agreeable gestures from the crowd. Even the children become mesmerized by his forceful, sharp expressions.

The crowd has never heard such powerful speech, promising those who follow The Speaker a life of utopia.

A tiny, frail man wearing an oversized sports jacket slowly makes his way to the altar.

THE SPEAKER:

You're sick.

LARRY:

I -I'm dying of cancer. *cough* I'm dying of cancer.

THE SPEAKER:

Have we met? Do I know you?

LARRY:

No. We-we've *cough* No, we've never met. *cough*

THE SPEAKER:

Your name's Larry. Am I correct?

The man looks with a surprised expression before throwing a surrendering hand at The Speaker.

LARRY:

Yes! I-I'm Larry.

The Speaker's assistants help Larry onto the platform.

THE SPEAKER:

I tell you, believe in me, Larry! Believe in the power I possess! Believe, Larry! Believe in me, Larry!

LARRY:

I believe in you.

The Speaker lays hands upon Larry's chest.

THE SPEAKER:

Come out of him, cancer! My power denies you, cancer! Come out! Come out! I command you!

Larry jerks and chokes. He vomits a tannish-brown slimy chunk of meat into The Speaker's hands.

The Speaker reveals the slimy substance to the crowd.

Larry raises his hands in reverence to The Speaker.

LARRY:

I'm-I'm healed. I'm healed! Thank you! Thank you! You healed me! You healed me!

The crowd cheers, tearfully shouting praises and calling to the great healer.

The Speaker wraps the cancer in his handkerchief and throws it to the trailer floor.

Suddenly, a furious stranger yells over the loud cries of the congregation.

DOCTOR:

You're a phony! I'm a doctor. This is impossible!

The wailing crowd quiets.

THE SPEAKER:

Who spoke words of nonsense?

DOCTOR:

I did. You're a fraud!

THE SPEAKER:

I have no need to prove myself. However, Kenneth Turner's presence will confirm me otherwise. Please, Mr. Turner, will you raise your hand?

Ken's hand slowly raises. He is astounded that a man he has never met or heard of knows his name.

THE SPEAKER:

Kenneth, may I call you Ken? Come. Come join me.

The Speaker kindly directs Ken to the stairs leading to the platform.

THE SPEAKER:

How many of you know Kenneth Turner?

The people from Seven Mile raise their hands.

THE SPEAKER:

What's our acquaintance, Ken?

KEN:

There's never an acquaintance. I don't know you.

THE SPEAKER:

Precisely. The woman you sit next to this evening, Farrah, she's your wife?

Ken cocks his head. He stares at himself in the reflection of The Speaker's dark sunglasses.

KEN:

Yes, sir, she is my wife.

THE SPEAKER:

And your three boys, Joe, Jerry, and Jack?

KEN:

Yes, they are my boys.

THE SPEAKER:

When I tell the crowd things impossible for me to know about you, you assure the folks to trust in me. Can I trust you to do this for me?

KEN:

Things like what?

THE SPEAKER:

Ummm - your telephone number, your address, perhaps even your social security number.

KEN:

You know my social security number?!

THE SPEAKER:

Two. Eight. Five. Three. Six.

KEN:

STOP!

Ken's perplexity permeates the crowd, validating The Speaker's abilities.

Everyone rises to their feet, praising The Speaker and jumping into the air. Everyone except for one lonely woman resting in a wheelchair.

KATHERINE GAMBLE:

What about me? I can't walk. What about me? Help me!

She lowers her head, tears falling onto her lap.

THE SPEAKER:

What's your name, ma'am?

KATHERINE:

Katherine. Katherine Gamble.

THE SPEAKER:

You ready to use your legs again, Katherine? You believe in me; you walk tonight, woman. You walk now!

KATHERINE:

Oh yes! I believe in you!

THE SPEAKER:

Why wait, woman? Stand on your feet and walk! Walk, Katherine! Come on, walk!

Katherine grunts in pain but cannot rise.

THE SPEAKER:

Rise, Katherine. Rise! You must rise, Katherine!

Katherine pushes, using her trembling arms as she struggles to her feet. The crowd clenches their hands in anticipation.

THE SPEAKER:

Come to me, Katherine. Come on. Come, Katherine. Run, woman! Run, woman!

Katherine slowly runs to the altar. The crowd collectively loses its mind, bellowing and applauding with tremendous excitement.

KATHERINE:

It's a miracle! It's a miracle! I can walk! Look at me! I'm walking! I can dance! I can dance now! I can dance! I can dance!

Ken looks on in amazement from his position on the platform, overwhelmed by The Speaker's magnificent miracles.

The cancer on the trailer floor catches Ken's attention, and he questions if he has ever seen the familiar-looking substance.

Upon exiting the platform, Ken notices a small plastic container in a trash can behind the stairs. Printed on the lid, CHICKEN LIVERS. He puts the cancer and the container together. He's not so impressed anymore.

Farrah notices Ken's look of apprehension as he ventures to his seat.

15

The Speaker beckons the ushers forward to receive the night's offering.

Farrah burrows into her purse, but Ken stops her from unsnapping the wallet's fastener. He shakes his head.

The Speaker holds several one-hundred-dollar bills towards the enthusiastic crowd, demanding his flock dig deep into their pockets to show Seven Mile their blessings of generosity.

THE SPEAKER:

Prosperity and good health to all who contribute.

DOCTOR:

Gladly! I'll give some land I own.

CONGREGANT 1:

Hell, I'll give my whole bank account. I believe in what's goin' on here. You guys are - You just gotta believe in this shit. It's some shit now. I tell you - you got to.

CONGREGANT 2:

Well, yeah! I'll give you my Cadillac.

CONGREGANT 3:

And I'll give you my home!

CONGREGANT 4:

Here, take my wallet!

CONGREGANT 5:

You can have my kidney!

The offering baskets overflow their brims.

The boys' choir sings a spine-chilling song to close the service. Ken focuses on the eerie words which assure him he must act on what he has witnessed.

Salvation eternal or
Damnation infernal?

He's our man
Will you follow him?

He's our shepherd
Leads us from sin.

He's our healer
Protecting his kin.

He's our god
He'll take us to heaven.

Life we will enjoy
Sins we will avoid
Forget your tribulations and your trials

Follow to his voice
Utopia rejoice
And leave this unjust world behind

Congregants from the church mingle persuasively with the folks of Seven Mile, uplifting their Speaker and insisting everyone join their newfound hope.

Ken whispers to a few friends that The Speaker is bogus, a devil. They blow him off as paranoid.

Cautiously, Ken makes his way to the trashcan, fishing the lid from the bloody chicken liver container. He swoops by the trailer's edge, carefully collecting the slimy "cancer," and stuffs the evidence in his pocket.

Ken hastily gathers his family and rushes them to the car.

KEN:

Farrah, The Speaker's running a scam. Drop me at the woods' edge, take the kids home and lock the doors.

Farrah is frightened and confused by Ken's agitation, but she reluctantly honors his command.

Ken stays hidden until the congregation clears the cove. He observes The Speaker, Larry, Katherine, the angry doctor, and the three gorillas laughing and talking in front of the altar.

DOCTOR:

Did you see everybody? We made it! We made it! We stole it all!

And I told you I was a doctor and I could do it. I told you! I told you! We did it! We stole it all.

KATHERINE:

laughs Did you see their faces? I-I can walk. I can dance! I can dance! Oh, I just was so good. I just raked all that money. I'm better than that phony doctor. I'm soooo good. *laughs*

LARRY:

laughs That was so easy. Like taking candy from a baby. You were so good.

KATHERINE:

It was so fun!

LARRY:

But you know what? I think I want to be in the wheelchair. I think I could do that better than you.

KATHERINE:

Oh no! I don't want cancer.

LARRY:

What? I can dance. I can walk.

KATHERINE:

Yeah, but not as good as me.

LARRY:

Well, maybe you're right, but I'd still like to try it.

KATHERINE:

Well...maybe, but I don't think so.

LARRY:

Ok. I'll talk to the boss.

KATHERINE:

Go on.

Ken approaches.

GORILLA 1:

Hey, hey, hey! Hey guys! Guys! Somebody's comin'. Hey. Hey! Settle down - somebody's comin'!

THE SPEAKER:

How may I help you, my friend?

Ken pulls his pistol.

KEN:

My friends aren't thieves! Give me the scratch you con artists drained from those poor, vulnerable families!

Larry and the Doctor, both vying for an extra cut of the night's take, make a foolheaded attempt to disarm Ken.

An expert marksman in his 4-H days, Ken fires two precise shots hitting Larry and the Doctor square in the chest before they can even get within an arm's reach.

LARRY:

Ugh! They got - they shot me!

KATHERINE:

shrieks Oh no! I'm outta here!

Katherine takes off like an Olympic sprinter, leaving the group behind and quickly disappearing into the surrounding forest.

Larry and the Doctor writhe in pain and agony before finally succumbing to their fatal wounds.

DOCTOR:

What?! They shot me? They shot me. They shot meee-oh *dies*

LARRY:

chokes I'm dyin'. I'm really dyin' *chokes* *dies*

One of the gorillas moves his hand towards his pocket.

KEN:

You pull that biscuit, and I swear, I'll shoot this phony right square in the middle of his brain... if he has one. Get your hands in the air, NOW! Before I blast this crook's thinker off!

THE SPEAKER:

Obey.

KEN:

THE CASH!

I'm returning this money and exposing your stinky sham. Seven Mile is an honest town, and I will make sure it stays that way!

Ken holds The Speaker hostage, directing him into the woods and daring anyone to move.

He releases The Speaker and disappears into the dense trees.

The Speaker's voice echoes through the cove.

THE SPEAKER:

I DECLARE THIS COVE, DEVIL'S BACKBONE! I WILL BUILD MY KINGDOM RIGHT HERE!

CHAPTER TWO

Thanks, Mom

Careful not to shuffle ground cover or rattle tree limbs, Ken hides late into the night, watching The Speaker's goons hunt the area. Eventually, he slips unnoticed through the backwoods to his home.

Ken slides into bed fully dressed, remembering the phony clan had gotten his address. He borrows Farrah's thigh for his pillow, placing both feet on the floor with no plans of closing his eyes.

Ken unintentionally dozes off.

He's abruptly awakened by a creaking sound. Footsteps from the loose planks of his front porch, he thinks. Drowsy and not sure he truly heard a noise, he lays still.

Seconds later, The Speaker's three goons take to their job, hatcheting the entry door into shards.

Ken and Farrah scramble to the front room. Their three scared children rush to the commotion as well.

Jack is nabbed by one of the droppers, who quickly places a knife to his young throat, holding him hostage.

East coast mobster "Mofo" Mickey Matos is the man in charge. He holds two guns, pointing one at Farrah and one at little Joe's head. Ken is outnumbered. He drops his piece.

"MOFO" MICKEY MATOS:

Give us the spinach you nicked from the grifter, or the ghetto bird becomes a lamp post missing her shade.

Ken moves to retrieve the loot.

"MOFO" MICKEY:

Not you, hero. The dame!

Farrah freezes.

"MOFO" MICKEY:

I'm not here to bump gums. Get them gams moving. Any funny business, and your old man here finds deep sleep and your kid a Harlem Sunset. Move it!

Farrah doesn't know the gab but gets the picture. She quickly retrieves a leather satchel and hands over the stash.

FARRAH:

You'll never get away with this. Never!

Instantly, the third hired hand splits Ken's dome with his hatchet.

Blood sprays onto young Joe's face. Joe doesn't flinch, however. He stares straight at the hatchet man as his father's warm blood slithers down his face.

Ken gives up the ghost. His large shell slams onto the hardwood floor. His spirit exits his body, floating in the room and crying out to deaf ears.

Ken's soul fights the spirit world that is beckoning him into the light, but his will to remain with his family is stronger than their attempts to carry him into the afterlife.

Mofo Mickey notices Farrah is a looker. He violently rips her panties from her, bending her forward, raping her like a just-released convict.

Farrah goes numb. She doesn't dare fight for fear of her children's lives.

The twins watch in horror, but Joe remains unemotional, staring into his mother's distressed eyes as Mickey continues his business. Joe's bravery tells Farrah a day of revenge belongs to her young son.

Mickey zips his pants.

"MOFO" MICKEY:

Thanks, Mom! They don't call me "Mofo" Mickey for nothin'.

He violently grabs Farrah's hair.

"MOFO" MICKEY:

If ya ever want to see your kid alive and you don't want me doing to him what I just done to you, your sweet lips better stay zipped.

The three goons abduct Jack and head into the night.

YOUNG JACK:

No! Huh. Ah. Ouch! Help me!

Farrah falls on top of her dead husband, clutching his bloody body. Frightened and confused, little Jerry clings to his mother. Brave little Joe stares at the two with no reaction.

Ken's spirit cries in pain as he watches his family suffer. His spirit hopelessly searches for a resting place.

Young Joe senses his father's presence and raises his hands high above his head.

Ken's spirit spins like a top, forcing its way into Joe's body. Joe's ten-year-old frame jolts as the spirit finds rest.

Suddenly, Farrah hears Joe's voice. She stops crying. Farrah and Jerry look at Joe in amazement because little Joseph doesn't often speak.

YOUNG JOE:

Mommy, it will be okay. Daddy lives inside of me now. I named him Jo-Ken. Don't worry - we will find Jack.

FARRAH:

Oh, Joseph. Oh, baby.

Farrah finds peace. She knows the truth lies within little Joe.

Ten Years Later

It's been ten miserable years in the Turner household since that dreadful night. Jerry and Joe have grown up and moved on with their own lives as best they can.

All alone in her empty house, Farrah's only reason for living is the hope of one day seeing her son Jack alive.

ACT ONE

CHAPTER THREE

The Trucker and The Intruder

A newer model Peterbilt's shiny coat glistens from the loading dock's security lights while gently touching the rubber dock pads at U.S. Dynamite. The driver releases the air brakes and sets the parking brake, then journeys inside.

Lurking in the shadow of a forty-yard dumpster, a nineteen-year-old female waits patiently for the driver to disappear. She makes her move, limping with each stride to the truck's cab. She suffers a sprained ankle, a compound fracture on her left forearm, a deep cut on her forehead, and her left eye is swollen shut.

She pulls herself onto the tractor steps using her unbroken arm, grunting in pain with each step while doing her best not to leak traces of blood.

She opens the driver door, grabs the steering wheel, and pulls herself onto the seat. Desperately, she musters enough strength to climb into the tractor's sleeper. The sleeper curtain is mostly open. She figures best not to disturb the truck's interior surroundings. She scrunches herself into the sleeper's dark back corner, trying to clear herself of The Trucker's view.

The Trucker returns, pours his thermos cap full of java, takes a healthy swig, and drives away.

After a few hours of the dark early morning haul, the sun peeks its shining face across the base of the Santa Cruz Mountains. The truck thunders down a steep grade, nearing the small town of Gilroy.

The Trucker ignores the "No Jake Brake" sign he clearly sees and gives himself a thrill engaging it anyway. The mighty rumble possibly woke the dead from a deep grave but for sure opened the eyes of a sleeping smokey waiting to capture a guilty lawbreaker.

THE TRUCKER:

Well, shit!

The old cherries and berries shine brightly in the tractor's side-view mirrors.

The Trucker pulls his rig off the road into a local café's parking lot.

The officer cautiously approaches the driver door.

The Trucker rolls his window down and smiles at the officer.

THE TRUCKER:

Ya got me.

The officer finds The Trucker's comment easy-going and slightly entertaining.

OFFICER NOLAN:

What ya hauling?

THE TRUCKER:

Dynamite.

OFFICER NOLAN:

It's against the law to haul dynamite without notification.

THE TRUCKER:

I know. That's why I haul it.

OFFICER NOLAN:

Where are you heading, youngster?

THE TRUCKER:

Youngster?! You're the one with the babyface.

OFFICER NOLAN:

Yeah, but I got a deep voice. Scares big fellas like yourself.

THE TRUCKER:

Yep! I'm sure I look worried. I'm scared shitless of you, Officer... Nolan.

OFFICER NOLAN:

I somehow doubt that. The roar of your pickle cart sounded like you were doing at least double-nickels in a three-five. License, please.

The Trucker hands Officer Nolan his license.

OFFICER NOLAN:

Well, I'll be damned. You're from Seven Mile!

THE TRUCKER:

And you're from somewhere other than the US.

OFFICER NOLAN:

The hell I am! I'm from Cali-for-ni-a. My great gramps was a gold prospector in this sparkling state.

THE TRUCKER:

Yep! And I'm from Seven Mile. Where else would I be haulin' dynamite from?

OFFICER NOLAN:

I'll be headin' your way next week. Gonna interview for the county detective job where you're from.

THE TRUCKER:

Then your crooked ass knows I'm haulin' dynamite.

OFFICER NOLAN:

You don't pull no punches, do ya? Cough up your log and permits, please.

The Trucker performs a fake cough and smiles at the officer.

The young lone ranger glances at The Trucker's smiling face shining from the morning sun and finds favor with him. He pulls himself to the top step of the rig, balancing with the grab handle.

The Trucker holds his smile.

The officer looks past his grin and suddenly loses interest in his popping personality. He becomes more concerned with the blood-stains smeared on the steering wheel.

OFFICER NOLAN:

There's blood on your steering wheel. Are you injured, sir?

The Trucker glances at the blood; scans his hands and body, searching for where the blood may have come from. To his surprise, a bloody youthful face reflects in his visor mirror. The Intruder pleads with a desperate hush signal.

THE TRUCKER:

Oh! There was a buck lying dead in the middle of the road back a few miles. Big wheels struck the big boy. Blood everywhere. I collected some, I reckon. Figured it was best to remove the bloody carcass before it causes an accident. Looked like about a nine-pointer. Still warm. Lotta good meat if you're interested.

The Trucker's mysterious passenger lets out a silent sigh.

The underpaid cop ponders the feather he might receive for writing The Trucker a ticket. He also imagines how many jars of Gerber 'a few large' buys his newborn.

The officer leans in, grabbing the door's interior panel, pulling close as he notices The Trucker's wallet chain attached to his belt loop.

OFFICER NOLAN:

Hey buddy, this small-town gig is not enough to pay the power bills, let alone feed a newborn. If I don't get the detective's position, I'll be looking to the system for help.

THE TRUCKER:

If you get the detective job, trust me, you'll be working for the system, better known as 'the organization.'

OFFICER NOLAN:

At least I'll be able to feed my child.

Officer Nolan glances at The Trucker's wallet chain again and goes for it.

OFFICER NOLAN:

Hey pal, you wouldn't have a few founding fathers resting in that folded piece of leather in your right rear pocket, would ya?

THE TRUCKER:

You catch on fast. Well, just so happens I ran into a few of them fellers on Tuesday at the bank. Matter of fact, two of them gentlemen want to meet ya.

The Trucker pulls out two one-hundred-dollar bills. He gently slides them into the officer's fingers which are resting in a taking position on the interior door panel.

THE TRUCKER:

I'll put a good word in for you at the courthouse.

Them fellers on those greenbacks told me to tell ya when you come up north; you better remember your old trucker buddy if you know what's good for ya.

Nolan nods at The Trucker and steps down from the rig.

OFFICER NOLAN:

I'm gonna cut you a break on the racket this morning. You drive safe and watch out for them deer.

The Trucker quickly draws his forty-five.

THE TRUCKER:

You're outta time, young lady.

The Intruder stares down the long barrel with her one un-swollen eye.

THE INTRUDER:

My drunken boyfriend beat me. He tossed me over his deck. I laid waiting for him to kill me. Lucky for me, he passed out.

I kissed our two-week-old baby boy goodbye. I'm so sorry I've left him.

THE INTRUDER (CONT'D):

He's beat me so many times.

I stole his car. The car ran out of gas alongside the fence at U.S. Dynamite. Please help me. He'll kill me. My arm's broke-

THE TRUCKER:

More than your arm is broke. What's your name?

THE INTRUDER:

Kami.

THE TRUCKER:

Joseph Nathaniel. Pleased to meet you.

THE INTRUDER/KAMI:

I need to get to Tijuana Regional Hospital. My aunt's a nurse there. Will you please take me there?

THE TRUCKER/JOE TURNER:

I can get into a lot of trouble smuggling you across the border. I'll do it, but if I ever see you again, you owe me a favor.

Joe and Kami both nod in agreement. They have a deal.

CHAPTER FOUR

First Generation (Lunch-room Jive)

Frank Thomas and Sam Spicer live on the poor side of the Russian River.

Chester Miller and Jerry Turner live on the other 'not so poor' side of the river.

These four best friends recently graduated from Seven Mile High and went to work for U.S. Dynamite alongside Joe Turner, Greg Fowler, and Brett Michaels, who graduated a few years earlier.

It's lunch break.

Greg and Brett sit catty-corner from the four friends. Joe sits alone. But close enough, he can hear the boys reminisce and brag about their recent high school football success.

Joe was captain and star defensive lineman for Seven Mile, feared by all who came against him, so he enjoys the boys' gab.

Greg warmed the bench a few years in middle school. His lack of talent and drive steered him to drinking and smoking pot but bullying the weak became Greg's strongest means of easing his insecurities.

Jealous of the four boys, Greg tires of their jock gush.

GREG FOWLER:

Why don't you shut these superstars' flapping traps before I do, Joe?

JOE:

They're not hurting anyone. Jerry's my little brother. Best stay clear if you ever want to look in a mirror again.

Greg blows Joe off. Not a choice most people choose.

It's rumored throughout the town of Seven Mile that Joe Turner enjoys all-inclusive vacations several times a year trucking illegal explosives south of the border. Joe is extremely feared and respected.

Greg pushes his luck with Joe and hassles the four boys anyway.

GREG:

Yeah, yeah. Look what playing high school football for the Seven Mile Vikings landed you super jocks - a minimum wage job making firecrackers. You're a nothing! I bet not one of you ladies can shoot and skin a deer. Not even uhhhh rabbit.

The four boys' smiling faces turn into threatening scowls.

Sam, who is always playing the tough guy, forcefully pushes himself away from the table.

SAM SPICER:

What's your game, big mouth? You got a problem?

GREG:

Ohhhh! Look who just grew peach fuzz. Snipe hunting, asshole!

Jerry overhears Joe chuckle.

JERRY TURNER:

Hey, big brother. What's so funny? Do you run with this loser?

JOE:

I don't run. I walk... alone. You know that.

SAM:

I ain't never heard of no snipes. What's in it for me when I whip yo ass at your own game, punk?

GREG:

Whoever wins eat the snipes the other one catch. WINNER TAKE ALL. Best meat you ever tasted. Better than chicken or steak. Go ahead, ask Brett.

Brett Michaels' claim to fame is dating the hottest girl in California - the ultra-provocative sex goddess, Sunny Shade.

Brett was also the star forward for the Seven Mile Vikings basketball team. Too bad no one cares about basketball in Seven Mile. It's football or nothing in this town. However, Greg was one of the few spectators who came to watch him play, so Brett pretends to like Greg out of pity.

Brett wants no trouble from Joe, so he ignores Greg. Greg huffs at Brett with disappointment.

GREG:

sigh Fuck you, Brett.

Greg points deviously at Sam and the other three boys.

GREG:

It'll take you and your lady friends to beat me. You girly scouts want to play?

JERRY:

When and where, asshole?

GREG:

Why not tonight, anus munch!

Chester Miller is a big, tough, cautious guy with nothing to prove. He doesn't trust many people, least of all Greg Fowler.

CHESTER MILLER:

Not on a Friday night, boys.

GREG:

Mommy's little girls still sucking gooey breast milk?

Greg sucks his thumb towards them.

Mommy's little girls hits a little too close to home for mama's boy Frank Thomas. He shoots Greg a nasty look.

FRANK THOMAS:

We're on!

SAM:

What about Mary Jo?

FRANK:

Mary's babysitting my baby sister tonight. It's cool.

Frank looks for any excuse to not hang out with his girlfriend, Mary Jo.

GREG:

You punks meet me at Devil's Backbone Cove.

Joe notices Jerry swallowing hard at the mere mention of Devil's Backbone Cove.

GREG:

Say... five-thirty? Snipes don't like the dark, so don't make me wait.

Greg steals a smoke from Sam's cigarette pack sitting on the table.

CHESTER:

Hey! Smoking's against company policy.

GREG:

I don't smoke. The cigarette does. Rules only apply to minimum wagers like yourselves.

See you losers tonight. Don't forget to change your feminine napkins, sissy boys!

Greg puts his cigarette out in Chester's soup.

Greg exits the break room. Chester glares at the floating cigarette in his cup of noodles.

CHESTER:

Smells like sardines to me, guys.

SAM:

That pussy didn't even make water boy four years straight. I'm going!

FRANK:

Me too.

Jerry has always looked up to Joe since their dad's murder.

JERRY:

You schooled with him, Joe. Tell us something.

Joe walks past the boys to the trash can, kind of ignoring the question.

JOE:

I'm not a cozy one. If you knew my friends, Jerry...

Joe catches himself.

JOE:

Snipe hunting's harmless. However, I'd never play cards with the guy.

JERRY:

That means he doesn't trust him. You ever snipe hunt, big brother?

JOE:

One time.

CHESTER:

Did ya get any, Joe?

JOE:

No, but they're plentiful. They're in heat right now. You guys stick together. Let me know if Greg steps out of line.

Twelve-thirty. Back to work, fellas.

Concerned, Joe pulls Jerry to the side.

JOE:

You sure you want to do this, little brother? You've not seen the cove since Dad died and they snatched Jack. You want me to go with you?

JERRY:

It's time for me to face my fears, big brother. The guy is safe to be around, though, right?

JOE:

He's no threat. Go have some fun.

CHAPTER FIVE

Momma's Kitchen Knives

Work ends.

The boys meet at Frank's parents' house. They pack into Frank's old pickup and head for Devils Backbone Cove to beat Greg at his own game.

Chester is nervous.

CHESTER:

I don't like this, guys. Like Sam said, I've never even heard of a snipe, let alone seen one. What happens if we get bit by one? That sniper will bury us!

SAM:

That's all the more reason to carry one of these!

Sam pulls a butcher knife from his boot, flashing it in front of the boys.

Jerry leans away from the knife.

JERRY:

Whoa!!! Where did you get that, Sam?

FRANK:

Hey! That looks like my Mom's knife!

SAM:

That's because it is.

Sam sly eyes the boys.

FRANK:

What the shit?!

Frank slams the brake, throwing the boys into the dash.

FRANK:

I'd rather get a root canal than take the beatin' momma would hand me for stealin' one of her good kitchen knives. Mary Jo better not catch you with it either. She'll tell.

What's your fascination with knives, anyway?

SAM:

I just like to cut things.

FRANK:

I oughta whoop your ass!

SAM:

Stop worrying, toddler! Mom and Daddy's going dancin'. Momma's knives'll get tucked in their crib before they get home, so screw you, Frank!

CHESTER:

Dancing? I heard your parents went to that devil's church in Ukiah. They believe in dancing?

FRANK:

Don't talk like yer parents are some kinda gosh damn saints or something. They act like angels when they're in the pews sucking the devil's rod. Horns and pitch forks ain't got shit on our parents once they leave their fucking cult friend, and you know it. So shut your cakehole before I make it a shit box and shove my dick in it.

JERRY:

Well, that sure was a queer thing to say.

Jerry doesn't approve of conversations concerning church.

JERRY:

My dad's dead, and my brother's missing because of that devil cocksucker. We don't go to their demon fuckin' show, so you better watch your words. You're just pissed off because Sam stole your momma's kitchen knife.

FRANK:

Damn straight! What the hell got you into stealin' from my house, anyhow? I oughta whoop your ass!

SAM:

You're gonna piss the shit right out of your pants now. **chuckle**
Look at this!

Sam pulls three steak knives from his other boot.

SAM:

Here's one for each of you tiny pussy holes. Now stick 'em in
your boot and shut your dick-sucking lips.

Chester can't believe his eyes.

CHESTER:

Well, lick my greasy ass. Why in the hell didn't you just steal the
whole fucking rack? You stupid kleptomaniac!

SAM:

Cause my boot's only a size twelve - like my dick, sweetheart.

The boys place the steak knives in their work boots.

SAM:

Relax, pussycats, you're with me.

CHAPTER SIX

Here, Snipes! Here, Snipes!

Frank, Chester, Sam, and Jerry finally reach Devil's Backbone Cove, where Greg is impatiently waiting.

Jerry closes his eyes as his traumatizing memories of the cove come rushing back into his mind.

Frank pulls his truck next to Greg's car and honks to get his attention.

GREG:

Shut that noisy fart can down! Get in the car and keep quiet!

The four boys pile into Greg's backseat. He provides each of them a chunk of chocolate and a piece of a candy bar.

GREG:

Here's your bait, gentlemen. Snipes love sugar. Once they smell the sweet from your breath, it's like monkeys on bananas.

Greg encourages them to eat the "bait" by munching on a candy bar of his own.

GREG:

Okay, youngsters, we wait. Once I see the little bastards, I'll get you your begging stick and a bag. Keep your eyes peeled.

JERRY:

What's a begging stick?

GREG:

Good question. You attract the snipes by tapping a stick against the bag I brought ya while calling, "Here, Snipes! Here, Snipes!"

Snipes are horny little bastards. They fuck more than rabbits. They believe it's their mate calling. I'll show you once I see one.

Chester is still concerned about their safety.

CHESTER:

Do they bite?

GREG:

Best question of all. They can, and they will. That's what makes this a man's sport. You close the bag tight and once they're inside - then beat 'em with the stick! I'm telling you, boys, best meat you'll ever beat. *laughs*

CHESTER:

laughs I'm feeling weird.

Greg's cue.

GREG:

I just saw one run out in the woods. Follow me, children.

Greg quietly opens the trunk and gives each of the boys a bag and a stick.

GREG:

Watch a professional, ladies.

The boys watch with anticipation.

GREG:

Here, snipe! Here, snipe! Here, snipes! Here, snipes!

Greg pretends a snipe ran into his bag. He walks past the boys wearing a cunning grin, beating his bag.

He opens the trunk, tosses the bag inside, and quietly closes the lid.

GREG:

That's how she's done, humans of the female gender. Watch for briar patches. Don't want ya gettin' a runner in yer pantyhose.

Greg climbs into his car and prepares to watch the comical charade.

SAM:

laughs Man, I got to shit!

FRANK:

laughs Me too!

The boys manage to embark on their hunt.

FRANK, SAM, CHESTER, & JERRY:

Here, snipes! Here, snipes! Here, snipey snipes. Here, snipes. Here, snipey snipes…

Jerry loses his begging stick. He pulls the steak knife from his boot, using it instead.

The boys' mysterious hysterics make it virtually impossible for them to walk, let alone bend over and hunt for snipes.

Greg laughs uncontrollably, watching the boys being duped by his well-planned prank. Basking in his brilliance, he reminds himself why all of this is so funny.

GREG:

Laxatives and acid. The perfect combination for a perfect prank. *laughs*

Ten minutes of hysteria is enough fun for Greg.

GREG:

starts car Enjoy your trip to the moon! If you don't shit your brains out, suckers! *peels out and drives away*

The boys come together. Their hysterics barely allow them to speak. Finally, Sam proudly announces...

SAM:

Oh man. I believe I've shitted my fruity-balloons plum full, fellers.

Chester notices the brown stain shining through Sam's light-colored painter's pants.

CHESTER:

Well, poo poo and doo doo! Tough guy has muddied his drawers. What the hell? Woo, I'm drunk, fellas.

Chester loses his balance, crashing into Frank's truck.

JERRY:

laughs That son of a bitch drugged us with those candy bars. He fuckin' pranked us! There's no such thing as a motherfuckin' snipe!

Jerry stumbles towards the trees.

SAM:

Where you goin', Jerry?!

JERRY:

laughs I gotta shit! You wanna wipe my ass for me?

SAM:

Only if I could use your tongue!

Jerry trips over a stump.

CHESTER:

Hey, guys! Somethin's wrong with Jerry!

Chester notices Jerry is lying in a fetal position and not moving.

CHESTER:

Hey! Straighten up, you guys! I'm serious! Somethin's wrong with Jerry!

They stagger to Jerry.

SAM:

Oh man. Oh crap! What's wrong with him?

FRANK:

Holy shotgun! He shit himself! He's bleeding!

CHESTER:

Bleeding?! From where?

FRANK:

From his stomach!

Chester rolls Jerry onto his back.

CHESTER:

You okay, buddy?

Frank is filled with paranoia.

FRANK:

I'm freakin' out! We gotta get outta here!

CHESTER:

We just can't leave him here, Frank!

FRANK:

I don't give a shit! I'm blitzin' out of my fucking mind! I've gotta get Momma's kitchen knives back in the rack!

Chester tackles Frank, pinning him to the ground.

CHESTER:

You and Sam just had to prove yourselves, didn't ya? I told you guys that this was a bad idea!

Chester draws a fist to strike; then punches the ground beside Frank's head.

He puts his fist in Frank's face.

CHESTER:

Get your shit together before I use this!

FRANK:

Okay! Okay! I give!

Chester helps Frank to his feet.

SAM:

crying If I hadn't taken them fuckin' knives! Someone get over here! Man, Jerry's gonna bleed to death if we don't do somethin'! Please, please help him! Chester, I'm sorry, man! It's all my fault!

CHESTER:

Frank! Pull your truck over here.

FRANK:

Pull my truck over here?! I can't even see the truck! Let alone drive it right now!

CHESTER:

Sam, can you drive?

SAM:

Man, I can't drive no fuckin' stick! I don't even have a license, man!

CHESTER:

That leaves you, Frank! Pull your truck over here, NOW!

Frank reluctantly stammers over to get his truck.

CHESTER:

Okay, Sam, I'm hitting the trees to take a steamer. Take care of Jerry. I'll be right back. And DON'T pull the knife out. It only makes it worse. Got it?

Chester runs to the trees, holding his butt shut.

Frank clumsily guides the truck over to Sam and Jerry.

There's only one thing on Frank's mind - Momma's good kitchen knives.

FRANK:

Let's get outta here, Sam.

SAM:

No way, Frank! I can't leave him here. He'll die.

Frank's fear of disappointing his mother leads him to jerk her steak knife from Jerry's stomach.

JERRY:

screams in pain

FRANK:

Let's go, Sam!

Sam doesn't want to leave Jerry. However, he also doesn't want to deal with the situation in his stoned state of mind. Sam freaks out and jumps in the truck with Frank.

Chester sees the truck rolling and tries to run, but his pants around his ankles trip him. He lays buck naked, beating his fist on the ground.

CHESTER:

Come back here, you coward bastards!!

Betrayed by his best friends, Chester weeps.

JERRY:

painful screaming

CHESTER:

I'm coming, buddy!

JERRY:

sobbing Please, don't let me die here! Not at Devil's Backbone! Please, god! Not here! Not here!

Using his shirt, Chester applies pressure on the wound while comforting his friend.

CHESTER:

Lay still. I'm gonna run to the nearest house for help. You'll be okay.

Sam's paranoid bickering makes it hard for Frank to keep his truck on the road.

SAM:

Dude! Slow down! You're goin' way too fast, man!

FRANK:

What?! I can't hear you!

SAM:

Slow the fuck down!

FRANK:

Slow down?! How fast do you think I'm going? I'm only doing forty-five!

SAM:

Sounds like we're doin' a hundred 'n fifty, man!

Frank is so high he doesn't realize the truck is redlining.

He finally notices his tachometer is pushing over eight thousand RPM.

FRANK:

laughs Oh shotgun! I'm still in first gear!

Frank forgets the clutch and jams the shift lever into second gear.

SAM:

That's better, dumbass! Be careful 'fore ya put us in the hospital, fuckhead!

They finally pull into Frank's driveway. Sam's guilt won't leave him alone.

SAM:

Frank, man - we gotta go back, man. Jerry's gonna die if we don't.

FRANK:

No, he won't, ya smelly prick! If ya hadn't taken the knives, we wouldn't be in this mess! It took all I had just to get us here, so shut your fuckin' cumdump!

They run inside. Mary Jo leaps to her feet, witnessing the bloody knife in Frank's hand.

MARY JO:

Shoo-we! Did you stab one of them snipers to death, Frank?

Mary Jo smells Sam's messy pants and grabs her nose.

MARY JO:

Those snipers smell like cow shit.

Frank stares at Mary Jo with his glassy, stoned eyes. Mary Jo places her hand over her mouth.

MARY JO:

What the hell is wrong with you?! Are those Momma's good knives? What have you done, Frank?!

Frank dashes to the kitchen to wash the knife.

MARY JO:

Someone! Please! Tell me what's going on!

Frank dries his hands and grabs Mary Jo's arms.

FRANK:

Listen, baby. That prick Greg pranked the shit out of us, literally! There ain't no such thing as a snipe. He drugged us and fed us diarrhea pills or something. We're fucked out of our gourds. And we shit all over ourselves.

Mary Jo stomps her foot and clenches her fists.

MARY JO:

Dammit, Frank! I warned you he's a bully! *growl*

FRANK:

I've got no time for this shit, Mary Jo! Jerry's in big trouble. He fell on Momma's kitchen knife, Sam stole. He's bleedin' to death, hurry! Call the ambulance before Jerry dies! Hurry, Mary Jo! Hurry! I'm freakin' out!

MARY JO:

They're on their way, Frank.

As he is running for help, Chester hears sirens and flags down the ambulance. He leads the EMTs to Jerry, and both of them are immediately rushed to the hospital.

HOSPITAL INTERCOM:

All doctors to the ER.

Farrah and Joe arrive to find Chester at Jerry's hospital bedside.

HOSPITAL INTERCOM:

All nurses to the nurses' station.

Joe notices Chester's swollen pupils. He's sure Chester is high.

Jerry insists the accident is Joe's fault for allowing Greg to prank him.

HOSPITAL INTERCOM:

Security to the ER.

Noticing Jerry is upset with Joe, Farrah recommends Joe and Chester leave Jerry to rest and recover.

Jerry flatlines

HOSPITAL INTERCOM:

Code blue, room 305. Code blue.

DEFIBRILLATOR:

Stand clear.

CHAPTER SEVEN

Zip Your Lips

Joe gives Chester a lift home.

*When Joe gets rattled, Ken's spirit living inside of him takes over,
something he can't control. Joe refers to him as Jo-Ken.*

JO-KEN:

Hi, Chester. I'm Jo-Ken. The truth, Chester! One word of bullshit,
and I'm pulling this truck over!

*Chester is speechless. He recognizes that wasn't Joe's normal voice
he heard. Cold chills tickle his spine.*

Chester pulls himself together and rats Greg out.

77

Joe, being Seven Mile's resident drug dealer, knows that Greg purchased eight hits of LSD after work, confirming Chester's confession.

Joe pulls into Chester's drive and drops him off. He leaves him with some threatening words.

JOE:

The river's deeper than wide. Better warn your friends. They best keep their mouths closed if they know what's good for 'em. I'll handle this.

Chester rushes inside to call Frank.

Mary Jo answers the phone.

MARY JO:

Hel - hello?

CHESTER:

Put your boyfriend on the phone, NOW!

Mary Jo points the phone at Frank. He shakes his head.

MARY JO:

Uh - uh, he's in the restroom, Chester.

Chester grunts loudly, beating the phone's receiver into his chair cushion.

CHESTER:

Uuuuughhhh! Uuuughhhh! Listen, you little bitch. If Frank's not on the other end of this phone in two seconds, I'm coming over there and burnin' his fucking house to the ground with you and Frank's little sister in it!

Now, put that coward on the fucking phone!

MARY JO:

Chester has to talk to you, Frank. It's an emergency.

FRANK:

sighs Hey, Chester.

CHESTER:

Listen close, you son of a bitch.

CHESTER (CONT'D):

Jerry's in the hospital. If one word leaks about tonight, Joe Turner promises the catfish will toothpick our flesh from their teeth. You got it, coward?

FRANK:

Got it, Chester.

CHESTER:

Joe Turner knows something and promises to handle the situation. Pass this to your shitty-pants, betraying friend. And tell your momma, if she wants her knife, it's tied to my dick!

slams the receiver

CHAPTER EIGHT

Cats and Rats are Born

The gang is in the lunchroom, minus Jerry. Greg enters, unaware of Jerry's accident. He strolls to Frank and Sam, drumming the side of his lunch bag with a spoon.

GREG:

Here, snipe! Any of you infants need a diaper change?

Greg walks on.

Joe moves a chair in Greg's path and places a bag in his hand.

Greg hesitates before taking a seat.

JOE:

Lunch is on me today.

GREG:

Uh - I'm not hungry, Joe.

Joe pushes a box cutter into Greg's side.

JOE:

My little brother is fighting for his life because of your little funny. Trust me. You're starving!

Greg is terrified of Joe.

GREG:

What happened? I didn't mean no harm!

JOE:

Eat your lunch.

GREG:

Joe, please tell me what happened. I-I'm sorry.

Jo-Ken takes control.

JO-KEN:

You're gonna eat every bite of your lunch special, or I will cut your guts out, dopehead!

Greg hears the clicks from Joe's box cutter. He eats his double dose - two chocolate laxatives and a candy bar laced with four hits of acid.

JOE:

I'm taking Greg home, Chester. He's experiencing illness. How does he look to you?

Chester is shocked and flattered Joe Turner even spoke to him.

CHESTER:

Oh! Well, looks like he's about to shit himself to me, Joe.

Joe respects Chester for not abandoning his brother.

JO-KEN:

Chester, handle your friends at the end of the table before I do.

Joe stops at Frank and Sam.

JOE:

I'm ashamed of you two boys.

Joe exits the lunchroom with Greg.

Like most people, Frank and Sam are fearful of Joe.

FRANK:

Just what in the fuck was that? Was blood drippin' from Joe's eyes?

SAM:

It-it sure as shit looked like it to me. And what happened to Joe's voice? He plum scared hell into me, and I ain't afraid of nothin'. Someone's gonna pay big time!

Chester makes his way to Frank and Sam.

CHESTER:

Kinda scary, huh, fellas? How are we gonna settle this issue?

Frank and Sam won't look at Chester. He claps his hands.

CHESTER:

I'm talkin' to you two cowards! I'll tell you one thing. You're better off to settle with me than Joe Turner.

Sam gets in Chester's face.

SAM:

Don't you threaten me!

CHESTER:

Sit! Before I hurt you real bad, Sam.

I've heard of two left feet, but damn I've never heard of two left hands! What, did your parents mix their cheap liquor with polluted Russian River water, or what? *laughs* How did you ever throw a football with that clubbed hand anyway?

None of the boys have ever brought up the fact that Sam was born deformed. However, his betrayal has brought war.

Sam takes Chester's advice and sits, but doesn't approve of anyone making fun of two left hands. Sam evil eyes Chester with the intent of getting even.

CHESTER:

Smartest thing you've ever done, Lefty. Let's give Jerry a month to heal. I'm sure he wouldn't want to miss an opportunity to get even with the pukes who left him to die.

Sam flies to his feet.

SAM:

I'm tired of your big mouth, motherfucker!

Chester grabs Sam's hair, setting him back in his chair.

CHESTER:

I told you to sit, and I mean it! I'm done playin'. Your braggin' mouths shut today.

Chester leans onto the table with both hands.

CHESTER:

Neither one of you cowards could carry my jock - so here's the deal. Put together a football team from your side of the river. I'll put together one from mine. Backyard style! No helmets. No pads. Just my head crackin' your head.

Chester is big and bad. However, Frank and Sam's pride knows no limit.

FRANK:

What's the trophy?

CHESTER:

Don't worry about a dust collector, Frankie boy. I just want to tattoo some serious pain on two of the town's biggest momma's boys.

Sam slams both of his left hands on the table.

SAM:

You're on, bitch! And we're the Jets!

CHESTER:

Like the New York Jets want you, huh, Sam? You keep on believing your embarrassing fairy tale. We see right through your
imagination, don't we, Frank?

Frank attempts to end Chester's grind.

FRANK:

We'll call our team - um - the River Rats! Yeah, the River Rats!

CHESTER:

Sounds about right. A large rodent living on the trash side of
town? Fits ya for sure.

The Blue Cats. Yeah, I'm callin' my team the Blue Cats.

SAM:

laughs Blue Cats? 'Cause you're a bunch of pussies, that's why.

Chester lets Sam's mouth slide.

CHESTER:

Blue Cats. As in the blue channel catfish. Like from the Mississippi River, boys. Game on, cowards!

CHAPTER NINE

Dopehead

Joe directs Greg into his pickup. Greg immediately tries to escape and goes for the door handle.

Joe pulls his .45.

JOE:

Go ahead! Try out running a bullet. I'd stake my life the bullet crosses the finish line first. If you're a good boy, I'll let ya pick out your own diggin' stick.

Greg slowly releases the door handle.

GREG:

Joe! I swear! I never meant no harm to none of them boys. I was just ticklin' feathers. You know that.

JOE:

Does this tickle?

Joe backhands Greg in the face, keeping him in line.

JOE:

You believe drugging a kid is funny? You're a sick little bastard, aren't ya? My little brother promised to never touch a drug. You broke his promise to me.

GREG:

I'm sorry, Joe. Please, I've got a baby boy - Chandler.

JOE:

Chandler can thank me when he's a man. No more apologies.

Greg is drenched in sweat.

JOE:

You're pouring enough sweat to float the Titanic. My history book told me that big bastard is sittin' at the bottom of the ocean.

Joe flashes his eyebrows at Greg.

GREG:

Please! Joe! Not the river. At least allow my family to find me.

JOE:

I might not kill ya, but you're gonna wear a reminder somewhere. Payback for my innocent little brother.

GREG:

Joe, I got to shit.

JOE:

laughs I know, better hold it. You shit in my truck, and a hot chili pepper feels cold on them hemorrhoids compared to the burning lead I'll plug your nasty asshole with. We're almost there.

Jo-Ken is awakened as Joe pulls into Devil's Backbone Cove.

JO-KEN:

I'm Jerry's dad. Call me Jo-Ken. This place got me murdered. Walk to the woods, dopehead.

Greg freaks out at the sound of Jo-Ken's voice.

GREG:

No. Joe! No! Please don't shoot me! Please! Please don't! No!

JO-KEN:

I told you - I'M JO-KEN!

Joe smashes Greg with the butt of his pistol, opening a cut above his eye.

GREG:

I'm sorry, Jo-Ken. I'm sorry! Gosh damn! Please don't strike me again. Please!

JO-KEN:

Joe told you sorry is in someone else's dictionary. Walk, dopehead!

The laxatives hit Greg hard. He barely clears Joe's door before he loosens his belt.

JO-KEN:

In your pants. Just like Jerry, dopehead.

Greg fills his work pants. He falls, shedding tears.

JO-KEN:

TAKE OFF YOUR CLOTHES!

Greg can't move.

JO-KEN:

I SAID, TAKE OFF THEM CLOTHES! And for not listening, you're gonna wear your panties as a hat. DOPEHEAD!

Greg puts his underwear on his head. Diarrhea oozes onto his shoulders.

JO-KEN:

Who's the infant now? Catch Jerry a snipe. There goes one!

Joe kicks Greg in his naked ass.

JO-KEN:

Get it, dopehead! Call 'em, dopehead! Come on! Get 'em!

Joe chases Greg, continually kicking him while Jo-ken enjoys the whimper in Greg's voice.

GREG:

whimpers Here, snipes. Here, snipes. Here, snipes. Here, snipes.

JOE:

Get it, dopehead! Get it! Get it, dopehead! Get it!

Joe kicks Greg, knocking him to his knees.

JOE:

Stay on your knees, Greg!

Joe stands over Greg with his legs spread and his crotch level to Greg's face.

GREG:

No, Jo-Ken! No!

JOE:

Wrong me, ya stoned fuck.

Joe and Jo-Ken enjoy keeping Greg confused.

JOE:

Open your mouth!

GREG:

No, I can't. I won't. Please, Joe.

JOE:

Open your mouth, or I'm blowing a hole clear through your shit-filled beanie.

Greg slowly lifts his hand towards Joe's zipper. Joe jerks his crotch back.

JOE:

laughing I'm not queer. You're not gonna suck my dick, you ignorant briar hopper.

Jo-Ken is not jokin'.

JO-KEN:

Last chance, dopehead. Open your mouth.

Greg hears the click from the pistol's hammer and unwillingly opens his mouth.

JO-KEN:

Suck your thumb just like your baby boy.

Greg sucks his thumb. Joe sticks the pistol to his gut.

JO-KEN:

Jerry's turn, Greg. Bite your thumb off!

Greg is so stoned and scared he is balling his eyes out.

GREG:

crying You promised you would not hurt me if I did what ya told me.

JOE:

No, I distinctly remember saying a good boy picks his own shovel.

Jo-Ken returns.

JO-KEN:

BITE YOUR FUCKIN' THUMB OFF, DOPEHEAD!

Joe fires the pistol into the ground.

The acid reminds Greg who is in charge. Like an attack dog, he viciously bites his thumb, leaving it hanging by a thread. Blood runs from his mouth, covering his neck. Joe pleasures seeing Greg cry in pain and embarrassment.

Greg lifts his head. Joe kicks him square in the face with his steel-toed work boot, knocking him unconscious.

JOE:

That hurt, didn't it, dopehead?!

Joe rips Greg's dangling thumb from his hand and sticks it in his pocket. He ties the wound with Greg's undershirt and leaves him for the buzzards.

CHAPTER TEN

Gonorrhea Greg

A short time later, a couple of the town's stoners pull into the cove to enjoy a buzz.

The passenger Ted, alias Tarred, packs a bowl for his driver friend Buck, alias Bucket.

Bucket takes a big hit and blows the smoke into the filthy windshield, then passes it back, but before the hooch ignites, Bucket's hit clears. The boys freeze. Twenty yards away stands a naked man with blood, snot, and slobber covering his face and body. He's wearing diarrhea-filled underwear on his head and a bloody t-shirt wrapped around his hand.

Tarred slowly lowers the bowl from his lips.

TARRED:

What the fuuuuuck is that, Bucket?

BUCKET:

stoner cough That's a zombie, Tarred.

TARRED:

Ca - can they hurt you?

BUCKET:

Uh -uh - hell yeah! They eat your face and your intestines and shit, man!

TARRED:

Umm - mm- maybe - maybe we should leave, Bucket.

stoner cough

Bucket fires his beast. He floors it, slamming into Greg, sending him tumbling into a tree. The stoners peek through their squinting eyes.

TARRED:

Fuuuuck. Did we kill it, Bucket?

BUCKET:

Yeah - I buh - I believe so, but we gotta make sure, though.

TARRED:

N-no way, dude! That zombie's not givin' me gonorrhea. N-n-no, sir!

BUCKET:

H-how can it give you gonorrhea, man? It hasn't gone nowhere. I-it's right in front of us.

Tarred slides Bucket a baseball bat. The stoners take a hit and lightly bump foreheads in agreement.

TARRED:

You're right, man. We gotta kill this intestine-eating alien before it gives us both gonorrhea, Bucket.

BUCKET:

Yeah, let's kill it before it pops my mom's cherry pie.

TARRED:

Huhhh?! Your mom baked a pie?!

BUCKET:

Awww yeah, man. That sounds gooood. Poppin' some cherries or somethin' right now? Oh man, I'm starving!

TARRED:

You popped your mom's cherry? She's so hot. That's rad…rad… dude.

They creep in on Greg. Unexpectedly, Greg moans.

Bucket cocks the bat. Greg raises his bloody hand. Tarred freaks.

GREG:

moans

TARRED:

Fuckin' kill it, man!! Kill it!

Bucket whacks Greg in the face, knocking him out.

The stoners race, diving through the windows. Bucket hits the ignition. The rag backfires, sending smoke signals as the clunker sputters from the cove.

CHAPTER ELEVEN

Sunny and Her Honeys

The cove glows slightly dim.

Brett Michaels and girlfriend Sunny Shade visit their usual parking spot for a quick romp. The young adults live at home, and they've been warned; any adulterous activity, and they're booted from the house. Their possessed parents believe virginity belongs to their devil cult leaders.

The attractive couple is deep in love...with lust. Sunny is a bright, young, full-figured tease. She's blessed or cursed, depending on how you look at her. She confidently enjoys flaunting her luscious playboy body. A mere glance at this doll-baby and the purest heart becomes a filthy lust bucket.

Brett encourages Sunny's flirtatious conversations with the attractive town cocks who fantasize about a chance to satisfy her sexually while waiting in the long line to visit her bank teller window.

The insanely jealous women employed at the bank trade whispers that she's just a dirty whore. Too bad for them.

Daddy owning the tiny little bank - that somehow draws the cream all the way from Hollywood - gives her a free pass to flirt with whom she pleases. She infuriates her co-workers by purposely dropping objects and bending over in her tight miniskirts for their customers' viewing pleasure to steal them away.

Ironically, the male employees never complain.

Sunny struts her heavenly shape in style. She proudly displays vibrant signature silk scarves around her neck, ensuring fleshly compliments from her horny patrons. Unknowingly to them, their filthy intentions create tiny orgasmic shivers to her sweet spot, triggering torrential floods of voluptuous feminine perfumes she accumulates in what she calls her sex panties - which she saves for Brett. He relishes her fragrant memento deep into his lungs. Her delightful scents bring him erections that satisfy his egotistical masculinity.

Brett embraces her shameful stories and, when in the moment, whispers persuasively, he would enjoy an actual kinky encounter. Her seductive obeyance brings him multiple explosive orgasms, but when the fire's out, he must restrain his anger from the one who lies beneath him.

SUNNY SHADE:

dials in cheesy 70's porn music on the car stereo

Sunny guides Brett's roaming hand from her scrumptious breast to her long, silky, shaven legs.

Brett presses hard against the perfect pattern of her swollen vagina, appreciating the seeping passion while massaging her sopping crevice.

Sunny's lazy bedroom eyes seduce as she glides her sex panties slowly to the tip of her foot, flipping them effortlessly to her hand before Brett's begging eyes.

BRETT MICHAELS:

Oh please, babyyy. Give me what fucking belongs to me. Give me your lust. Fuck me, Sunny! Fucking fuck me!

Like the great Houdini, his present disappears as she stuffs the sodden undergarment between her legs, generating a tease to satisfy his fantasy yearnings.

Inside the glove compartment lies a pair of Brett's tube socks they've sacredly kept for sex play since Sunny lost her virginity to Brett in the eleventh grade.

Sunny brings Brett into submission, tying his wrists to the steering wheel until he howls. She ties the other sock around his erection.

He's fond of her slapping his pulsating mushroom to create mounds of foreplay semen.

She passes his seeping secretions, moistening one another's thirsty lips while pleasuring herself for Brett to view.

SUNNY:

Look at me! My stud devil fuck buddy came to tease me with his enormous cock again today.

BRETT:

Confess, my beautiful whore! CONFESS!

SUNNY:

I fucked them all. Every big dick that came to my teller window left dripping wet from my sopping whore hole.

BRETT:

Confess to me, my duchess. Fuck the devil hard! Fucking dirty little fucking whore!

SUNNY:

Oh! Yeah! You like hearing about him, don't ya?!

I fucked that devil just to piss you off. You'll never fuck me like my demon.

BRETT:

Tell me, you dirty goddess! TELL ME!

SUNNY:

He removed his sunglasses and fucked me hard with his fuck-me eyes. *moans* I tasted the sweat from his forehead while he throat fucked me with his mind. He begged me with my tits in his drooling mouth.

BRETT:

Fuck him, Sunny! Fuck his big throbbing love stick!

SUNNY:

He shoved his tongue hard into my tight ass.

BRETT:

On your knees, slut! Take it up your hot ass! Take it! Take it! TAKE IT!!

SUNNY:

He slid a hand full of his hot juice onto my hand, and I rubbed him in my panties. It's yours now, Brett! Take his juice, Brett! Eat it, Brett! EAT IT!

Sunny forces her semen-stained panties into Brett's mouth.

BRETT:

gags and chokes

SUNNY:

Taste his cum, baby. Please taste it, baby.

BRETT:

You whore!

Sunny only calls Brett by his first name when she's being honest.

Brett tries to break free.

SUNNY:

You made me this whore, now fuck this horny whore.

DEVIL'S BACKBONE: THE INVISIBLE WALLS OF SEVEN MILE

This is what you wanted. I like the way the devil's cum tastes. He's inside of me, Brett. Fuck me with his hard cock! Fuck me!

Brett breaks free and forces Sunny's sweet lips onto his throbbing monster, filling her mouth with pre-cum, throat fucking her deep until he releases.

Out of breath, dripping with sweat, confused Brett waits for an explanation.

SUNNY:

Yes, it happened. Just like you wanted, baby. Should I be sorry, baby?

They become uncontrollably exhilarated.

Sunny ties a sock around Brett's neck, and he grasps the ends of her neck scarf, choking each other purple, releasing the pressure just before entering unconsciousness.

Brett's jealousy forces Sunny to the back seat. She receives his half-erect boner, deviously grinning inside, getting off on his competitive grudge fuck.

Their sex noise drowns sounds of Greg pulling himself to Sunny's open window.

Spotting Greg's silhouette, Sunny begs Brett to remove himself.

111

SUNNY:

Get off! Get off!

BRETT:

I'm trying! I'm trying, baby!

Greg passes out onto the windowsill. The blood from his wound drips onto Sunny's sweaty, terror-stricken face.

SUNNY:

There's a monster! Get off!

BRETT:

The monster's ready, baby! I'm getting off! I'm getting off, baby! BAAAABYYY!

SUNNY:

Get off of me, asshole! Get the fuck up!

Brett realizes something's wrong. He observes the monster's bloody head.

The two dash to the opposite side of the vehicle.

BRETT:

What in tarnation is that?!

GREG:

whimpering Help me, Brett. Help me, Brett. Help me.

Eventually, they recognize the monster is Greg and rush him to the hospital.

CHAPTER TWELVE

4 Fingers and 3 Thumbs

A local police officer visits Joe's home after speaking with Greg in the hospital.

JOE:

Is there a problem, officer?

OFFICER CRANK:

I got a few questions for Joe Turner concerning Greg Fowler.

Joe picks up on his East Coast accent.

JOE:

I know the police in town. You're not a familiar face.

Joe observes the officer's name tag.

JOE:

Officer...Crank?

An unusual name for an Italian-sounding voice, Joe thought.

JOE:

I'm Joe Turner. Who sent you?

OFFICER CRANK:

My second day. I sent myself. We need to talk - let's talk inside.

Joe stops the officer before he can enter.

JOE:

I live a private life. No reason for you to enter my home. Do you have a warrant?

OFFICER CRANK:

Do I need one? The question makes you sounds guilty.

Jo-Ken feels uneasy about Officer Crank.

JO-KEN:

You do if you want to enter my home.

Joe tries keeping Jo-Ken calm, but Jo-Ken can't stay cool.

JO-KEN:

Unless you plan on putting me in cuffs, keep away from this residence!

Officer Crank becomes frightened by Jo-Ken's voice and notices the loaded gun in Joe's hand. He realizes this is not a good time.

OFFICER CRANK:

I'm coming back, ya son of a bitch!

Joe slams the door in the officer's face. He questions the officer's east coast accent to himself. Joe takes "I'm coming back" as a threat. And being called a son of a bitch? Well, that's unkind to his mother.

Joe remembers Handsaw Henry from Compton owes him a favor.

Two days later, Detective Nolan receives an envelope. Inside, he finds Officer Crank's name tag - a name Nolan's not familiar with, along with four fingers and an intriguing three thumbs. He remembers Greg Fowler's police report stated he was missing a thumb. He also knows Joe Turner is somehow involved in Greg's beating.

DETECTIVE NOLAN:

Well, well, if it ain't my old trucker buddy from the past. I owe ya one, my friend.

Detective Nolan shakes his head with a smile while filing the envelope into the trashcan.

After a brief investigation, police find Greg delusional, and no arrests were made. Joe caught wind Officer Crank is working underground in a wine field outside of town.

Six feet under, to be exact.

CHAPTER THIRTEEN

Seven Mile Showdown

Weeks pass.

Confusion became anger, and anger turned into hatred.

Jerry has finally healed from his grievous wounds and is ready to get even with the pukes who left him to die.

Chester and Jerry have put together a team of bruisers from their side of the river, and Sam and Frank have done the same from their side. Chester and Jerry's team, the Seven Mile Blue Cats, wear flashy jerseys sporting an evil catfish with the word "BLUE" printed in the center of the fish. While Sam and Frank's team, the Seven Mile River Rats, wear jerseys that humor their fans with a smiling rat flushing a catfish down a toilet.

The Cats and Rats backyard game of football may seem trivial to some. However, anyone who's lived in a small town will quickly agree; a small-town scuttle can become big-time trouble. Lies move faster than Bob Munden can draw his six-shooters. Rumors spread swifter than a raging forest fire in a sixty-mile-per-hour wind.

The stadium is full, and the town is empty. Generations of lifelong friends with newfound hatred for those that live on the "other side" stand shoulder to shoulder, staying loyal to their side of the Russian River.

The crazed crowd begins chanting their team's chosen name, which quickly turns into rancid, demonic words of anger. Flying fists fill the air.

There are no refs. There are no rules. Shirts tear, noses bleed, and bodies break. Quickly, the free-for-all backyard game is in disarray.

Frank takes the ball around an end from Sam's lateral, presenting Chester his opportunity to get even. Frank runs out of bounds; however, this doesn't slow Chester. Charging like a raging bull, he power-drives Frank into the crowded sideline, pounding his face.

Jerry joins the fray, kicking Frank's rib cage and stomping his groin.

Both teams lock horns as fans clear the bleachers.

The fight quickly escalates into an all-out war. Glass bottles become jagged blades, wooden bleachers become tinder for a raging fire, and the goalposts become nothing but heavy steel beams, crushing bodies as they fall to the ground.

The crowd hurls any object they can get their hands on, screaming and fighting to the death.

After being assaulted from a flying object to his jaw, Joe exits the stadium.

While digging for his truck keys he is blindsided by two large men. One assailant removes his brass knuckle belt buckle and brutally beats Joe, while the second sticks a knife in his gut.

"MOFO" MICKEY:

This is for my brother from the wine field.

MOBSTER 1:

Come on, Mickey, he's dead. Let's go!

Mofo, let's get out uh here! He's blue! He's blue, Mofo! Let's go! Come on!

Joe is set on fire and left for dead.

Joe wakes in the hospital with Chester by his side. He is badly burned with a fractured skull and internal bleeding.

The doctors were able to save his life and his eyes, but his face will be scarred forever.

Joe will repay Chester one day for saving his life, but for now, he has only one thing on his mind… kill Mofo Mickey.

The riot marks the day of the Great Seven Mile Divide. A culmination of works unknown and fervent pride have boiled over, leading to the creation of two Seven Miles.

No longer just citizens of Seven Mile, the inhabitants of each side of the river now identify themselves as only Rats or Cats. The once heavily traveled bridge has been barricaded on both sides, ensuring the Rats and the Cats remain sealed in on their side of the Russian River.

These infamous events occurred ten years to the day that Seven Mile became possessed and Russian River Cove became Devil's Backbone Cove. July tenth, the day all devils howl.

CHAPTER FOURTEEN

Stevie Snitchie Snatchie

Mofo Mickey's East Coast accent remains locked in Joe's memory since the day Mickey raped his mother when he was ten.

Joe made no mistake; it was Mofo's voice he heard beating him alright. He follows Mofo's accent, hiring a couple of door-knockers in Providence.

For the West Coast, Joe knows a guy who knows a girl who pledges only two excuses justify her failure; incinerators and oceans.

For a small pot of gold, Stevie Snitchie Snatchie will find a piss-ant hiding in the tall grass of a thousand-acre farm.

At first glance, Stevie may appear incompetent. Rose-colored glasses hide her gooey glass eye, her bald head is speckled with blue stubble, and her voice is so deep she sings bass in a barbershop quartet. Chewing an unlit cigar is not much help either.

However, one glimpse of her smooth ski slopes and bulging camel toe and the rest becomes an oversight.

Joe provides Stevie the bullion. Two days later, she delivers a van carrying East Coast hitmen, Mofo Mickey and his brother Red, gagged and hog-tied.

Stevie surprises Joe with a surprise. A bonus body! Mofo Mickey's mother.

JOE:

Make yourself at home, Stevie.

STEVIE SNITCHIE SNATCHIE:

Thank you. I will.

Stevie takes a seat at Joe's dinner table, adjusting her camel toe before speaking.

STEVIE SNITCHIE SNATCHIE:

Before we commence words, sweetie.

JOE:

Give it to me.

STEVIE SNITCHIE SNATCHIE:

I used my snatchie to get the snitchie. Extra service comes with extra fries, Joe.

Joe knows the business. He's always prepared for a bump. He slides Stevie the lettuce plus a couple bones for Mickey's mom.

STEVIE SNITCHIE SNATCHIE:

Thank you. First off, sweetie, Mickey's last name is Matos. So's his two brothers, Tom and Red.

The three plug-uglies visited your parents in Sixty-five. They gained popularity on the West Coast when laboring for a cult leader to flip the light out on your dad.

Stevie spits a cut off her cigar onto Joe's floor.

STEVIE SNITCHIE SNATCHIE:

That's why you keep spreading the butter on the East Coast to find the three headshots, right?

JOE:

That's correct. They're slick. Seems like no one can catch 'em. I've spent a fortune tryin' to kill these bastards. Continue.

STEVIE SNITCHIE SNATCHIE:

The snoops you hired back east passed wind. They rolled over on ya. A bullet was more comfortable than torture. Mickey sent Tom disguised as a cop to assassinate you.

JOE:

I knew the bastard wasn't a cop.

STEVIE SNITCHIE SNATCHIE:

Handsaw sliced Tom Matos - he's fertilizing a wine field. Am I correct again?

Joe agrees.

STEVIE SNITCHIE SNATCHIE:

Mickey and Red came hunting in Tom's honor. They searched you out in a high school parking lot, believing they put you to sleep. The grapevine told them Handsaw chopped Tom.

I needed a little help. I slid Secret Asian Man a few rice patties.

He looked through some cracks. Spotted a speck of dust. Mom had come along with her boys. She wanted a piece of your ass herself for burying her kid in the wine field.

JOE:

No shit?

STEVIE SNITCHIE SNATCHIE:

I guess her old man's not so hot in the sack.

Secret Asian Man snapped a few photos of her and the local priest doin' the nasty.

Secret Asian Man shared the snapshots with her legs in the air. She squealed on her own kids so her old man wouldn't cast her into the swamp for spreading for another man.

JOE:

How do you know Secret Asian Man if he's a secret?

STEVIE SNITCHIE SNATCHIE:

There are no secrets in the killing business. That's why we don't live long. The best of us stick close. We spread the love - keeps us alive.

Caught 'em in Compton before they could thwack Handsaw.

JOE:

You've done me a great justice. Anything else?

STEVIE SNITCHIE SNATCHIE:

Yeah. My face ain't much, but my body's my temple. Red, the jaw-flapping brother in the van is the one I had to screw to get the dealio.

My pussy's so good he squeaked like a mouse.

He got out of line when he asked me to remove my eye to skullfuck me. Not happening, I told him. That's reserved for the apple of my eye. To get even, he put his smoke out on my sweet little tuchus while attempting to fist-fuck me. Left a scar. Keep that in mind when you do the cocksucker in.

Stevie refunds Joe his Gs.

CHAPTER FIFTEEN

Slayer's Matos Sauce Recipe

Joe purchased a few acres seven miles south of Seven Mile along-side the Russian River. He spends his spare time building a log cabin on the river's edge. Recently, he finished his hobby workshop, which turned out to be a lovely little hotel for his precious cargo.

Joe arrives. He's greeted by a tall, muscular man who slides the workshop door open, directing the van inside.

Hard-working business parents raised Dalton Slayer, a.k.a. Slayer Coo Coo, in a wealthy neighborhood. Slayer was beaten and gang-raped when he was only fourteen while watching his mother and two younger sisters receive similar treatment for his dad's only mistake, being born black.

Joe heard Slayer carries a story similar to his, which is why he felt Slayer was best for the job.

Eventually, this harrowing experience helps Slayer find his niche in his own business, Slayer's EnterSurPrises.

The mob uses Slayer's services to entertain child molesters, rapists, and rats.

He prefers two types of torture. The more attractive receive Slayer's slayer-sized slayer, filling their doo-doo dungeon to the max.

His preference is the pear of anguish, a medieval torture device. Turning the key to this utensil opens four pear-shaped metal leaves decorated with sharp protrusions that shred as the device tears and splits human orifices wide open.

Joe drags Mofo Mickey's mom center stage, placing Mofo and Red as her audience.

Suddenly, a hatchet floats slowly through the air. Sparks fly as the hatchet glides itself across Joe's grinding wheel.

Slayer 'bout dumped his dirty dumplings.

SLAYER COO-COO:

Woah, hold on, Joe! Our agreement ain't say nuthin' 'bout no axe floatin' shit now.

JOE:

We believe an eye for an eye 'round here. We call that instrument a hatchet. You don't want Jo-Ken to miss the show, do ya? He's the reason I hired ya.

Jo-Ken! Say hello to your new friend.

JO-KEN:

Hello, Slayer Coo Coo. *chuckles* I'm expecting a fabulous performance.

SLAYER COO-COO:

And I'm expecting me a strong muthafuckin' drank.

Joe pours three triple-bangers. The three glasses collide.

Slayer's hand is trembling.

SLAYER COO-COO:

Cheers... I think.

The three tip their glasses. Slayer's and Joe's drink hit their bellies; Jo-Ken's hits the floor.

JOE:

Happens every time. *laughs*

Joe bends to Mofo Mickey.

JOE:

I believe in formality. Trust me, the pleasure's all mine. We met once in my parents' front room and again in the parking lot.

Mickey Matos, I'm Joe Turner.

Joe turns to Slayer.

JOE:

Mofo's the scum who believed he got away with raping my mother.

Joe grabs Red by the hair.

JOE:

And this must be Red Matos. He believed he got away with hatcheting Jo-Ken.

Their brother Tom Matos is slurping grape juice from the grave.

Joe turns himself to Mama Matos.

JOE:

I'm not sure how Stevie Snitchie Snatchie rustled this one - it's a secret.

SLAYER COO-COO:

If it's a secret, then it's got be Secret Asian Man. That fella's good wit a camera.

JOE:

What's your name, ma'am?

Mama Matos spits at Joe. Joe pulls his knife, cutting her long black Italian hair, stuffing her mouth full.

The hatchet floats in front of the Matos boys.

JOE:

The guy you can't see is Jo-Ken. Say hello, Jo-Ken.

JO-KEN:

I'm not here to split hairs... maybe chop a few Red Matos. I hear they're real good with mobster tail. *laughs*

Slayer is keeping his eyes on the suspended hatchet.

SLAYER COO-COO:

I do my best, Joe. I ain't git paid by no hours. Let's git rollin'.

Slayer addresses Mama Matos.

SLAYER COO-COO:

You disrespected my boss! Yo' name!

Slayer removes his belt, swinging his large steel belt buckle.

SLAYER COO-COO:

Yo' name!

Mama Matos won't answer. Slayer violently beats her.

MAMA MATOS:

pained screams

Red can't stand the sight of his mother's torment.

RED MATOS:

Cherry!

SLAYER COO-COO:

I should uh known. We got us a fuckin' tomato garden. What's the husband's name, Roma? Gonna make some good sauce, Joe.

Ironically, her husband's name is Roma.

Slayer Coo Coo drops his trousers; he hangs a record holder.

Slayer performs like a jackhammer, sodomizing Cherry. Slayer, the sadist, enjoys Cherry's screams.

He reserves his fountain of love exclusively for her two adorable children, covering Mama's crybaby boys with his joy juice.

MOFO MICKEY:

NOOOOO! RED!

Joe can't handle Mofo Mickey's loud, threatening mouth. He figures the pear of anguish might calm him a bit.

Joe shoves the apparatus to the back of Mofo Mickey's throat, turning the key, splitting his cheeks, and breaking his jaw.

Red keeps his mouth shut.

Slayer Coo Coo slowly carves Cherry's back with a scalpel giving access to her ribs which he breaks upward, giving the illusion of wings.

MAMA MATOS:

horrific screams

SLAYER COO-COO:

Look! I turned Mama into a birdie. Spread yo' tiny wings and fly away - aww fuck me into a gallop, I plumb forgot, turkeys can't fly.

The Matos boys refuse to watch Mama Matos take her torture.

SLAYER COO-COO:

Joe paid big money fo' them seats y'all's sittin' in. I'm a comedian; y'all supposed to be laughin'. At least give the man common courtesy and watch my muthafuckin' show!

Joe wants his money's worth.

JOE:

Like I commented earlier - eye for an eye. Either one of you close your eyes again, and I'll pluck your mom's eye and pay Slayer Coo-Coo to skull-fuck her brains out - pop her cherry.

You'd like that, huh, Red.

For the final blow, Slayer pulls Cherry's lungs through her back, draping them over her ribbed wings. The rotten Matos watch their mother's lungs expand their last pocket of air.

Slayer plugs Mofo Mickey's poop canal with the pear of anguish, expanding the device to full capacity.

Joe can't handle Mofo Mickey's screams. He grabs his staple gun, stapling Mofo Mickey's broken jaw shut.

SLAYER COO-COO:

Which one a y'all wanna go next? Any volunteers up in da house?

Jo-Ken floats the hatchet near Slayer.

JO-KEN:

Red does. He belongs to me.

136

SLAYER COO-COO:

You got no argument comin' from me fo' sho'! Hell no! I ain't never not seen any shit like dis befo'.

Jo-Ken teases Red with power blows but doesn't strike. The mental torture sends Red over the edge; he jerks and screams for death.

Slayer hangs Red from the rafters.

Joe takes Red's iconic brass knuckle belt buckle and beats Red in the kidneys, then allows Jo-Ken some pleasure.

Slayer Coo Coo had believed he'd seen and done it all. But an invisible man beating a man with brass knuckles tops all he's never not seen.

After a few broken ribs and some nasty knocks to Red's kneecaps, Jo-Ken puts the hair-splitting hatchet to work. Lingchi... death by a thousand cuts.

Joe follows, closing the wounds with a butane torch, making sure Stevie Snitchie Snatchie gets her money's worth.

SLAYER COO-COO:

Hold on, fellas. Before dis one crosses da otha' side - it's time to add the meatballs.

Slayer rips the staples from Mofo Mickey's mouth.

He slices Red's bean bag open and removes Red's chandeliers, stuffing them into Mofo Mickey's mouth.

MOFO MICKEY:

gags and chokes

Joe fires the butane torch and burns Red's bald-headed yogurt slinger from his body. Red slowly bleeds out.

Slayer saves the best for last.

SLAYER COO-COO:

Aww, Mofo Mickey, the rapist. My specialty.

Red's meatballs spicy enough fo' ya? Wait till ya try my Matos sauce recipe. Even yo' Italian ass be impressed.

MOFO MICKEY:

gags

SLAYER COO-COO:

What? Ya like a little mo' seasonin'? Fresh pepper comin' yo' way.

Slayer removes the pear of anguish from Mofo Mickey's anus, leaving him a canyon-sized gaping hole. He continues by filling Mickey's gash full of hot pepper flakes. Mickey can't scream; the pain is too excruciating.

SLAYER COO-COO:

Whew! Dat's a hot tamale!

Damn Mickey, by the look on yo' face, I overdone my favorite recipe. I swore the recipe called for that entire bottle of them red pepper flakes. Let me take some out.

MOFO MICKEY:

You fuckin' nigga!

Slayer grins, wondering why it took so long for the stereotypical racism to come forth.

SLAYER COO-COO:

Name callin' leads me to believe yo' beggin' to die. I'm nobody's boy. I'm just gonna allow them peppers to simmer a bit mo' time.

Slayer slides a metal opera glove comfortably to his elbow.

SLAYER COO-COO:

Ti strapperò le viscere.

Didn't know you's talking to an educated nigga, now did ya?

MOFO MICKEY:

VAFFANCULO!

JOE:

What's all this mean? Speak English in my house.

SLAYER COO-COO:

I'm sorry, Mr. Turner. I use colored slang due to the fact people of ghostly pigment expect a large colored man such as myself not to have a formal education. Let alone speak four foreign languages fluently. They expect ignorance, if I may. My survival does not depend on this fool's game. I inherited my family's riches. I'm a wealthy man of color. I play for the sport of it.

Joe doesn't know if he's angry or impressed.

JOE:

I'm the one sorry for underestimating your nature and your mind.

What did you say to him?

SLAYER COO-COO:

"I'm going to rip your guts inside out." And if I understood him properly, "fuck you!" Which is exactly what I'm about to do.

The metal opera glove contains sharp flesh-tearing studs, Slayer's very own fascinating torture innovation.

He inserts his arm inside Mofo Mickey's rectum using an excruciating twisting motion. Once he's up to his elbow in anus, he grabs what innards he can grasp.

SLAYER COO-COO:

La vita è una cagna!

Unhurriedly, Slayer turns "No-Mo" Mickey inside out. He calmly removes his glove and gives Joe a look of pride and accomplishment.

SLAYER COO-COO:

Just in case you were wonderin', Mr. Turner. I'm confident of your thought. "Ain't life a bitch!"

ACT TWO

Twenty Years Later...

CHAPTER SIXTEEN

Second Generation

Twenty years have passed, and the scars from the infamous riot show no signs of healing.

The Great Divide forced U.S. Dynamite to branch to both sides of the river, filling the company's needed labor pool. This gave the Rats side funds to develop their own schools, shops, and even their own bank. Independent of the world, proud, you might say.

The towns of Seven Mile are famous nationwide for the ugly rivalry between the Seven Mile High School Blue Cats and the Seven Mile High School River Rats. Crossing the Seven Mile Bridge means death except for the one day a year the two teams meet on the football field.

Chester Miller, Jerry Turner, Sam Spicer, Frank Thomas, Brett Michaels, and Greg Fowler all have senior high children of their own.

Joe Turner has distanced himself from Seven Mile and is rarely and only ever seen floating cargo up and down the river.

One week from now, the Blue Cats and the River Rats face each other for a shot at the state title. To the parents, losing is not an option.

The possessed parents of Seven Mile live vicariously through their children's success on the field. Win, or suffer mental and physical torment.

CHAPTER SEVENTEEN

Are You Insane?

Jerry Turner's son, Austin, nicknamed Preacher, longs to see the town reunite. He dreams of someday building a church and preaching the gospel of his Lord and Savior, Jesus Christ.

Brandon Michaels, the school genius, became the Blue Cats water boy after a football injury, leaving his right arm paralyzed. His sister Jackie and he suffer serious evil abuse from their despicable parents, Brett and Sunny.

Brandon and Austin are hanging in Austin's basement, their weekend tradition.

AUSTIN TURNER:

Hey Brandon, do you suppose the River Rats get abused as much as we do?

BRANDON MICHAELS:

Yep! Sure do.

AUSTIN:

I don't know. I can't imagine it's as bad across the river. Do you suppose they live in fear like we do?

BRANDON:

Yep! Sure do. Come on, Austin, if our parents are devils, so are theirs. They're just as abused and scared as we are.

AUSTIN:

So many students have lost their lives - nobody cares. We've got to end the abuse before someone else dies.

BRANDON:

Yep, sure do. I guarantee someone will die after the game Friday night. They always do.

Brandon points a phone book at Austin.

AUSTIN:

I know the look, Mr. Brainiac smarty pants. What do you want from me?

BRANDON:

Remember when we played the River Rats last year?

AUSTIN:

I'll never forget that game. I missed one tackle. My drunken dad woke me with a razor strap, beating me black and blue, while he and mom tee-tee-tee'd, whatever that means. I wet myself.

BRANDON:

Tee-tee-tee? My devil parents make the exact, crazy, scary noise every time Jackie and I get tortured.

Hey! I'm just the waterboy. Because the Blue Cats lost that game, Jackie and I were drugged, woke up stripped with our hands tied with tube socks, and choked with mom's silk scarves while getting scalded with boiling water. The same torture they handed us when we were babies.

Jackie and I saw the devil for sure that night.

AUSTIN:

Man, we've got to come up with something! Anything! You got any ideas, Brainiac?

BRANDON:

I remember hearing the field sports announcer, "tackle by number thirty-two, Lucas Spicer," so many times I've never forgotten his name.

AUSTIN:

Yeah, he's a mean linebacker for sure. But, so what? He plays for the Rats. How's that gonna help us?

BRANDON:

I noticed he's missing a finger. Let's just say abuse caused the missing finger. He might be our guy.

AUSTIN:

Come on, man, I don't need the labor pains. Give me the baby already!

BRANDON:

Look up "Spicer." I heard my dad mention Lucas's dad. What was his freaking name?

Dad said he likes to cut things. S - S. That's how I remember things. Sam Slicer. That's it! Look up "Sam Spicer." Maybe he's his dad. Let's give Lucas a call.

AUSTIN:

Are you insane?! Call a Rat?! No way! That boiling water couldn't melt a bag of ice compared to the pain our parents would inflict on us for such an act. No way, you go ahead!

BRANDON:

How bad do you want it, Austin?

Austin finds the number just to appease his friend.

AUSTIN:

Sam Spicer, right here, now what?

Brandon raises his eyebrows, triggering Austin to dial the phone.

ring

AUSTIN:

hangs up I can't do it. I'm too scared!

BRANDON:

That's cool, hand me the phone.

AUSTIN:

Okay, one more try. I'm not hanging up this time.

ring

ring

ring

ring

ring

ring

ring

AUSTIN:

No one's home.

LUCAS SPICER:

picks up Spicer residence, Lucas speaking.

AUSTIN:

Lucas, don't hang up! I need to talk to you.

LUCAS:

Who is this?

AUSTIN:

Austin Turner. I play football for the Blue Cats.

Lucas's eyes expand. Though his dad's not home, he nervously looks around the room for him.

LUCAS:

I know the name. Why did you call here? Are you insane, or just have a death wish?

AUSTIN:

I guess I am. We really need your help. We're getting murdered over here.

LUCAS:

Oh, sweet Jesus, so are we.

AUSTIN:

Now you're speaking my language.

Lucas never knows when Sam might show. He locks the front door.

AUSTIN:

Every game we lose, someone dies over here. We've got to come together. The next beating may be our last if you catch my drift.

BRANDON:

Did you say that? Did you really say that?

LUCAS:

We get caught crossing that bridge - we'll drift all right. Do you have a plan?

Brandon nods his head yes. Austin does a double-take.

AUSTIN:

Uh - yes - we do.

Austin's not sure why he said that, knowing there's no plan.

LUCAS:

Go to the foot of the bridge Monday morning at seven, before school. My dog Tippy Toes will retrieve the plan. I'm in, but please never call here again; my dad owns a body bag. Don't get caught!

hangs up

AUSTIN:

Well, what's next, Brainiac?

BRANDON:

I gave you the connection. It's your turn, and it better be dang good.

Austin is disappointed with Brandon's answer.

BRANDON:

Come on! Of course I have a plan. *draws a circle* There's your plan! I'll see ya Monday at school.

AUSTIN:

Wait! That's it?! A stupid circle?!

BRANDON:

Yep! I'm sure that's all you'll need.

AUSTIN:

Well, thanks, buddy, for nothin'.

After praying, Austin paces the floor. He continuously peers at Brandon's circle and places a pen to the paper, closing his eyes.

The pen glides across the page.

Austin has received his plan and is ready to obey.

Monday arrives.

Tippy Toes, a large jaw flapping pit-bull, approaches the Cats side of the bridge. Austin places his plan in Tippy Toes' mouth. She sprints the plan to Lucas.

Lucas spreads the news to the River Rats student body. Austin does the same for the Blue Cats. Everyone's sworn to secrecy.

CHAPTER EIGHTEEN

Holy Firewater

Several Blue Cat students meet Austin on the street corner before school each morning to hear him talk about his friend Jesus in secret. This particular morning, he's rudely interrupted by teammate Rusty Miller, Chester Miller's boy.

RUSTY MILLER:

Hey, Preacher! Sprinkle some holy firewater on me so I can pass my science test and remain eligible.

BRANDON:

Like being eligible matters to this school. You can run with a football - everyone knows you're the town's golden boy, Miller.

Austin blows his words off; Rusty's soul is his concern.

AUSTIN:

Faith without works is dead faith, Rusty. You need to pray and believe. You don't need water. Just believe. Can I pray with you?

RUSTY:

There's one thing I believe for sure, Turner.

AUSTIN:

What's that, Rusty?

RUSTY:

You're full of shit!

school bell rings Don't make these fine people late for class because of your sewage. Remember, the cat's still in the bag - at least for now.

The two teammates exchange fierce looks as Rusty threatens Austin's plan.

The Cats are having their last practice before the big game against the River Rats. Rusty keeps tensions high as Coach Holland rides his players.

COACH HOLLAND:

Run the same play! Tincher, ya gotta block! Miller can't score unless you do your job! Let's go!

Rusty steps to the line, pointing a threatening finger at Austin.

RUSTY:

Hey, Preacher! The devil's getting the ball, and it's on fire. I'm gonna run it right down your throat!

Austin ignores Miller's threat and takes his position.

COACH HOLLAND:

Last play! Let's go! Make it real!

Rusty runs the ball directly at Austin.

Austin pile drives Rusty, slamming him to the ground, looking directly into his eyes.

AUSTIN:

There's that holy firewater you asked for this morning! Fire's out!

The two throw punches. Coach Holland steps in.

COACH HOLLAND:

Break it up! You're on the same team - act like it! Anger loses games! Focus, Miller! This entire town is counting on you two tomorrow night.

Get dressed, team!

Not another word from either of you two! Got me?

The team meets on the gym bleachers. Coach Holland gives his annual cautionary speech.

COACH HOLLAND:

All right, gang, settle down.

There're three things the Cats and Rats have in common. One, they manufacture dynamite. Two, they love football. Three, they hate each other. Twenty years of heated competition - ten wins for us, ten wins for them.

You must win to protect the innocent on this side of the river.

The players glance at one another because of Coach Holland's slip of the tongue.

COACH HOLLAND:

Sorry, guys. I didn't mean to say that. Do any of you know why I wear this glass eye?

Rusty's heard this story too many times. He loves pushing Coach Holland's buttons.

RUSTY:

Come on, coach. You're just changing the subject. Too afraid to say we're all in danger. We all know why you wear a glass eye.

Bryan, the new kid, sitting next to Rusty, wonders what happened to Coach Holland's eye.

RUSTY:

Come on, Bryan. Coach don't wanna relive that. He just doesn't want to tell us we're gonna die.

Rusty punches Bryan in the leg, not wanting to hear the story.

COACH HOLLAND:

That's enough, Miller. I asked. It's only fair I answer.

Ten years ago, I played for the Blue Cats. We headed over the dreaded Seven Mile Bridge to take on the Rats. The bus got bombarded by rocks. One flew through the window and caught my right eye.

Listen, we know we're headed into dangerous territory. I'm here to teach football, not put your life in danger. I will excuse your absence if you opt out. Those of you willing to take part, you're to put your helmets on and place your head between your legs once we come to the bridge. Got it?

PLAYERS:

Yes, sir!

COACH HOLLAND:

Does anyone have questions?

Austin raises his hand.

AUSTIN:

Just one, Coach, may I lead the team in a word of prayer before we leave?

COACH HOLLAND:

Don't see why not.

Rusty observes his teammates all with bowed heads. Shame fills his heart.

Austin concludes his prayer.

Rusty runs down the bleachers to catch Austin before he leaves.

RUSTY:

Hey, Preacher. Coach is right. We're on the same team.

They shake.

CHAPTER NINETEEN

Big Mouth Drunk

Across the river, the Rats finish their last practice before the big game.

Lucas enters his front door. He's trampled by the smell of alcohol and fears his dad's usual drunken behavior.

SAM:

Howuz pwactice, Lucas?

Lucas is not fond of his abusive, obnoxious dad. He knows in his heart Sam's responsible for the absence of his mother. Sam has indicated his mom died when he was a baby. He doesn't believe Sam, but it's a subject he dares not touch.

LUCAS:

It's good, Dad. Good girl, Tippy Toes.

Lucas engages his dog, trying to avoid conversation.

SAM:

You're gonna be a Jet boy. Be a Jet just like your old man was.

LUCAS:

Yeah, a Jet who never saw one play.

SAM:

The fuck you say, boy? You might think I'm a fool, but you can learn a lot more from a fool than you can a clever man.

Sam grabs Lucas's arm as he tries to escape to his bedroom.

LUCAS:

Yep, a New York Jet, just like my daddy was.

In the corner, three pit bull puppies in a box have been driving Sam crazy.

SAM:

Didn't I tell you to get rid of those damn whining-ass pups? Where the fuck you get them dogs anyway?

Lucas knows his dad is not fond of animals. He fears for the pups.

LUCAS:

Someone dumped 'em at the river! I will this weekend, I promise.

SAM:

If you don't this time, I'm gonna feed the current.

Shut the fuck up, ya stupid hounds!

puppies whimper

LUCAS:

I got studies, Dad. I'm going to get some rest for the game.

SAM:

Yeah, boy, get some rest. And you better not embarrass me tomorrow night, ya hear? This game's gonna play on the radio and on cable tv.

Sam pours two shots of whiskey. He raises the shots to Lucas.

SAM:

Come on, have a little early celebration shot with your old man before you whoop some bottom feeders' ass tomorrow night, huh?!

That's exactly what Lucas tried to free himself from.

Because Sam can't let go of his past, he's a demon alcoholic, and Lucas despises him for it. The more Sam drinks, the more abusive he becomes.

LUCAS:

Come on, Dad, please! I gotta stay sharp.

SAM:

Boy, don't make me shove it down your nuckin' feck! Drink it! Cryin' outhouse! Can't a man get any repect?

Lucas shoots the shot, makes his typical whiskey face, and heads to his bedroom with Tippy Toes.

CHAPTER TWENTY

Shattered Dreams

It's a tradition for the demon parents on both sides of the river to start their perpetual gameday partying the day before the Rats and Cats meet.

The Turner family is having dinner. Austin's parents dream of watching him play professional football. Austin has other dreams.

Jerry, and wife Sandy, have indulged in a few shots before Austin came home from practice.

Austin sits at the table. He gives thanks to God for his blessing. Normally, this brings an uproar from his demon parents, hissing and such, making a mockery of Austin's beliefs. However, tonight, they stay calm to persuade Austin to follow their dream.

JERRY:

You know, tomorrow is one of the biggest games of your life, Austin.

AUSTIN:

Bigger than you know, Dad. Bigger than anyone knows.

Austin normally carries strong rebuttal towards conversations concerning football. His mild response leads Jerry to believe he's getting through.

JERRY:

Oh my, do we have a change of heart this evening?

AUSTIN:

Come on, Dad, we're not going through this again, are we? Please?

JERRY:

Son, there'll be scouts from all over the country around the field tomorrow night, and they're comin' to watch you. Please act interested. Or how 'bout this? Respect the time and listen to what they have to say.

AUSTIN:

Please, Dad, I've told you, I'm going to seminary school. This town needs a church, not another football player.

The demon parents get fueled just hearing the word church.

Jerry pours another drink.

JERRY:

Church, huh?! We tried that at the Russian River Cove, remember?!

AUSTIN:

How can I remember? I wasn't even born.

JERRY:

Church killed your Grandpa Ken, and your Uncle Jack was missin' for a long time. We're lucky they didn't kill him too. Is that what you wanna be? Huh, is it? A phony preacher gettin' people killed. Well, is it?!

AUSTIN:

I'm a child of God! He's a devil, like my parents!

Jerry clinches his fist and pushes away from the table, shattering his whiskey glass into the kitchen cabinets.

He grabs Austin, leaning him back in his chair.

JERRY:

You better get this Jesus thing out of your head before I beat it out of you. You will play football! Do you hear me? HUH?! DO YOU?!

SANDY TURNER:

Ohh, Jerry, why don't you slap him around like the dog he is?

Jerry slaps Austin's face. Austin turns the other cheek.

JERRY:

Arrrggghhhh!

Jerry doesn't strike again and slowly sets Austin back into position.

SANDY:

We only want what's best for ya, Austin.

We don't want ya endin' up like your loser Uncle Joe - livin' alone, driving a semi, floatin' a stupid boat up and down the smelly ol' river. Football is best for ya.

AUSTIN:

You're both always too drunk to know what's best for me! I love my Uncle Joe!

SANDY:

Eeeeeyaaah! Don't ya ever say that name again!

Sandy squeals like a pig just from the mention of Joe's name.

Jerry grabs Austin by the throat, grinding his teeth.

JERRY:

You don't even know your Uncle Joe. What do you mean you love your Uncle Joe? That loser set me up. I almost died because of that bastard. Don't mention his name in my house ever again!

The idiot believes our dad lives inside of him. He's a known killer, and I better not catch you around him!

Austin escapes Jerry's grip.

AUSTIN:

I will win the game for you tomorrow night. You and this Satan-bound town - that's a promise. But I will never play pro football. You're living shattered dreams. Remember what I said. The game tomorrow night's bigger than you know.

Austin walks to his bedroom.

Jerry breaks his dinner plate on the floor.

JERRY:

Arrrggghhhh! Son, there will be consequences!

CHAPTER TWENTY-ONE

The War Zone

It's game night.

The Blue Cats load onto the bus. A long line of Cats fans follows closely to do what no one dares but once a year - cross the Seven Mile Bridge. Tension is high, and violence is expected once the bus crosses.

Coach Holland tries not to show the team his nerves as the bus comes to a stop in the middle of the bridge.

COACH HOLLAND:

This is it! We're entering the war zone. Helmets on and heads between your legs.

The players put on their helmets.

The bus driver's wearing a catcher's chest protector; he puts on a motorcycle helmet with a full-face shield.

Coach Holland stands at the bottom of the bus entrance steps protecting himself with an arm shield pulled to his nose, keeping a sharp eye, expecting an ambush.

COACH HOLLAND:

Stay put until I say!

Coach slowly lowers his shield as the bus stops at the end of the bridge.

COACH HOLLAND:

What in the hell is going on?

The bus rolls slowly off the end of the bridge.

The team raises their bodies and removes their helmets. They are astonished by banners planted on the right side of the road. The friendly vinyls flash happy Rats smiling and hugging blue catfish with red hearts that read, "Welcome Blue Cats," "You are home," "Good Luck!"

The last banner reads, "Friends," with kiss lips.

Dumbfounded, the fans following become skeptical. They sneer at the Rats' kindness.

Brandon taps Austin's leg with the back of his hand. They grin.

Rusty Miller is sitting across the aisle, smiling, shaking his head.

The team is moved by the Rats' secret yet expected, elaborate greeting.

CHAPTER TWENTY-TWO

Fondue Gambled

Decked out in their team's apparel, the parents chant, striving to raise their volume louder than their opponent.

The students are dressed in everyday wear, embarrassed by their parents' silly actions. They feel sorrow for the players, knowing the abuse the losing team will suffer from their stoned, evil parents.

Pregame warm-ups end, and both teams move to the sidelines.

The River Rats Marching Band enters the field. The students rise, cheering louder than the evil parents beside them.

The Rats students' genuine pride lies in the school's marching band. They hold the Bands of America National Championship title three years running.

Band is foolish to the parents. They couldn't care less. Uppers, downers, and the flasks secretly tucked on their person bring these demon-stricken parents bliss, but nothing compares to their top priority...winning a Seven Mile high school football game against the Blue Cats.

The percussion brings it, slapping a cadence on the rims of their drums.

The parents go silent, angry that the students are cheering for the band. The students' expressions of joy are highly impermissible unless pertaining to the football team.

The members of the Rats Marching Band differ none from the players on the field; they have grown tired of their parents' demonic torment.

Tonight, fear has no hold.

Fondue Gamble, the Rats Marching Band drum major, has concocted a plan of her own to surprise the inconsiderate, intoxicated, demon parents. Motionless as a statue, the band members stare into their repulsive, pathetic parents' eyes.

The band continues their silent performance, bringing their impatient parents to a boil.

RATS FAN 1:

You gonna play?! Or you just gonna stand there?! Play the school fucking fight song or something! And whoever hung them banners is gonna get butt-fucked!

The band purposely ignores the parents' insisting requests. The students have become immune to such actions and language, even though they know plenty of them will receive such torture.

The Field Announcer senses the tension and takes to the mic.

FIELD ANNOUNCER:

Fondue Gamble, three-time national champ drum major, will lead the Seven Mile River Rats in tonight's band performance titled, "Dark Days Will Come."

Hmm...interesting...

Fondue's plan to delay the game tortures the parents. They go insane while the students secretly gloat.

RATS FAN 2:

Your day's about to end! Play or get off the field!

Fondue and company have enjoyed their little stint. She motions horns up and tosses her baton over her shoulder, high into the air, landing it deep into the impatient crowd.

The whiskey-wasted parents shriek from her outlandish maneuver.

Fondue knows the repercussions from her possessed parents will be devastating, so she completely lets loose, savoring the performance of her life...or possibly her death.

The championship band plays like they have never played before. Their renowned perfect pitch and timing is replaced with horrific screeches and off-tempo percussion. The cacophony of sound is all part of Fondue's masterful plan to bring the band their well-deserved attention, even if it's not the desired type.

The students laugh hard inside but don't dare show any emotion.

The vindictive Fondue turns to face the flabbergasted crowd. She enjoys watching them cram their fingers deep inside their ears to block the horrible screeches. Their squished faces indicate her plan is going well as the band roams the field recklessly out of line.

Smiling from ear to ear, Fondue conducts the band's horrible squeals ever so elegantly while gracefully flying two angry birds directly into the parents' stunned faces. This is the first time these rotten parents have ever shown interest in the band's performance.

Much to the parents' delight, the horrendous performance finally ends.

The band stands in disarray.

RATS FAN 3:

Woo! Great devil in Hell! Call da doctor. My ears, they won't stop bleedin'.

The band collects themselves and marches in perfect unison towards the Cats side of the field, crossing enemy lines. The band gives a warm, unexpected, smiling, cheerful wave intended only for the students.

181

The Cats adults hiss and cuss at them, while the Cats students risk it all and wave back.

RADIO ANNOUNCER:

Please stand and remove your hats for the playing of our National Anthem.

drum roll

CHAPTER TWENTY-THREE

Circle of Love

The Anthem ends.

The students give a standing ovation to Fondue's outstanding performance. The parents stare, astonished as the band dances perfectly in step to the percussion's exiting cadence.

Intrigued and confused, the Radio Announcer handles the mic.

RADIO ANNOUNCER:

Captains Rusty Miller and Austin Turner for the Blue Cats, along with Lucas Spicer and Scotty Thomas for the River Rats, take center field for the coin toss.

The four captains gaze into one another's eyes, waiting for someone to speak. Austin leans in.

AUSTIN TURNER:

You guys read the plan. Guys, are we sure we want to go through with this?

SCOTTY THOMAS:

Does a cat have a climbing gear?

AUSTIN:

And Lucas?

LUCAS:

Let's do this.

The other three captains are worried. Will Rusty carry out the plan?

AUSTIN:

What about you, Rusty?

RUSTY:

I'm all in.

Austin smiles, but he is still not confident that Rusty is trustworthy.

Meanwhile, two students, one from each side of the river, climb the ladder into the announcer's box. The radio announcer is uneasy with the students joining him in the box but continues with his job.

RADIO ANNOUNCER:

The River Rats won the toss but have deferred. These two teams, known across the country for being the biggest rivals in high school football, have shown remarkable sportsmanship here tonight.

The two teams are set for kick-off. The adults in the crowd howl, waiting for the ball to fly.

RADIO ANNOUNCER:

Chandler Fowler, number six, will boot for the Rats this evening. The return man, Rusty Miller, number thirty-two, rests deep for the Cats.

Greg Fowler is his normal, loud, drunken, obnoxious self.

GREG:

That's my boy! That's my motherfuckin' boy kickin' the ball! Man! Wooo!

RADIO ANNOUNCER:

We're underway! Fowler sends it deep. It's a dandy! Miller fields the leather on his own one-yard line!

Austin's plan goes into action.

Rusty places the ball on the ground. His team forms a straight line. The Rats form another straight line. Both teams take hands and approach the center of the field.

crowd boos

RADIO ANNOUNCER:

I do not understand what's taking place. No one's carrying the ball, and both teams appear to be marching towards each other. This is absolutely one of the strangest things I've seen in my twenty-year announcing career.

The two teams meet on the fifty-yard line and form a circle. The players on the sidelines take a knee.

Holly Thomas, Frank and Mary Jo's daughter and Scotty's sister, is one of the students who climbed into the announcer's box.

HOLLY THOMAS:

Good evening, I'm Holly Thomas, class president for the Seven Mile River Rats.

DONNIE LEWIS:

And I'm Donnie Lewis, senior class president of the Seven Mile Blue Cats.

For twenty years, the town of Seven Mile has suffered division. Divided by a game called football.

HOLLY:

As parents and adults, you've shown us, your children, how not to act.

Frank and Mary Jo rage in anger from embarrassment.

DONNIE:

Your drunkenness and beatings we've received because of this sport need to stop tonight before another life is lost.

HOLLY:

We have all agreed to forgive and forget.

The parents get surprised by Holly's words. We have all agreed?!

The parents recognize students broke the cardinal rule. Death to those who converse with anyone from across the river. Demonic moaning and grumbling comes forth from the devils in the bleachers.

HOLLY:

We have all agreed to forgive and forget, but you will need to do the same. You've come to see what you live for - a football game.

DONNIE:

We're here to tell you - until one adult from each of the stands meets in the circle of love and shakes hands, we will stand firm on our protest. There will not be a football game this evening.

Evil fills the air. Donnie wishes he had not given his name. Donnie's Dad doesn't approve of his son's lecture.

DONNIE'S DAD:

Trust me! You won't be standing when I get a hold of ya! Don't dare come home! I'm gonna murder your traitor punk ass!

The crowd won't cave.

ANGRY FAN:

I'm not joining shit! You better get your asses playing ball!
Circle these, bitches!

The Angry Fan grabs his crotch and tosses his drink.

HOLLY:

Please. Please. We beg you. This is a time of peace - a new dawn.
A time to put aside your differences and reunite Seven Mile.

*Austin takes to his knees. Both teams go to their knees, following
their leader.*

*The fans hiss and growl from Austin's audacity. They crave the
sound of hitting pads.*

An Angry Rats Fan pushes his way through the crowd.

ANGRY RATS FAN:

Oh hell, I'll go. But I'm bringin' my drink with me. Get the fuck
out of the way. I came to see a fuckin' football game - this shit!

A Callous Cats Fan makes his move as well.

CALLOUS CATS FAN:

Let's jus' - let's just get this over with!

The students and players clap, watching the fans make their way.

The two fans meet in the circle of love and shake hands. Both wipe their hands in disgust and head back to their seats.

The students continue clapping.

HOLLY:

On behalf of the River Rats student body -

DONNIE:

And the Blue Cats student body -

HOLLY AND DONNIE:

We thank you!

Knowing their courage will bring trouble and a war like no other, the two teams decide to appease the devils and continue the game for everyone's safety.

CHAPTER TWENTY-FOUR

Poop Hits the Fans

Water boy, Brandon Michaels, hobbles around the Cats sideline squeezing water shots, fearing the worst for his team.

RADIO ANNOUNCER:

As if this evening's not been interesting enough, the Blue Cats called time out.

The pigskin lies on the Rats four-yard line with only two ticks remaining. The Rats lead the Cats by four - a field goal does the Cats no good. They must find a way into the end zone on this play to go to the state championship game.

CATS QUARTERBACK:

Buck gut slam twenty-two on two. Buck gut slam twenty-two on two. Break!

RADIO ANNOUNCER:

The Cats set for the snap.

Rats' Lucas Spicer has keyed on the expected Rusty Miller the entire game. I don't expect this play to go any other way.

Miller takes the handoff! Spicer meets him head-on! Miller's still on his feet! Miller crosses the line - he is in the end zone!!

The Cats have defeated the Rats twenty-six to twenty-four. The Seven Mile Blue Cats will travel to Oakland for the state title. From the great football towns of Seven Mile, I'm Eaton Beaver. Drive safe. Goodnight, and God bless!

The score of the game, along with the announcer's send off, "God bless," sends the demon Rats into a frenzy, but none more than Sam Spicer. He detests the word "God."

The adult Blue Cats fans jump with joy one second and snarl from the announcer's send-off the next.

The students wear no expression. They don't even appear to know who won the game.

Sam Spicer turns his anger toward the referee.

SAM:

He was offsides ten days ago! What side of the river you from, ref? You better hope that flag's glued to your pocket, buddy! 'Cause I'm coming for your ass!

Frank Thomas joins the fracas.

FRANK:

You're blind as a blindfolded bat! Twenty-two held the entire play, you lousy no good sandy beaches!

Frank attempts to hold Mary Jo back.

MARY JO THOMAS:

You're gonna pay with your lives, you rotten mudsuckers!

The Rats fans collect bags of rat poop throughout the year for such an occasion. They sprint to the exit gate, showering the Cats fans as if they were throwing rice at a wedding.

Back on the field, both teams line up to shake hands. The players share whispers as they pass one another.

CATS AND RATS PLAYERS:

See ya tonight, spread the word.

Spread the word.

Spread the word.

See ya tonight, spread the word.

Much to Austin's surprise, Rusty is on board with the plan.

CHAPTER TWENTY-FIVE

Forbidden Bus Ride

The Cats load onto the bus.

Brandon Michaels makes his way to the back seat toting the team's ball bag. He prepares to heave his load when bright eyes capture his sight. He seats himself, being careful not to bring attention.

The Mystery Guest motions to Brandon.

FONDUE GAMBLE:

Are you going to the cove tonight?

BRANDON:

Yes, for sure.

FONDUE:

Take me with you. I can't go home until I figure something out. My parents will kill me.

BRANDON:

What's your name?

FONDUE:

Fondue Gamble.

Brandon remembers hearing her name over the loudspeakers at the game.

BRANDON:

Oh shit! You're that band girl. I'm Brandon. Okay, stay put and keep quiet. I'll take care of you.

FONDUE:

Someday I will marry you for this, I promise.

Brandon delicately places the ball bag over top of her.

The coach gives his congratulatory speech before the bus approaches the bridge.

COACH HOLLAND:

Guys, you've made your parents proud. I can't say enough about-*crash* What the fuck?!! Get down! Get down!

The coach is interrupted by thunderous sounds of breaking glass from a hailstorm of rocks pelting the side of the bus. The players assume their position.

The irate Rats parents continue insanely firing rocks.

SAM:

Stay on your side of the river before I cut your fish stick off, motherfucker!

Frank Thomas cuts a hole in the friendly catfish's mouth. He hangs his genitals through the hole, hunching the air.

FRANK:

Here's ya some bait! Suck on this, ya stanky anchovies!

Mary Jo is flying the bird with one hand and hurling rocks with the other.

MARY JO:

We're gonna kill you all! Die, you moby dick-suckers!

The bus driver grips the steering wheel, showing white knuckles, daring anyone to move into his path.

The bus hits the on-ramp of the bridge. Players fly everywhere as the driver continues with his foot on the gas.

The lingering Cats fans catch the wrath of the distraught Rats, doing whatever possible to make it back across the bridge.

CHAPTER TWENTY-SIX

Dick Twitchier with Harry Sachs

Joe Turner returns home after a late run, eager to learn the results of tonight's football game. He hits the remote, grabs a cold one, and flops inside his recliner just in time for the news.

DICK TWITCHIER:

Good evening, I'm Dick Twitchier standing live where the Battle of Seven Mile High football game took place this evening - Seven Mile's big event of the year. What makes this year bigger? The winner will face the Oakland Red Devils for the state title.

DICK TWITCHIER (CONT'D):

Though both teams gave a stellar performance, the River Rats fell short twenty-six, twenty-four - led by the Cats running back, Rusty Miller, in the last seconds, sending the Blue Cats to Oakland.

JOE:

Yes!!

Joe is happy Austin is safe.

DICK TWITCHIER:

The teams' unusual show of good sportsmanship sent the fans spiraling - not witnessed this bad since the town dividing riot took place twenty years ago.

Standing next to me is Greg Fowler, parent of Rats kicker number six, Chandler Fowler. Tell us, Greg, what does this game mean to the parents of these kids this evening?

GREG:

Well, for one thing, my boy's leg was soft. He didn't kick worth a stankin' shitty diaper. Not one kick went into the end-zone for a touch-backer. Therefore, he's got him a fuckin' beating comin'.

Greg violently jerks the mic from the broadcaster, slurring his words.

GREG:

And that little circle-jerk scene you senseless fucks displayed did nothing but bring out the devil in every one of us. You're all gonna pay! Tee, tee, tee, tee.

DICK TWITCHIER:

wrestling for the mic Let's - Let's look inside - Harry Sachs back at the station. Harry!

HARRY SACHS:

Good evening, I'm Harry Sachs at six and nine.

Other news this evening - confirmed from across the river. High school class president Donnie Lewis, representing the Seven Mile Blue Cats, was found hanging from the River Rats goalpost. Police discovered the word "TRAITOR" carved into young Lewis's back and chest area. Police also reported Lewis's right foot was found hanging from his mouth.

Lewis's parents were spotted leaving the school parking lot, when pulled over. Police found bloody objects which possibly were used in Donnie's death. When police asked if Donnie Lewis was their child, the parents responded, "we don't have any children." Police also reported when the Lewises were asked to step from their vehicle, their response was, "no Rat will ever touch me."

HARRY SACHS (CONT'D):

They were found later with gunshots to the head. Though no firearms were found, police are ruling this as a double suicide.

Filma Wang has tonight's leading story.

FILMA WANG:

Dick Champion grow large cucumber late in fall season. The ladies go crazy over Dick's omega pickle. What his secret? Miracle-uh-growin'. Dick's been growing large -

Joe hits the remote.

JOE:

It's a good thing that girl's got big sweater cows. I can't understand a word she says.

When cucumbers become a top story over a high school student's death, there's a problem. He's not the only person who'll die tonight. I better get the boat heading north.

CHAPTER TWENTY-SEVEN

Loser and the Traitor

Frank and Mary Jo are slugging whiskey while impatiently waiting to take the Rats' losing out on Scotty and Holly.

The two children make it home, hoping to find their sloshed parents passed out. Unfortunately, there's no escape. Frank badgers them before they make it through the door.

FRANK:

Well! If it ain't the loser and the traitor.

Scotty bows his head in shame.

SCOTTY:

I'm sorry we lost, Dad.

FRANK:

Sorry doesn't change the score of a football game, now does it?

What?! You and your chubby-chasin' buddies faggots now? I thought you and your tongue-to-bung teammates were gonna skip to the lou my little fuckin' darlin' the way you fairies held hands. I better not find out who's responsible for that shit. Whorely!

Frank sly eyes Holly.

Mary Jo downs a shot and wipes her mouth on her sleeve.

MARY JO:

Yeah, just what in the hell was that shit? I'm Holly Thomas, ass president, shit! Whoopdy fuckin' doo diddly doo! You in love with the Blue Cats now? Well, give the winner a brain, Johnny! Get this through your ignorant skull; we hate those smelly fr- ish. They're our renemies. And as an adult, I'll show you how I act, bitch!

Mary Jo swings the wire end of a fly swatter. Holly blocks her blow and sails it across the room.

HOLLY:

Not tonight, demon!

Normally she submits, taking the horrible abuse. Tonight's different. Mary Jo slaps her face. Holly stands her ground.

MARY JO:

Frank! Frank! Did you see what this bitch just done what to me?

Scotty barely keeps from laughing from her drunken mixture of words.

FRANK:

Since Fuck and Fucker don't give a rat's ass about the shame they've caused.

Ohhhhh, hold the fuck on! Wait a short minute! Not one of you sandy beaches are worthy enough to be called a Rat. Now we gotta drink all night to get over our disappointment. Get your losin', stinky asses to bed before I cut your head off and throw it at your dying ass.

Those were the words Scotty and Holly hoped to hear. They head to their respective bedrooms across the hall from each other.

Scotty fluffs his pillows and blankets, creating a dummy. Holly does the same.

Frank and Mary Jo continue raving in the kitchen, trying to out-drink the fish in the river.

FRANK & MARY JO:

unintelligible drunk conversation

Scotty sneaks into Holly's bedroom.

SCOTTY:

Are you - are you sure about this?

HOLLY:

I'm positive. Let's go.

They sneak out Holly's bedroom window, scurrying along a long dark path, fighting to remain on course. They run into three more students also battling their way to the river. Knowing the plan, they keep silent, slipping and sliding the steep riverbank to a small cove where other students cautiously wait.

They anxiously watch as a boat cruises slowly to the bank.

Several terrified Rats quietly board the large vessel. It slowly sets sail towards a vast bonfire across the river where Cats students excitedly wait for their arrival.

CHAPTER TWENTY-EIGHT

Bond Fire

The captain flashes the boat's security lights, alerting the Cats he's approaching.

The boat pulls to shore. Austin, Brandon, and Rusty are the front-runners helping the students from the boat.

The fire's light shows abuse on many of the Rats' faces as they make their way to introduce themselves. The last student off the boat is Lucas.

LUCAS:

You guys look different without your football helmets on. We did it, Austin. This is not a dream.

Rusty gives a warm grin, thinking from within how wonderful the gathering is and how he almost missed the magnificent occasion.

The captain is none other than Big Joe Turner. Austin and Uncle Joe hug.

AUSTIN:

Uncle Joe, I'll never forget what you've done for us.

UNCLE JOE:

You're a great kid. Remember our deal. If your dad finds out...

AUSTIN:

You can trust me, Uncle Joe.

UNCLE JOE:

I'll see you in about two hours. Have fun.

AUSTIN:

I love you, Uncle Joe.

UNCLE JOE:

I love you too, Austin.

Uncle Joe backs the boat out of the cove.

Austin turns and finds Rusty waiting for him.

RUSTY:

Who was that? I've never seen him or his boat around here.

AUSTIN:

That was my uncle, Joe. He built a cabin seven miles downstream after the riot. He hates Seven Mile and all it stands for.

RUSTY:

Oh my gosh, that's Joe Turner! My dad's Chester Miller. He brags about saving your uncle Joe's life the day of the riot.

AUSTIN:

Yeah, my dad holds Uncle Joe responsible for the riot. I'm dead meat if my parents find out he helped pull tonight off.

RUSTY:

What's your uncle do?

AUSTIN:

According to my dad, he kills people for a living.

RUSTY:

Ohhh, interesting.

AUSTIN:

Just kidding.

RUSTY:

laughs

AUSTIN:

He moves dynamite with the big boat you just saw. None of this is possible without him, for sure.

RUSTY:

Well, please thank him for me. Come on, let's mingle.

Austin is pleased that Rusty is talking to him.

As they make their way towards the fire, they run into Holly and Scotty. Rusty puts his eye on Holly right away.

RUSTY:

I'm Rusty Miller.

SCOTTY:

Scotty. Scotty Thomas.

AUSTIN:

Man, that sure was a heck of a game tonight.

SCOTTY:

Yeah, and I've got the bruises to show for it.

AUSTIN:

laughs I'm Austin Turner. They call me Preacher.

HOLLY:

So, you're the mastermind behind all of this. I'm Holly Thomas.

AUSTIN:

Lucas Spicer and I had a lot of help.

HOLLY:

I'd like to thank them.

RUSTY:

I believe he's referring to his friend, Jesus. That's why we call him Preacher.

HOLLY:

Jesus?

RUSTY:

Yeah...God?!

Austin is very impressed. Rusty knows Jesus is God?!

HOLLY:

Imagine a church in this town.

AUSTIN:

Holly, I promise, one day, Seven Mile will have a church. Or I'm not Austin Preacher Turner.

Holly glances at Rusty.

HOLLY:

We live right across the river, and yet we've never met. How can that be? Imagine if we came together.

RUSTY:

Imagine the football team we'd have.

Rusty laughs at his own joke. Holly smiles.

HOLLY:

I will own an ice cream parlor and grow sunflowers and daisies here someday - ice cream full of wild berries.

SCOTTY:

The Holly Berries Ice Cream Shop.

214

RUSTY:

Sounds famous. I like the Daisy Duke part.

Rusty makes an advance on Holly.

RUSTY:

It's nippy. You can wear my flannel.

Holly smiles, looking to Austin, trying not to be obviously interested in Rusty.

HOLLY:

Preacher, tell me about your friend Jesus.

AUSTIN:

You know - the boat'll return in a couple of hours, and judging by what I'm seeing and hearing, that'll come pretty quick. You'll know Jesus before the boat arrives. Come on, guys, let's leave those two mudpuppies alone.

Holly blushes.

HOLLY:

Wow, I'm embarrassed. Am I that transparent?

Rusty offers his hand.

RUSTY:

Do you need a dance partner?

HOLLY:

I've never danced.

RUSTY:

Neither have I.

HOLLY:

There's no music.

RUSTY:

Hey! Let the crickets make the music. Maestro Cricket! Strike up the band.

Holly's nerves shoot through the roof, but she's not about to resist her invitation.

They awkwardly hold one another.

RUSTY:

Do you live on the river?

HOLLY:

Right across the way.

RUSTY:

I've never been on that side of the river, except to play football.

HOLLY:

None of us have. If my parents even suspected where I am, they'd literally beat Scotty and me to death.

RUSTY:

We've all taken our share of beatings. I presume the only thing keeping us from war is the river.

HOLLY:

The only thing keeping us AT war is the river... and football.

Holly cozies to Rusty.

Frank is standing on his back porch glaring at the bonfire.

Mary Jo finds Frank holding the porch rail, keeping his balance with one hand and steadying his glass of whiskey in the other. His anger grows with each flicker of the flame.

MARY JO:

Whatta you lookin' at, Frank?

FRANK:

I'm looking at those Blue Cats celebratin' they shitty cheating celebration. That's what I'm looking at, woman!

MARY JO:

Let's go to bed, Frank. I'm drunk.

Frank ignores her - he is seeing red.

FRANK:

I don't get it - I'm the one who's gotta wake up with my head hurtin' like a cut worm because Scotty can't play football. I'm not willin' to just let that go. He's gonna wake up with a headache!

Frank chugs the glass of whiskey and fires the glass at the flames across the river.

He stomps towards the children's bedroom. Mary Jo throws herself at him.

MARY JO:

smacks Frank No, Frank! Frank, no! Don't do that, Frank!

Frank chokes Mary Jo.

He watches her face turn blue, then throws her to the floor. She lays coughing and gasping for air.

FRANK:

Damn it, woman! You get in my way again and that vow I made, "till death do us part," gonna come real soon! You hear me, bitch?!

MARY JO:

Please! Please, don't do that! Please, Frank! Please, leave 'em alone!

Frank stomps into Scotty's bedroom, dragging Mary Jo from his shirttail. He yanks the covers and finds the pillow dummy, then rushes to wake Holly.

FRANK:

Holly! Where's Scotty? You little traitor!

Frank sees Holly is missing also. He wrings her pillow like a dishrag.

FRANK:

You imaginin' what I'm believin', woman?

MARY JO:

whimpering There's no way, Frank. No way. They're not over there, Frank!

FRANK:

Well, I'm damn sure gonna find out. Get your shoes and my pistol. We're gonna cross us a river, woman.

Back at the cove, Rusty and Holly continue dancing in the warm firelight.

RUSTY:

Do you ever fish the river?

HOLLY:

CCF. I'm a catch 'em, clean 'em, and fry 'em girl.

RUSTY:

Wow! Am I a good catch?

HOLLY:

I don't know. Are you?

Holly melts into Rusty's arms. They both kiss their very first kiss.

Holly notices Rusty's passion. She presses herself firmly against his erection.

HOLLY:

You feel like a great catch to me.

Holly's soft lips take Rusty's hormones over the moon. He slides his hand between their bodies and adjusts himself.

RUSTY:

I'm sorry. I've never danced before. I'm losing control.

HOLLY:

This is my first anything. I'm soaked. When you're ready, I'll go with you.

Silent moans escape their kiss. They do their best to go undetected as they secretly climax together.

RUSTY:

That was incredible.

HOLLY:

That was beautiful. I love dancing.

Enviously, the other students watch Rusty and Holly. They long for what they see.

RUSTY:

Have you ever been in love?

HOLLY:

I've never felt love in my life, ever, until now.

Rusty holds her tight.

RUSTY:

You have the most beautiful white hair. Is it natural?

HOLLY:

Rusty, my hair was brunette. Due to the constant fear of being beaten or worse, my hair turned solid white. I'm glad you like it, though.

RUSTY:

That's it! We have nothing to lose. Let's do it! Let's catch some blue cats together.

HOLLY:

Rusty, we can't cross that bridge.

RUSTY:

I'll swim downstream and cross. They'll never see me.

HOLLY:

They will shoot an arrow in your back! We can't... I lo-

RUSTY:

A beating's worth the chance to hold you again. I'll wear my old man's River Rat hat. He used it for target practice, so it's got a few holes in it.

HOLLY:

Yeah, we've got a dummy Blue Cat with a noose around its neck. Sick!

RUSTY:

No one'll ever know. Everyone on both sides of the river will drink till the sun comes up and sleep their hangovers off until the sun goes down. I'll meet you at the foot of the bridge at ten.

HOLLY:

Please, don't get caught. The Rats will beat you to death.

RUSTY:

I won't. Promise me you'll meet me.

HOLLY:

I wouldn't miss it for the world.

Rusty glances over Holly's head.

RUSTY:

There's a boat coming right at us.

HOLLY:

Just a night fisher.

RUSTY:

Not at that speed!

HOLLY:

Oh shit! It's my dad!

Frank's boat is speeding towards them at full throttle. The boat crashes violently onto the shore.

Holly hides behind Rusty.

Frank falls out of the boat from his drunkenness.

FRANK:

Scotty! Holly! I know you're here! Get your asses over here!

Holly slowly walks towards the boat, covering her face from embarrassment. She tries to sneak around Frank, knowing he will have no problem beating her in front of everyone.

FRANK:

You little traitor bitch!

Holly runs to the side of Frank, but even in his drunken state, he's too fast. He jumps in front of her backhanding her in the face. She falls, crying.

FRANK:

You little bitch!

HOLLY:

No, Daddy, please! No, Daddy, please!

Frank punches her wherever his fists land. Scotty comes to her rescue.

SCOTTY:

Get off her, you demon child beater!

Scotty tries to wrestle Frank off of Holly. Frank flips him from his back like he's a flea. Frank punches Scotty in the face, knocking his front tooth out.

Scotty heads to the boat, holding his mouth.

Rusty tries his luck.

RUSTY:

Hey!

Holly sees Frank pull his pistol.

HOLLY:

No, Rusty! Stop! He will shoot you!

Rusty stops dead in his tracks.

FRANK:

Come on, boy! There's nothin', and I mean nothin', I'd rather do than fillet me some Blue Cats!

Frank glares at the gathering crowd of students.

FRANK:

I'll kill every one of you sandy beaches. Stay the fuck back!

Oblivious, Mary Jo leans over the side of the boat and vomits.

MARY JO:

Frank! Let's go, Frank! I'm sick.

Frank holds the students back with his gun and drags Holly by her hair.

FRANK:

Fuck all y'all! Bunch of traitors! I'm tellin' yer parents to set out the Rat poison, fuckers! Tee, tee, tee, tee!

CHAPTER TWENTY-NINE

Man Overboard

Frank heads the boat back towards his side of the river. Scotty and Holly sit nervously in the back of the speeding vessel.

In secret, Scotty chews a long piece of fishing line from one of Frank's fishing poles and stuffs it into his pocket. He scoots over, putting his arm around his sister.

SCOTTY:

I love you, Sissy.

Scotty plunges himself into the river. Holly yelps, but not loud enough for Frank to hear.

She's too afraid to move. She figures Scotty is better off dead than to suffer what is coming. She bends her face into her hands, juddering in tears.

Frank recklessly docks the boat. Holly leaps onto the dock and runs inside.

Frank attempts to wake Mary Jo, but she's too intoxicated to move, so he leaves her on the boat to sleep off her drunkenness.

Frank stumbles up the dock stairs. He's so wasted he doesn't realize Scotty is missing.

FRANK:

I'm killing both of you turncoats!

Frank enters the house to find Holly stark naked, standing firm and bleeding from her nose.

HOLLY:

Tonight, you can kill me. I want you to kill me, Daddy! Just like you killed Scotty.

To satisfy their inner demons, Frank and Mary Jo have beaten Scotty and Holly, even tortured them with rat-poison-laced food just to watch them suffer.

Frank is uncomfortable with Holly's nudity. He hands her an afghan to cover herself.

Frank slaps Holly wicked hard in the face. She falls to the floor, staring at Frank with hopes of dying. Her fear of death no longer exists.

FRANK:

You don't deserve death. You deserve pain. Get your ass in bed! I'll deal with you tomorrow. I've got to let the neighbors know their children are traitors. Tee, tee, tee, tee.

Frank kicks Holly. She runs to her bedroom, and he runs to the front porch screaming to the neighborhood.

As Holly lies crying in her bed, she swears she hears a faint tap on her window. It's Scotty!

She throws the window open, and he climbs through, shivering in his damp clothes. Holly comforts him under her warm blanket.

HOLLY:

What are we going to do, Scotty? I can't live in this hell very much longer.

SCOTTY:

Can you keep a secret and promise not to hate me, no matter what I tell ya?

HOLLY:

I promise.

SCOTTY:

We all know Fondue's plan, right?

HOLLY:

Of course - kill our parents.

SCOTTY:

Remember, she said the only thing that can stop her is if her mom and dad kill her first.

HOLLY:

There's no forgetting that. We know she's going to float the river after flipping those devils off, and no one will ever find her. She's just another missing teenager.

SCOTTY:

Fondue's wicked smart, literally. She knows how the devil thinks for some reason. There's gotta be a reason for what she's done.

HOLLY:

So, what's the big secret, Scotty?

SCOTTY:

Remember, you promised not to hate me.

HOLLY:

I could never hate you. You're my brother.

SCOTTY:

I went to Fondue's house.

HOLLY:

What?

SCOTTY:

I told Mr. and Mrs. Gamble I fell into the river chasing Fondue and that she's in danger and I know where she is. I told them I would take them where she is.

We loaded into their vehicle and drove to the river. I wrapped fishing line around my hands several times as we drove towards Devil's Backbone cliff. I strangled Mr. Gamble and dove out of the car before it plummeted into the river over the cliff. I watched the river swallow the car with both of them in it.

Scotty and Holly hold one another.

SCOTTY:

Holly, say something, anything, please.

HOLLY:

Fuck 'em!

Scotty is shaken to his core.

SCOTTY:

What?

HOLLY:

Fuck! Them! Consider it an early jump on Fondue's plan. All of these devils deserve to die.

CHAPTER THIRTY

Confession

Meanwhile, back at the bonfire, the students gather around, petrified of what will come if Frank squeals.

Rusty finds Austin alone, praying, and places his arm around him.

RUSTY:

Hey, Preacher, tell me about your Jesus. I want to know him.

AUSTIN:

This is all my fault, Miller. I'm sorry. Rusty, I'm just too upset right now. You'll know Jesus tomorrow, I promise.

RUSTY:

Okay, friend.

Jackie Michaels approaches. She is never seen without her signature scarf around her neck. The other students have always assumed she was mimicking her sexy mother, Sunny, who is never seen without her own signature, silk scarves.

JACKIE MICHAELS:

That was brave of you, Rusty.

RUSTY:

Thanks. I'm sorry, but he had a gun.

JACKIE:

What we just witnessed is our house. Cold, abusive, and like yours, demon-possessed. My brother Brandon once told my dad he saw a rat in the barn. He took a beating just for saying the word rat. I can't take it anymore!

AUSTIN:

Go ahead, get it off your chest, Jackie. Maybe this is a time for all of us to come forward.

JACKIE:

Thank you, Austin. I will.

Jackie boldly removes her scarf and tosses it into the air. The cool night breeze carries it perfectly into the fire.

JACKIE:

Free at last!

Much to everyone's surprise, Jackie is branded with a long, thick scar across her throat.

JACKIE:

This scar around my neck - my brother Brandon got clotheslined in a game, paralyzing his right arm. My parents told Brandon he better get back on the field for the Cats if he wants to live in their house - or live at all. I made the mistake of laughing when Brandon got injured.

When they brought Brandon home from the hospital, they went to slamming shots. They told me they have a special surprise, just for me. I was so excited.

I rode my bike to the top of the hill just like they told me. They waited for me at the bottom. I took off pedaling hard.

JACKIE (CONT'D):

When I got within a few feet, they raised a wire tied to T-handles they were holding. The wire caught my neck and flipped me to the ground. They stood over me, laughing hysterically, repeating the letter "T" while I begged for air.

BRANDON:

She almost died. They didn't care. They hate her for being a girl.

JACKIE:

It's okay, Brandon.

Jackie rolls up her sleeve to share more scars. The students stare, but not in disbelief - they all wear such horrible scars.

JACKIE:

Every game night, Dad sprays me with acid because Brandon's not on the field playing. He blames me for laughing.

LUCAS:

That's crazy, man! I assumed that kind of shit only happened on our side of the river until Austin called me.

Everyone around the fire freaks out in disbelief that someone called across the river.

LUCAS:

That's right, he called me. That's how we got here.

The students extend a gracious thank you to Lucas and Austin.

Everyone has always wondered about Lucas's scarred hand and missing finger, and for the first time since it happened, Lucas feels comfortable sharing his tragic story.

LUCAS:

Before I lost my hand, I was a running back. I fumbled at the end zone costing our team the game.

My dad told me it was the Fourth of July, but I knew it wasn't. We went to the backyard. *sniffle* He made me hold an M-80 in my hand until it exploded.

He took me inside, beating me, calling me fumble fingers. Strangely enough, I can remember him laughing, repeating the letter "T." He poured whiskey on my wound and sent me to bed. I can't describe the pain.

Lucas shows his scars to the crowd.

LUCAS:

See the results? That's why I'm a linebacker. *sniffle* I can't hang on to the ball.

The students sob, but for the first time, they recognize the warmth of compassion. Some vibrate from fear as they replay their own abuse in their minds.

CHANDLER FOWLER:

Hi, everyone. I'm Chandler Fowler. I have only a few physical scars, but here goes. I missed a game-winning field goal last year, not to brag, but it was the only field goal I've missed since I've been kicking a ball. I'm sure many of you took a beating for my mistake. I'm sorry for that.

My coach slapped me. I told him to go to Hell. Coach ratted me out to my dad.

Chandler hangs his head in shame.

CHANDLER:

Sorry, but this is graphic. He drugged me. I woke tied to his recliner - I had my mom's dildo in my mouth. He continuously slapped me while shooting shots of booze like a thirsty mule.

He kept screaming at me, "you gonna back talk a coach again, boy?" "How's your momma taste, boy?" "Tee, tee, tee, tee!" He laughed hysterically as he got off on his sickness.

I guess that wasn't enough. You know where he shoved that dildo next.

My mom's part Indian. She watched him abuse me while dancing a crazy, devil Indian dance in front of me naked. Bunch of drunks!

AUSTIN:

We got to do something about these sick fuckers.

Austin shocks everyone with his language, especially Rusty.

RUSTY:

Didn't know a preacher used that kind of talk.

AUSTIN:

My imperfections won't keep me from loving God - or him from loving me.

Rusty, these people pull their shades as if God can't see them. The devil is a deceiver; God sees all sins. I'm sorry I was angry. God invented anger - just never make him mad, my friend.

Austin moves close to Brandon.

BRANDON:

Fondue, this is my best friend, Austin.

AUSTIN:

Hey, I'm Austin.

FONDUE:

In some weird way, I'm aware of who Austin is.

Rusty remains curious about God.

RUSTY:

Can your God stop the abuse, Preacher?

AUSTIN:

Faith can move mountains, Miller, and it's our time to move.

Pulling into the cove to pick up the Rats students, Uncle Joe spots a large white object on top of the water's surface. He pulls alongside, and using his gaff, he drags the heavy object close and shines his light.

Uncle Joe guides his boat and the strange floating debris to shore.

Austin and Rusty stand on the riverbank, waiting to help Uncle Joe dock the boat.

AUSTIN:

Hey, looks like someone dumped the Rats' banners in the river. Why would they do that?!

They wade into the water to drag the banners onto the bank.

AUSTIN:

Man, these banners are heavy! Feels like somethin's in there!

AUSTIN (CONT'D):

Come on, pull, Rusty. Pull!

Curious to see what's inside, the two boys begin unwrapping the banners.

RUSTY:

What in tarnation is that?!

Wrapped inside the banners are two corpses. One has a crushed head and a referee's flag sticking from his slit throat, while the other has a microphone protruding from his anus and his guts missing.

Hearing the commotion, the other students come running.

The students turn from the grotesque scene, running and screaming.

This isn't Uncle Joe's first peep show; he's seen it all. He glances at Austin.

UNCLE JOE:

My assumption? Someone made a few terrible calls, and someone was talking out their ass.

AUSTIN:

That radio announcer should've never said "God Bless" in a town filled with devils.

Tied to the leg of one of the victims is a large sports cooler.

UNCLE JOE:

Kids, you might want to step away before I open the cooler - no telling what's inside.

The few remaining students return to the bonfire, heeding Uncle Joe's advice, fearful of what lies within. However, Austin is not going anywhere. He remains with Uncle Joe, feeling protected by his presence.

Uncle Joe pops the cooler lid. Out jumps enormous rats.

UNCLE JOE:

Whoa!

AUSTIN:

What the heck, Uncle Joe?!

Uncle Joe and Austin creep up to the cooler, holding one another's arms. Uncle Joe takes a distant peek. He stops Austin from witnessing the horror and slams the lid.

Buried inside the cooler is the severed head of the Rats coach with his headphones still attached.

UNCLE JOE:

You can't look at this Austin. You might want to sleep someday.

AUSTIN:

Uncle Joe, we've got to put these devils to rest.

UNCLE JOE:

Take it to your grave. When you figure it out, count me in.

It's time for the Rats to board Uncle Joe's boat and return to their side of the river. The students awkwardly hug during their goodbye, crying for their union to never end. This simple embrace is the only affection these deprived children have ever experienced.

Afraid of what torture awaits them, two Rats students, Fondue Gamble and Lucky Lackey, refused to board Uncle Joe's boat. They would rather take a chance on their own than return to their evil, abusive households.

The Cats wave goodbye, sobbing as their newfound friends disappear into the distance.

The Cats students know their parents will be out all night celebrating their victory, so they decide to return to the fire and spend the rest of the evening together.

Lucky approaches the fire, recognizing Fondue.

LUCKY LACKEY:

Oh my goodness, you're our drum major. I didn't recognize you without your shako. Wow! Wow! Wow! Your performance this evening, it was to die for. I never laughed so hard inside, not ever, never never.

FONDUE:

It probably will cost me my life.

LUCKY LACKEY:

Hello everyone, I'm Lucky Lackey, bench warmer for the Rats.

Austin is not thrilled to see Lucky or Fondue.

AUSTIN:

Why didn't you board the boat, Lucky? That was our deal. You and Fondue broke the rules. Explain yourselves. Now!

LUCKY LACKEY:

Look at me. I'm a hundred and fifteen pounds of nothin'. My proper name's Earl Lackey, but they call me "Lucky" because of their superstition. They believe I bring the Rats good luck, so they make me dress.

I've never seen a single play on any football field in the four years - well, actually, SIX years I've been on the team - on account a' they keep holding me back so I can't graduate. Trust me, I'll take the wrath for the Rats' loss tonight, for sure. They will kill me when they find me.

Lucky removes his shirt, showing the long, protruding scars covering his body that the students know could only be caused by a bullwhip. Some students' knees buckle from the gruesome sight.

LUCKY LACKEY:

I was sick and missed a game one night. I said nothing, but the same game, Chandler missed a field goal. Yeah! Lucky me! Lucky Lackey! The Rats lost. The townspeople took turns beating me in their satanic ritual held in my parents' barn.

We lost a big game tonight. Those two guys washed up on shore looked pretty compared to what I'm gonna look like, trust me.

Austin knows Lucky is right.

AUSTIN:

We're aware no one crosses that bridge and lives except on game night once a year. Those devils will kill you.

LUCKY LACKEY:

And yet, here we are, willing to take this enormous risk for just one night of freedom. My plan is to appreciate my last night of life with friends. Please, guys, allow me to enjoy this evening with you. Please?

Austin's heart softens from guilt.

FONDUE:

Lucky and I will suffer torture or worse when they find us.

I hopped the bus because who would ever expect anyone to cross the bridge. It was my only option.

FONDUE (CONT'D):

I'm sorry for the danger I've placed you all in. I'm not sure what to do. If I return home, the river will take me. I'll come up missing for sure.

Brandon squeezes Fondue's arm, assuring her that he will take care of her.

AUSTIN:

Okay. We're all in this together, and we've got to stick together. We knew the risk, but did I hear you say you would go missing?

FONDUE:

Yeah. Missing.

Do you guys want to hear a ghost story, a true ghost story?

RUSTY:

I'm not too sure I believe in ghosts.

FONDUE:

You will when I tell you my story. You'll want to throw a couple logs on the fire. This'll take a minute.

CHAPTER THIRTY-ONE

Fondue's Ghost Story

FONDUE:

Legend has it, looooong agooooo, there was a devil born in a tiny town in Indiana. As a young man, he gathered folks for his demon cult. He declared the Bible that Austin believes in false - and he's God's true prophet. He grew his flock to roughly one hundred and fifty devils.

RUSTY:

That's a hell of a lot of devils!

crowd laughs

FONDUE:

Just wait. You've heard nothing yet.

The Devil Cult Leader deceived his demonic following by convincing them there would be a nuclear attack and people would be much safer if they moved to Ukiah because of its high altitude.

JACKIE:

That's where all the Cats' parents go to church! Ukiah - only seven miles north from here.

FONDUE:

You're correct, Jackie. Strangely enough, the Rats go to the same church.

The Cats find her statement confusing. Rats and Cats going to the same church? How can that be, they wonder.

FONDUE:

The devil washed their brains into giving him property and possessions. To continue surviving and serving Satan, they followed their leader here to their new home. They're all around us.

The terrified students squeeze in close.

FONDUE:

A few years later, the devil outgrew this tiny area. He launched services in San Francisco - thousands attended. Some devils remained here to keep his cult alive.

Continuing to grow, he built a compound in Guyana, South America. His congregation sold everything they owned to follow him.

A few short years later, his flock was under siege and forced to drink a flavored concoction his gorillas laced with cyanide, where they met their final faaaaate.

A student moves close to the fire, pretending she's cold.

SCARED STUDENT:

We know this story. It scares me, though.

FONDUE:

Listen carefully to this. The devil is a pedophile. He adopted a teenage boy to rape and torture. The child cussed and spat at the devil, crying out for help! His agonized pleas only fueled the frenzied cult.

Wicked cult leaders hung this poor child by his feet over a large washtub. They sliced his little throat with the jagged edge of a crucifix. He hung for two full days dripping out his blood.

FONDUE (CONT'D):

He was sacrificed so his demonized blood could possess and enslave more unsuspecting souls.

Lucky grabs his queasy stomach.

LUCKY LACKEY:

Please don't tell me they drank his blood. I'll get sick.

FONDUE:

Not quite. But everyone else did.

Unbeknownst to the folks of Seven Mile, they poured his demonized blood into a large, galvanized trough, mixed with flavored water as a tempting refreshment for all in attendance at this very cove's service in 1965. Everyone who drank this bloody beverage became possessed by his demons.

This, my friends, is our parents. That's why this cove is called Devil's Backbone. It's haunted. The happening that took place here are the reason our parents beat and torture us. It's not because of football. They're full of the devil's spirit. It's a curse!

Many believe the cove we're standing in is the Devil Cult Leader's headquarters - including me.

The students lift their feet from the evil ground.

BRANDON:

Didn't the Devil Cult Leader die from a bullet to the head?

FONDUE:

That's the media talking. Here are the facts; there's a tombstone in a cemetery in Oakland with his name on it. They found the body of the cult leader, but they never found his head. His flesh is dead, but his spirit's alive. He's allll around us.

Everyone knows the story but have never heard it this way before.

FONDUE:

I know all of this is true because of who my grandmother is. Katherine Gamble.

JACKIE:

Who?

FONDUE:

She was part of his evil scheme.

FONDUE (CONT'D):

She played a cripple in a wheelchair during the 1965 gathering. A participant discovered their fraud that night. July tenth, a night all devils howl.

Everyone has heard and remembers the scary devilish howls that fill the air every year on July tenth, and now they know why.

FONDUE:

Rumor has it they found the participant with a axe in his head and his child kidnapped.

Austin knows she's talking about his grandpa, Ken, and uncle, Jack.

AUSTIN:

Where's your grandma, Fondue? I need to talk to her.

FONDUE:

That's impossible unless you can talk to the dead! She's buried in the same cemetery in Oakland as the devil. They forced her to drink the poison in Guyana.

AUSTIN:

I mean, how do you know all of this? It was long before your time.

Austin's question upsets Fondue. She turns into a black-headed praying mantis with long bloody fangs that, for some reason, only Lucky can see.

She scolds Austin.

FONDUE:

I told you my grandmother's Katherine Gamble! And also because…

Fondue makes sure everyone is paying attention.

FONDUE:

…my grandpa IS the Devil Cult Leader.

crowd gasps

The students swear Fondue's confession was not her voice.

Brandon tries to remove himself from Fondue's arms, but she holds on tight.

Lucky continues to see the evil in Fondue and runs with all his might to cross the bridge.

STUDENTS:

Lucky, come back! Lucky!

Fondue turns their attention to her.

FONDUE:

Please! Please, everyone! Here's what you must know, and what we must do to survive. When my grandma Gamble flew the coop to bum-fuck Guyana, my parents moved into her old house. She left her diary behind. I found it buried deep in her forbidden hiding place.

The devil knocked up my grandma early in the game. She hatched my retched dad. His demonic seed entered my mom. We're all going to become devils if we don't kill these demons before they enter us. He must die. The demons will die with him.

Brandon ponders Fondue's story.

BRANDON:

But he's buried in Oakland.

FONDUE:

Like I said, his corpse is rotting, but his spirit lives. We must destroy his soul.

BRANDON:

What I've learned tonight is our parents go to the devil's house in Ukiah with the same people they hate from across the river. That's weird.

FONDUE:

When they worship, they can't see faces. They only see the evil souls before them. They don't know who lives where.

RUSTY:

Ooooooh!

Rusty's getting more scared by the second. He's not sure what to believe.

RUSTY:

How do we know who the devils are? We can't just go killing innocent people.

Fondue points at Jackie.

FONDUE:

That's easy. Look at her neck.

She waves her hand around at everyone.

FONDUE:

Listen to their stories. The letter "T" we've all heard flow from these evil ones. Tee, tee, tee, tee.

SCARED STUDENT:

Oh my gosh, please stop that noise! Please! Please stop!

FONDUE:

It's the demons' signature laugh. They release the sound when receiving pleasure from the torture they give.

Our grandparents passed the baton to our parents. They're the devils - we're as innocent as sheep. We must make sure the generation of evil stops here before it's too late.

Rusty is not convinced by Fondue's jibber jabber.

RUSTY:

My dad's not a devil. He's a good man. He just doesn't like the Rats.

BRANDON:

Has your dad ever beat you?

Rusty shakes his head.

BRANDON:

Have you ever heard the sound we've all heard?

RUSTY:

Not from my dad, but was that the sound coming from Holly's dad when he was dragging her to the boat?

The students agree the sound has a connection to evil. Austin knows he must do something, even if it's wrong.

AUSTIN:

Then he shall live. That's the proof your grandparents or your dad didn't drink the blood at the gathering.

AUSTIN (CONT'D):

The truth is in us, and the truth will make us free. Protection will come from above.

Jackie becomes concerned for Fondue.

JACKIE:

What about you, Fondue? You can't stay on the Cats side. They'll kill you.

FONDUE:

I rest my case. Angels don't kill people.

Jackie takes Fondue's hand.

BRANDON:

She's right. We will shave your head and give you a mustache or something. You can hide in our outbuilding until we figure something out.

AUSTIN:

It's settled. I will pray and let the Lord show us his plan.

What about the Rats students, Fondue?

FONDUE:

We've already had this discussion. They're ready to kill!

CHAPTER THIRTY-TWO

Catfish Traitor Special

Lucky can still hear the students from the bonfire yelling and begging him to come back. His heart is racing faster than a scared rabbit. He imagines the devil praying mantis chasing him from behind, tingling his spine.

Too terrified to look back, Lucky stays on course, sprinting as fast as he can to cross the bridge.

Unfortunately for Lucky, he's Frank Thomas's neighbor. Frank spent his drunk night screaming from his porch, alerting the neighborhood that their traitor children snuck across the river with the Blue Cats.

The demon-possessed Rats' parents are now roaming the streets, howling and grinding their teeth in search of their missing children.

They are ready to devour their disobedient offspring with only the vilest types of torment.

Lucky is well aware, once he crosses the bridge, he will be tortured or worse.

Exhausted, Lucky makes it to the end of the bridge, but he can't escape the hidden townspeople waiting to capture anyone who crosses. He becomes nauseous from the sights before him and collapses to his knees.

Panting out of control, Lucky rolls over, surrendering to the demons that wait to bring him pain.

LUCKY LACKEY:

Kill me. Please, just kill me, but make it quick.

Lucky passes out from fear and exhaustion.

Out from the riverbank's thicket jumps Lucky's mom and dad, along with Greg Fowler. They snarl and growl like starving wolves, showing their evil teeth, daring anyone to bring harm to Lucky.

The next morning, Lucky is awakened by his mother's presence. She is standing over his bed, smiling.

Confused, Lucky slowly uncovers himself from his warm blanket. He examines his body, expecting to see scars and to suffer pain from the torture he thought he had received.

LUCKY LACKEY:

I can't believe this. I must be dreaming. I'm not bleeding!

Lucky sits up and stretches his arms far above his head.

LUCKY LACKEY:

I'm alive! I'm alive!

Lucky runs from his bedroom. His mom and dad are sitting at the kitchen table, smiling, eating buttered toast and enjoying a hot cup of tea. They give Lucky a happy good morning nod and continue with their morning, smiling.

LUCKY LACKEY:

Dad? Mom?

They raise their faces to Lucky, smiling.

LUCKY LACKEY:

This is the best day of my life. Thank you for keeping me safe. I'm going to work extra, extra hard at the diner today for ya.

You'll see. I will never cross the bridge again. Never. Not ever.
I promise.

They smile.

After a hot shower, Lucky skips merrily down the sidewalk, dragging a stick along the metal rail fence, enjoying the clicking noise as he strolls.

LUCKY LACKEY:

Yay! Yay! Yay! Yay! I'm so happy! Ah man! Ya! Woo!

sings a tune Nuh na nuh na nuh na nuhhh na nuhhhh.

Lucky makes it inside the front door of his family's restaurant, Lackey's Diner, when suddenly he hears the door behind him lock.

He slowly turns to find Greg Fowler and Sam Spicer sitting in the dimly lit corner booth, smiling, and sharpening their fillet knives.

Lucky raises his arms like wings, pondering a way to escape.

When he turns to run for it, he finds the kitchen help, along with his mom and dad, entering the dining room single file, smiling, and sharpening their knives.

LUCKY LACKEY:

No! No! I - I'm sorry! I said I was sorry! Nooo! Please don't! *stab*
Noooo! Ahhhh!! *slice*Ahhh!! *slice*Ahhhhhh!! *stab* Ahhh!

Lucky was deep-fried and served as a blue channel catfish traitor special at Lackey's diner that day. The townsfolk say Lucky was the best traitor they ever tasted.

Un-Lucky Lackey was never spoken of again.

CHAPTER THIRTY-THREE

Sam Dupes Lucas

The next morning, Lucas lies in bed, hesitant to leave for fear of the beating he knows Sam will deliver.

He and Tippy Toes ultimately make their dreaded entrance into the living room, where they find Sam comfortable in his chair, enjoying a cup of coffee. Much to Lucas's surprise, Sam's in a friendly mood, something Lucas has never witnessed before.

SAM:

Good morning, son. Would you like a cup of coffee?

LUCAS:

Morning, Dad. Coffee?

Sam's low, polite tone is throwing Lucas for a loop.

LUCAS:

I'm sorry we lost the game last night. I gave it all I had.

SAM:

Hey, it's only a game, right? No big deal.

LUCAS:

Dad, are you - are you okay?

SAM:

I'm great, son. I thought you and I might spend a little time at the river this morning.

Lucas longed to hear a kind word from his dad his whole life.

LUCAS:

For real, Dad? I'll grab my shoes. Come on, Tippy Toes!

Lucas believes his prayers for Sam to change have been answered.

Tippy Toes sits anxiously while Lucas ties his shoes.

TIPPY TOES:

*whimpers nervously**

She leads him to the missing box of puppies.

They dash to the backyard and find Sam holding a burlap bag.

LUCAS:

Sit, Tippy Toes. Dad! I thought you weren't mad.

Sam remains calm, part of his evil scheme.

SAM:

I'm not mad you lost the game, boy. You disrespected me. Didn't I tell you to get rid of them whining-ass pups?

SAM (CONT'D):

Well, ya didn't listen. And I don't believe for a second you gave it your all last night. You embarrassed the fuck out of me. You just got a little lesson coming to ya, that's all, boy!

LUCAS:

Beat me, Dad! Beat me! I cannot kill those puppies. Please, Dad.

SAM:

Here's the deal, boy. I'll give you two choices.

puppies crying

Sam pulls his pocketknife and raises a puppy in front of Lucas.

SAM:

Choice number one. I cut all of these three whining-ass pups' guts out for catfish bait, AND I get to put a little bullet in Tippy Toes' pretty little head. That leaves you with no dogs.

LUCAS:

No, Dad, please! I'll do anything. Please don't kill my dogs.

Lucas cries uncontrollably but then quickly realizes his tears will only bring Sam more satisfaction.

SAM:

Are you goin' all pussy on me right now, boy? Huh? Tee, tee, tee, tee.

Here's choice number two. You're gonna crush this little guy's head with a river rock, just like you should do to Miller.

Sam places the first puppy in the burlap bag and raises the second puppy.

puppy whimpers

SAM:

And this little guy - you're gonna leave him in the burlap bag, and you're gonna toss him far into the river as you can and watch him sink to the bottom, just like you should be doin' to Miller.

Sam places the second puppy into the burlap bag and raises the third puppy.

puppy yelps

SAM:

And this little fine specimen of a canine - you're gonna let it go. Give the coyotes somethin' to eat. Just like ya did when you had Miller all wrapped up at the end zone, and you just let him walk right in. Ya let him go! Sounds fair to me, boy!

Sam puts his knife to the pup's belly. Tippy Toes is not fond of Sam's behavior.

TIPPY TOES:

Growwwwlll

SAM:

Choice is yours, boy! Two doggies live, or four doggies die. What's it gonna be? Tee, tee, tee, tee.

LUCAS:

sniffle Let's go to the bridge, Dad.

CHAPTER THIRTY-FOUR

River Rock Rusty

Rusty makes it safely across the bridge to meet Holly for their ten o'clock date. He sits on the riverbank with the bill of his River Rats cap pulled over his eyes.

Nervously, he casts his line into the water.

Holly, with her black eyes and bruised face, sneaks from her bedroom. She's taken by surprise when she finds Frank awake, still drunk and still drinking. He badgers Holly right away.

FRANK:

Where ya going, ya little traitor bitch?

HOLLY:

I'm gonna catch you a fresh mess, Dad - clear my head from my ignorance. I don't know what was going through my thin head last night.

I'm sorry. I'll fix it! I promise.

FRANK:

You're damn straight you will! I better never catch you across that river again. You embarrassed the shit out of your mother and I last night. It's the least you can fucking do. I'll beat you and your brother later. Your mama slept in the boat last night because of you. Wake her and tell her to get her ass in here. I'm hungry.

Now get out of my face and catch me them cats!

Lucas and Sam make their way to the bridge. Rusty hears them shuffling towards him; he takes a glance hoping to see Holly. Noticing it's not her, he hides his face. Rusty's presence surprises Sam.

SAM:

Good morning. They hittin'?

Rusty stares at his line.

RUSTY:

Just put my line out.

Behind the scenes, Holly's making her way onto the bank when she spots the trouble. She lays her fishing pole down and hides behind a tree. She's scared but watches.

SAM:

Do I know you?

RUSTY:

Kevin. Kevin Reece, from over the hill.

SAM:

You know this Reece boy?

LUCAS:

Kid from school, Dad. I don't know.

SAM:

Good luck to y'all. We'll just go on away from ya.

Before Sam and Lucas can move, one of the puppies whimpers.

Not thinking, Rusty turns. Lucas recognizes Rusty.

LUCAS:

Miller?!

SAM:

Miller? Rusty Miller? Well, let me shake your hand, young man. What a fine performance you put on last night. It's an honor.

Hey! I played for the New York Jets.

RUSTY:

The Jets?! Wow!

I'm sorry I lied. They're not biting on the other side. Hey! I'm wearing your hat, though.

Rusty turns his head to his fishing line, hoping he's in the clear.

Sam finds a good-sized river rock and tries to hand it to Lucas. Lucas won't take the rock.

SAM:

Hey, Miller!

Rusty turns. Sam brutally bashes him in the head.

Rusty lies lifeless.

SAM:

See how it's done, boy? Get your ass over here. Hurry!

Holly sits behind the tree helplessly, biting her palm to keep silent.

Sam sets the puppies free. He turns, conjuring a way to dispose of Rusty's dead body.

Freaked out, Lucas stares at Rusty's lifeless, bloody face. For a second, he swears Rusty winked at him.

They place Rusty's upper body in the burlap bag with the river rock, hoping the rock will sink Rusty to the bottom of the river.

Together, they roll Rusty's corpse into the water.

SAM:

Let's get the hell out of here, boy!

Holly remains hidden, barely holding it together. Lucas spots her as Sam and he race past. Lucas and Holly lock eyes.

CHAPTER THIRTY-FIVE

Somber

Holly crashes through the front door, running straight into Frank.

FRANK:

You ain't caught no gosh damn cats already!

HOLLY:

No, Dad, I forgot my studies. I'm going to kill a couple of birds with one stone while I catch you them yummy cats I promised.

FRANK:

Yeah, yeah, just what in the hell you sneakin' about for?

HOLLY:

Nothing, Dad! I gotta line in. Gotta run!

Notebook in hand, Holly heads out the door. She circles around to the garage and removes the noose from the Cats dummy she told Rusty about. She grabs a roll of duct tape and heads back to the river.

Holly finds Lucas's puppies roaming the bank. While gathering them, she notices Rusty's fishing line in the water. She reels in the line. There's a tug; she's skilled enough to know whatever's on the end of the line isn't a fish. She pulls the object from the water and finds a large arrowhead with the words "I'm in love" inscribed.

She hears Rusty's voice in her head.

RUSTY'S VOICE:

I'm in love.

HOLLY:

No. Please. Please, God, no.

Holly crumples to her knees.

After a long, hard cry, she pulls herself together long enough to write her suicide letter. She uses the puppies for her audience as she reads aloud.

HOLLY:

Dear Mom and Dad,

I met a friend last night at the forbidden bonfire. I felt love for the first time. I'm thankful I had the opportunity to appreciate what you never allowed me to experience. I hope you realize how somber this letter truly is.

I can't live in hell for very much longer. I see your lies, promises disguised as truth. We know what's right for us. You beat Scotty and me, not because we crossed a river, but because of a score of a high school football game.

When they go looking for Rusty Miller, he's at the bottom of the Russian River. I watched Sam Spicer beat him to death with a rock by the bridge. They placed him in a burlap bag and rolled him into the waterway. I'm going to be with him.

I was going to hang, but this river will assure me you will never see me again. Tell Scotty to run hard to get away from you. Most suicide letters end with I love you, but I'm a product of you.

So, fuck you!!

Holly finds Rusty's cap. She brings it to her face, sniffing the fragrance of Rusty she so vividly remembers. She places it on her head, then wraps her feet and hands with the duct tape in hopes of drowning once she plunges herself into the river.

Looking out over the water, she prepares to end her life in the rushing current.

CHAPTER THIRTY-SIX

Ooooops!

Word that Rusty and Holly vanished in the river traveled fast because of Holly's letter.

Jerry and Sandy come home from an early night of drinking. They find Austin with his face buried in the couch, crying and praying over the death of his friends.

Jerry places his hand upon Austin's shoulder.

JERRY:

We heard the news. They knew better than to cross the bridge. How in the world did they ever mingle together, anyway? I'm just as concerned as you, Austin. There's no way the Cats can win State without Miller.

AUSTIN:

Do you have any idea how ignorant you sound, Dad? Two people are dead. Two people who begged me to tell them about Jesus. Two people that will burn in Hell because I didn't tell them, and now it's too late!

Sandy watches Austin grab a bottle of Mad Dog 20/20 from the cabinet.

SANDY:

Austin! Stop that! Put that bottle back. That bottle is mine! Stop him, Jerry! Stop him, Jerry, don't let him take my Mad Dog!

JERRY:

Oh, let the boy become a man. Let him drink the cheap shit. He'll never do it again. Besides, something tells me our little boy's been mingling with the dirty Rats himself.

SANDY:

Jerry, are you crazy? How in the world did you even imagine such a thing?

JERRY:

Weren't you listening? How can someone beg unless they're right in front of you?

SANDY:

Oh! That's right! I'll get the ties and the razor straps. Tee, tee, tee, tee.

Austin heads to the cove. He lights a fire and lies gazing at the stars. He glances at the bottle of booze. His Christian spirit warns him the bottle has no answer. The warm fire closes his eyes.

Austin hears a gurgling noise echoing from the cove, bringing him floating to his feet. Traces of his spirit slowly catch up to his body.

From the dimming firelight, he observes ripples forming on the calm water. Rusty and Holly's spirits slowly rise from the water, walking towards the bank.

RUSTY'S SPIRIT:

Preeeeeeacher...

HOLLY'S SPIRIT:

Auuuuustin...

RUSTY'S SPIRIT:

Preeeeeeacher... Preeeeeeacher...

AUSTIN:

Rusty?! Holly?! This can't be happening. I haven't touched that bottle. I haven't had one drink of that stuff.

RUSTY'S SPIRIT:

Are you suffering guilt because we see the bottle? Don't be a hypocrite, Austin. Didn't Jesus turn the water to wine, Pre-eeeeeacher?

AUSTIN:

Yes, he did, Rusty.

HOLLY'S SPIRIT:

Didn't Jesus drink the wine, Preeeeeeacher?

AUSTIN:

Yes, he did, Holly.

HOLLY'S SPIRIT:

Then what makes you any better than Jesus? Drink the wiiiine, Preeeeeeacher.

Austin twists the cap, tips the bottle, and chugs a few swallows.

AUSTIN:

Ohh, that stuff's good!

RUSTY'S SPIRIT:

You brought Holly and I together, and now you will bring this town together once and for all. We love you, Preeeeeeacher...

The spirits walk into the river and slowly dissolve. Austin's shuddering body opens his eyes.

AUSTIN:

Okay, Lord, I promise. I will unite this town once and for all.

Austin returns home, eats dinner, and hits the bed. He's awakened by two flailing razor straps striking his bound body.

Jerry and Sandy beat Austin black and blue.

SANDY:

Tee, tee, tee, tee. Ohh, that's right!

JERRY:

laughs maniacally

CHAPTER THIRTY-SEVEN

Never Fight a Ghost

AUSTIN:

panicked breathing

Austin awakens drenched in sweat, his body covered with welts.

He finally musters enough strength to get out of bed, for on this particular morning, he feels led to go see his uncle, Joe.

Austin pumps the tires on his old ten-speed and pedals away, doing the best he can with his aching body.

Uncle Joe spots Austin on his lane. He quickly rushes a box with three pit bull puppies he's fostering into the spare bedroom and heads to the front porch to invite Austin in.

Uncle Joe senses Austin's panic. He pours a glass of iced tea to settle him down.

AUSTIN:

panting

UNCLE JOE:

Relax. Take your time, Austin.

Austin collects himself and tells Uncle Joe Fondue's story and his plan.

AUSTIN:

Uncle Joe, this town's tainted with unclean spirits. The devil cult's demons float on their backs down the Russian River from Ukiah still today. It's them or us. Someone else will die, and especially if we lose the state championship game.

Come on! We've gotta do something, Uncle Joe, come on!

Joe doesn't question the bruises he notices on Austin's face.

UNCLE JOE:

Austin, you need not try to convince me. They possess Devil's Backbone Cove. Everyone knows the cove's a dwelling place for evil. How do you suppose it got its name?

Your friend, Fondue, her story's accurate. Austin, I believe you're a prophet, but before I commit to helping you, there's a lot more to this story that you must learn. This will get a little weird.

AUSTIN:

I need you more than ever. Tell me, Uncle Joe, please. Please tell me.

Uncle Joe leans forward.

UNCLE JOE:

Your grandpa Ken's spirit lives inside of me. My body is your grandpa's dwelling place. I refer to him as Jo-Ken.

Austin listens closely. He remembers his dad mentioned this recently.

Uncle Joe tells Austin the story of what happened in 1965. Austin's heard bits and pieces of the story from his dad but was unsure. He trusts his Uncle Joe, though.

UNCLE JOE:

Jo-Ken and I got into a terrible scuffle one evening. He tossed me around in his room like a rag doll. I tried kicking him in his ghostly crotch - my foot went clear through him straight in the air. I landed flat on my back. See the bullet hole in the wall? Well, that didn't work neither. "Did you just try to kick me in the balls," he asked me. He laughed hysterically. His playtime, I guess. It was like bringing a switchblade pocket comb to the O.K. Corral. I was no contest.

He told me he'd leave me alone if I'd go to Guyana and kill the Devil Cult Leader and bring Jack home alive. Just so happened, I have some trusting friends from Mexico who had an interest in going to Guyana to visit this devil.

Uncle Joe cracks a wry smile.

UNCLE JOE:

The devil's loaded! Our deal was, I help them get their treasure, and they help me bring back Jack. Austin, I'm affiliated with a lot of - let's just say, bad, powerful people. Do you know what I mean by that?

AUSTIN:

I'm sure the Holy Spirit leads me here for a reason, Uncle Joe. I need some bad people.

CHAPTER THIRTY-EIGHT

Operation Watercolors

UNCLE JOE:

Back in seventy-eight, nine of them extreme trained fellers from Mexico I mentioned, along with my best buddy Gary - who insists on being called Cross-Eyed Knife Warrior on account of being cross-eyed - boarded a private plane fueled by people you don't want to know and headed for South America.

AUSTIN:

Cross-Eyed Knife Warrior? Whoa, that's a cool name, Uncle Joe.

UNCLE JOE:

He also has the most unfortunate name in history, Gary Indiana, which he hates because he's from south Texas. Now, Gary may be cross-eyed, but for all I can say, he'd never had no use for a gun.

We did a night jump around two in the morning. Believe me, friend, you've not experienced dark until you've experienced Guyanese jungle dark!

military plane flashback

UNCLE JOE:

I led the platoon. We were dressed in ghillie suits and armed to the hilt. I swear Cross-Eyed Knife Warrior was carrying more knives than a fancy dinner party. *chuckle*

We crawled on our bellies for hours on that hot, muggy morning, drenched in sweat, covered with mosquito bites, fighting God only knows whatever snakes live there. We finally found the devil's compound just about the time the sun rose.

There wasn't much movement, except for a couple guerillas we spotted guarding a dimly lit larger building. My assumption? We'd found the devil's headquarters. We get him. We get Jack!

We needed to take out the two guards at the door.

Cross-Eyed Knife Warrior threw two machetes, if you can believe that. Machetes!

UNCLE JOE (CONT'D):

One from his left hand, one from his right - at the same time - landing two perfect bullseyes. Those guards dropped like a bowling ball, Austin.

Gary and I ventured inside while the rest of the team went to handle their business, which was pilfering the millions that nasty old devil stole from his flock.

steel door creaks open

UNCLE JOE:

Cross-Eyed Knife Warrior and I made it inside. The devil was sound asleep wearing a sleep mask, snoring louder than a drunken crowd at an L.A. Dodgers game.

Unexpectedly, Jo-Ken showed. His spirit lit the room. I fought him, but trust me, he always gets his way.

Cross-Eyed Knife Warrior can only see shadows, but the rest of his senses are top-notch. He sensed Jo-Ken's spirit and went to swinging and kicking like a crazed donkey.

Jo-Ken removed the devil's sleep mask, waking him. That old devil looked just like someone would if a ghost had woken them.

Jo-Ken grabbed him by his throat, squeezing the life out of him.

Grandpa wasn't playing. He wanted to know where Jack was.

The devil had stolen so many children he didn't know which boy was Jack. Besides, we weren't looking for a boy. Jack was a man by then.

Austin, that demon invented what I know today as human trafficking. He stole so many people.

The old devil didn't cooperate, so it was my turn.

Knife Warrior took my backpack filled with cyanide and dispatched the other warriors to action on the mission we called, Watercolors.

AUSTIN:

That's a cool name!

UNCLE JOE:

Yeah.

Jorge, one of our warriors, braved the open range and filled a large, galvanized trough full of the cyanide with a fruit-flavored drink.

We heard gunfire from a distance, which I later learned was at the compound's airstrip, killing a governor and some news reporters. It triggered an all-out war.

My men killed all the guerillas, or at least, I assumed they did.

Jo-Ken kept asking the devil, "where's Jack?"

"I don't know your son," the devil explained to Grandpa.

UNCLE JOE (CONT'D):

Knife Warrior held a razor to the devil's throat while I checked for Jack at the trough.

The Mexican crew forced all the followers to drink or take a gut shot until they gave us Jack. He watched as his flock drank the poison. His followers were choking and vomiting from the poison, falling dead right in front of us.

It was awful, Austin, but the devil didn't care. He just made the strangest sound, "tee, tee, tee, tee."

AUSTIN:

Uncle Joe? Are you telling me you killed those people in Guyana and not that Jimmy guy?

UNCLE JOE:

Unfortunately, yes, Austin.

AUSTIN:

Oh, my gosh!

UNCLE JOE:

We repeatedly called for Jack.

We were losing hope, watching one right after another drink the poison. No one was giving us Jack. We assumed they killed him.

After hundreds and hundreds had fallen dead, finally, a young man named Jack approached the trough.

JACK:

Well, I'm Jack.

UNCLE JOE:

Grandpa recognized Jack in his spirit. We'd found him!

Jack recognized me. He fell into my arms. Grandpa leaped into my body. The warmth of his son's arms made him weep.

AUSTIN:

You're making me cry, Uncle Joe.

UNCLE JOE:

It makes me cry, too, Austin.

But then, the strangest thing happened!

A young girl, a child, maybe twelve years old. I'll never forget her name, Rita, had climbed into the trough before we noticed. She cupped the poison in her hand, slurping it like she was dying of thirst in the middle of a hot desert.

UNCLE JOE (CONT'D):

It was as if she wanted to die, Austin.

I'll never forget the horrific voice of the Devil Cult Leader, "drink it, Rita! Hurry, drink it, honey! Tee, tee, tee, tee." He laughed as the poor child choked on her vomit, passing right before our eyes.

Joe slumps in his chair.

AUSTIN:

What happened then, Uncle Joe? I need to know.

UNCLE JOE:

Out of nowhere, bullets whizzed all around my head. We had no choice but to abandon Operation Watercolors.

Jack and I made it halfway through the jungle before I noticed Knife Warrior wasn't behind us. I wasn't about to leave my best friend.

I had Jack keep moving. I ran into the rest of the team in the heat of battle. I saw Knife Warrior about sixty yards out. I shouted his name, his keen sense of hearing picked up my voice through all the gunfire, and he made it to me.

We dropped about forty gunmen that day. We needed to get out of there quick. As we were running, I felt Knife Warrior slip something bulky into my backpack. I didn't have time to check.

Sorry to say, my men didn't get their fortune. I promised them a fortune, and I always keep my word, Austin. They've got one coming.

We landed safely on American soil unscathed. America's crooked media, and the help of a few dollars, wrote whatever story I paid them to report. America believes the devil took a bullet to his head.

AUSTIN:

Oh, my precious Lord. Fondue's devil grandpa is still alive, isn't he?!

UNCLE JOE:

No, Austin, I'm afraid not. When I returned home, I checked my backpack. I jumped ten feet in the air. Gary Indiana had given me a souvenir.

AUSTIN:

What was it, Uncle Joe?

UNCLE JOE:

I pulled the head of the Evil Devil Cult Leader from my backpack.

AUSTIN:

Was he dead?

Wow! That was a stupid thing to say, huh? *laughs*

UNCLE JOE:

Knife Warrior always gets his man. He literally twisted the devil's head from his shoulders like unscrewing a lid from a jar.

Austin remembers Fondue saying that the devil cult leader was buried without a head. He doesn't let on that he knows as he realizes Fondue was telling the truth.

UNCLE JOE:

Like I said, Austin, you're a prophet now. What's your plan?

AUSTIN:

Kill them. Kill them all, seven days from when I say.

UNCLE JOE:

Hold on, Austin. The Devil Cult Leader raped Jack. Grandma Turner drank the blood in sixty-five - they're unclean.

You sure you can kill your grandmother, your Uncle Jack, and your mom and dad?

AUSTIN:

It's not my plan, Uncle Joe. It's his.

Austin points to the ceiling.

AUSTIN:

Jesus was our sacrificial lamb, Uncle Joe. He took a severe beating and was nailed to a cross where he died for our sins and transgressions. If God is for us, then who can be against us?

Joe, not being a godly man, doesn't know scripture, but he has always respected Austin's belief in the God of Heaven and Earth.

UNCLE JOE:

I hate the devils of Seven Mile, you know that, but I'm gonna have to sit this one out. Sorry, buddy.

AUSTIN:

Uncle Joe?

UNCLE JOE:

Yes, Austin?

AUSTIN:

What happened to "I can take it to my grave?"

Uncle Joe remembers his commitment.

UNCLE JOE:

But they're your mom and dad, Austin.

Austin removes his shirt, showing Joe the scars from his severe beatings.

UNCLE JOE:

Who did that to you?

AUSTIN:

Like you said, my mom and dad.

UNCLE JOE:

Okay, get in touch with Chester Miller. Like me, he's clean. He's a friend.

AUSTIN:

That's Rusty Miller's dad! A devil killed Rusty, Uncle Joe, I just know it!

UNCLE JOE:

He's not…

AUSTIN:

He's not what, Uncle Joe?

UNCLE JOE:

Never mind. Chester's my inside connection at U.S. Dynamite. We will need him. Send him to see me today, and no later than today. He'll come. I'll get in touch with Mr. Indiana.

It's your mission, Austin. Give it a name.

AUSTIN:

I'm naming this mission... Saving Grace, Uncle Joe!

Austin hugs Uncle Joe's neck.

JO-KEN:

Mmmmmmmmmmmm...

AUSTIN:

What was that?

UNCLE JOE:

That was your grandpa. He says make sure you take care of Grandma Farrah.

AUSTIN:

I promise, Grandpa.

Uncle Joe walks Austin to the door.

UNCLE JOE:

I better not give you a ride into town. The devils thirst for my soul. But I can take you most of the way.

AUSTIN:

That's okay, Uncle Joe. It felt good to ride.

Austin has witnessed enough spooky encounters for the day. He pedals home.

UNCLE JOE:

You can come out now!

CHAPTER THIRTY-NINE

Daddy, it's the Fuzz

football highlights on tv

Two police officers, Nolan and Vance, knock on Sam Spicer's front door. Lucas peeks through the door at Officer Nolan.

OFFICER NOLAN:

Can I speak with your daddy?

LUCAS:

whispering Daddy, it's the fuzz.

Sam's lying on the couch watching television. He motions the officers inside.

SAM:

Come in, boys. Come on in. What's this all about?

OFFICER NOLAN:

Sam, let's turn that down a little bit.

SAM:

Can I get you guys a beer or somethin'?

OFFICER NOLAN:

No, thank you, Sam. We received a copy of Frank Thomas's daughter's suicide note, leading us to believe you might know something about the Miller boy's disappearance. We've got just a few questions if you don't mind.

SAM:

Who? I don't know no Miller boy.

OFFICER VANCE:

Come on, you know, Chester Miller's son?

Officer Vance tips his hat.

OFFICER VANCE:

The running back for the Blue Cats?

SAM:

Look, I don't know the boy. He was their running back? Damn shame. He's their top athlete, wasn't he?

Sam's giving an academy award performance. Nolan's not really buying it.

OFFICER NOLAN:

The letter used the word they, as in more than one person rolled his body into the river.

Nolan notices Lucas can't look him in the eye. He's more nervous than a child getting a shot.

OFFICER NOLAN:

I bet your boy knows something.

LUCAS:

Yeah, he's their back. That's all I know.

Nolan persists.

OFFICER NOLAN:

And Sam, you didn't hit that boy in the head with a rock, like the letter states?

SAM:

Been right here the whole time, just me and my boy. Gentlemen, this tree don't have no barkin' dogs. You can try someone else.

Officer Vance hates the Blue Cats.

OFFICER VANCE:

Miller's from the other side of the river. I mean, if Sam said he didn't do it, that's good enough for me.

SAM:

Well, that ought to tell you boys right there I did nothin' like that. I'd never cross that bridge!

OFFICER NOLAN:

They're gonna send some divers, Sam. You better pray if they find that boy, he's not wrapped in a burlap sack, and his head's in excellent condition, or you're gonna look mighty guilty.

SAM:

I don't pray, Cap'n Nolan, never needed to. Prayin's for people who did somethin' wrong. Chester Miller and I go way back. Sure do hope they find that boy.

Sam shows the officers the door. Captain Nolan stops and turns before exiting.

OFFICER NOLAN:

Found the referee in the river. Someone performed a juicy junction on his throat, and his head's crushed. You're a popular fellow for the knives, Sam. I noticed spots of blood on your van tires, too. Blood on the tires and a flat head - kinda fitting, huh, Sam?

SAM:

So's blood 'n coyote hair! They're thick around here. Thanks for remindin' me, though - I need to get the old hump-mobile washed.

The police exit. Sam and Lucas look at each other as if to say "that was close."

The phone rings. They jump out of their skin.

LUCAS:

Shit!

picks up Hello? Sp - Spicer residence. Lu - Lucas speaking.

AUSTIN:

Monday. The bridge. Tippy Toes.

Lucas recognizes Austin's voice and slams the receiver.

SAM:

Who was that, Lucas?

LUCAS:

Wrong number, Dad.

Monday comes soon. Lucas rubs Tippy Toes' head and gives the command.

LUCAS:

Tippy Toes, you know what to do, girl. Go see Preacher!

Tippy Toes takes off, running across the bridge to Austin.

TIPPY TOES:

barks confidently

Tippy Toes sprints the plans to Lucas.

CHAPTER FORTY

Cross-Eyed Knife Warrior

It's late at night. Uncle Joe and his old friend, Cross-Eyed Knife Warrior, have reunited, joining forces to do their part in Operation Saving Grace.

Joe cuts the motor from his boat, coasting into a cove where Lucas and Scotty anxiously await.

Cross-Eyed Knife Warrior's notorious shiny steel blades glisten in the moonlight, creating an aura around the mammoth of a man.

Lucas and Scotty stare at the goliath as if he were an alien.

UNCLE JOE:

Don't let him scare ya, boys. He's as gentle as a kitten. Let's move, fellas!

The boys and Uncle Joe unload many wooden crates marked DYNAMITE, while Cross-Eyed Knife Warrior stands guard.

Cross-Eyed Knife Warrior's incredible sense of hearing alerts him to a disturbance…a raccoon shimmying up a tree roughly twenty yards away. He fires a weapon he designed himself called a spatchet, half spear, half hatchet. It makes a scary whistling noise as it twirls straight through the raccoon's head, fastening it helplessly to the tree.

raccoon shrieks

The boys stop and stare. Joe shakes his head.

UNCLE JOE:

What did you do that for?

CROSS-EYED KNIFE WARRIOR:

Thought I hear'd an alligator, Joe!

Joe gives the fellas a speech before departing.

UNCLE JOE:

You boys better know what you're doing, or a lot of the wrong people will die. Not to mention your heads will look worse than the raccoon if things go south. This is not a movie. This is not a joke. This is your life versus their life. This is one game only our team can win.

Lucas is sweating pellets. Not sure what to say.

LUCAS:

We've been up three nights in a row studying Austin's plan - not a wink of sleep. I pray we know what we're doing too.

Uncle Joe hands Lucas and Scotty a vial of sleeping medicine.

UNCLE JOE:

Here, Scotty. Here, Lucas. I'm not sure what part of Austin's plan this is for - I'm not sure I want to know. Whoever drinks this will go under for about two hours. Be careful.

Joe and Cross-Eyed Knife Warrior set sail across the river. Knife Warrior is a bit concerned about Lucas and Scotty.

KNIFE WARRIOR:

I sure ain't no expert, but if I didn't know any better, that Lucas feller couldn't pour piss out of a boot with the instructions written on the heel. And that Scotty, he's so dumb, he could throw himself on the ground and miss. They ain't nothin' but a bunch of youngins, Joe.

CHAPTER FORTY-ONE

Don't Call Me That

Across the river, Austin and Brandon wait to receive their dyna-mite. Uncle Joe removes himself from his boat, greeting the boys.

UNCLE JOE:

Austin. Brainiac. Like I told the boys across the river, you better know what you're doing. Austin, are you sure?

Austin, surprised by Cross-Eyed Knife Warrior's size and glitter, doesn't hear Uncle Joe's question.

AUSTIN:

Woah! Is that - is that Gary Indiana?

KNIFE WARRIOR:

Who said that?!

Cross-Eyed Knife Warrior throws himself into a fighting stance and roars.

UNCLE JOE:

Remember?! I told you he hates that name!

KNIFE WARRIOR:

I will cut whoever called me that's tongue out and eat their shit for brains for dinner!

UNCLE JOE:

You better go to apologizing, Austin, before he sticks ya.

AUSTIN:

I'm sorry - I'm so sorry. Please forgive me, great and mighty Cross-Eyed Knife Warrior.

Brandon's so frightened he begs for Austin's life.

BRANDON:

No! No! Please don't hurt my friend! Please, Mr. Cross-Eyed Knife Warrior!

Uncle Joe and Cross-Eyed Knife Warrior bust out in hysterics at the boys' behavior.

KNIFE WARRIOR:

Well, butter my butt and call me a biscuit! That just dills my pickle. If we can't make a little fun outta killin' some devils together, then what's it good fer?

AUSTIN:

Aww, Uncle Joe, ya made me wet my britches.

They have a merry laugh at Austin's expense. Uncle Joe attempts to get back to business.

UNCLE JOE:

Nephew, before we unload them fireworks, are you sure you're ok with all of this?

AUSTIN:

Uncle Joe, I've got to set this town free. Brandon Michaels here - is a certified genius. He swore to me he can follow your directions perfectly. And besides, we have the Father, the Son, and the Holy Ghost as our support group. It can't get any better.

Austin and Uncle Joe unload the crates as Brandon stands watching. Uncle Joe pulls a flare gun from the last crate.

UNCLE JOE:

Here's your flare gun. Your timing will have to be perfect, Austin. And here's the sleep aids you requested. You've got two hours to rope and tie whoever, or whatever you're going to do with these drugs.

Uncle Joe glances at Brandon's arm.

UNCLE JOE:

How's Brandon gonna help you load with an arm like that?

AUSTIN:

A friend's bringing his truck. He'll be here soon.

KNIFE WARRIOR:

That boy's about as useless as a steering wheel on a mule, Joe.

UNCLE JOE:

Austin, this is our last time. If one bit of this plan gets off schedule over fifteen minutes, you will do what?

AUSTIN:

I'm to fire the flare gun straight in the air, Uncle Joe, straight above my head.

UNCLE JOE:

Correct. And if all goes as planned?

AUSTIN:

I'm to shoot the flare gun against the current, towards Ukiah, to carry out Operation Saving Grace.

KNIFE WARRIOR:

If this don't go as planned, I'm gonna slap you to sleep, then slap you for sleepin'.

Uncle Joe ignores Cross-Eyed Knife Warrior's dilly. He's frightened if he lets go of Austin's arms, the plan will actually go into effect. Joe considers the need for a higher power.

UNCLE JOE:

I don't know how to pray, but I'm damn sure gonna try.

Austin prays with the group. Uncle Joe releases Austin's arms.

ACT THREE

CHAPTER FORTY-TWO

Walk the Perimeter

The children of Seven Mile have accepted God's plan of salvation and have been born again in Christ. Their sins of before and their sins to come are covered by the blood of his crucified Son. The God who conquers evil tells their pure young hearts that anything is possible for those who believe, and the measure of faith dealt to each of them will move mountains. But still, they question. Will their tiny mustard seed of faith move the mountains standing before them? Will they take a beating or die once they cross the Seven Mile Bridge? Is it worth risking their lives for?

The newly christened Saints of Seven Mile are commanded to march the perimeter of their side of Seven Mile for seven days.

For each of the first six days, they will march one lap around their side's perimeter. On the seventh day, they will complete seven laps before meeting together on the middle of the Seven Mile Bridge.

Day one, the clock strikes noon. The God that cannot lie leads the Saints of Seven Mile from their chairs, lunchroom tables, restaurants, restrooms, wherever they stand or sit. They are beckoned to the call. It's time to march!

The Saints march with a stomp so intense each stride echoes into Heaven.

The Demons of Seven Mile, those tainted by the Evil Devil Cult Leader's influence, are placed into a trance by the virtue of the Saints' marching. The power vested in this procession miraculously freezes the Demons in their tracks as if they are mannequins. They will remain frozen until the saintly parade disperses.

Austin's spiritual march divides the wheat from the tares, the righteous from the evil, the Saints from the Demons. There is no longer a question in any of the Saints' minds; they now know who shall live and who shall be destroyed.

CHAPTER FORTY-THREE

Jo-Ken and Joe's Heart to Heart

The Saints have finished day five of their perimeter march.

Joe's taking in a little relaxation time before Operation Saving Grace begins. He's kicked back in his recliner, enjoying a cold one, and watching college football, while Knife Warrior is showing off for Joe's secret company by taking in some target practice on a few barn flies.

Joe notices Jo-Ken is restless and wants to come out and play, but Joe's not in the mood to converse at the moment. Joe pays him no attention, but Jo-Ken's not having it.

Jo-Ken floats around the room, doing his best to get under Joe's skin.

He rattles the mirror on the wall. He tickles Joe's feet and knocks on his forehead. Joe purposely ignores Jo-Ken, keeping his eyes focused on the game.

JO-KEN:

Joe-Joe! Oh Joseph! Do I need to turn off the tube and pour out your beer, or what? Or hey, I know.

In an instant, Jo-Ken lifts Joe from his recliner, bends him over his knee, and starts spanking his butt.

Joe squirms and kicks like a five-year-old but can't escape Jo-Ken's strong spirit hands, and just when Joe believes he's finished, Jo-Ken gives him one more good one to grow on.

JO-KEN:

That last one's for rooting for Alabama!

JOE:

Come on, Ken. I'm a grown man for crying out loud!

JO-KEN:

Aww, did Daddy hurt him little boy's feel-bads?

Jo-Ken takes big Joe in his arms, rocking him like a baby.

JOE:

Okay! Okay! Put me down! I'm sorry, let's talk, dammit!

JO-KEN:

Now, that's better. Listen, son, we need to have a heart to heart. You can't allow Austin's plan to destroy your two brothers. They're your brothers.

Joe's still upset because he's missing the game.

JOE:

Well, Ken, I believe if you hadn't taken your family into a devil meeting, I wouldn't have to kill anyone, now, would I?

JO-KEN:

It hurts me when you call me Ken. I'm your dad. Can't you call me Dad?

JOE:

Sure thing, Ken!

333

Jo-Ken bypasses Joe's sarcasm and gets to the point.

JO-KEN:

Well, this God Austin worships, this Jesus everyone's marching to, maybe He can do something - maybe change Jack and Jerry and take the devil out of them. *ugh* I don't know - redeem them or something.

I mean, what about your mother? I still love Farrah. Doesn't she mean anything to you?

JOE:

If she means that much to you, maybe you should go live inside of her and leave me the hell alone. I mean, come on, Ken! I can't have friends or a relationship with a girl because I know you're watching my every move, and who knows when you'll attack someone. Hell, I can't even jerk off for crying out loud! Besides, you're the one who got her raped!

JO-KEN:

Masturbation will make you go blind. *laughs*

JOE:

You should know! *chuckles* So, that's what happened to Gary's eyes. Leave me alone. I'm watching the game.

JO-KEN:

I'm sorry, son. I've been selfish. I'm ashamed. If there's any forgiveness, I promise I'll give your life back and look for another place to dwell if only you can find a way to save Farrah.

JOE:

Okay, but you promised me you'd leave me alone if I killed the devil and brought Jack home, remember?

JO-KEN:

I mean it this time. I swear on Farrah's life.

Joe always wanted to have this conversation but has too much respect for his dad. Joe goes soft.

JOE:

I can speak for Austin. That boy will have no problem killing his mom and dad. But I'm not sure how to contact my brothers or my mother - we've not spoken in years.

They're devils, Ken, but if I run into 'em, I'll give it a go. Fair enough?

JO-KEN:

That's all I can ask for, son.

Joe is being kind as usual, but in his heart, he knows he must find his family to rid himself of Jo-Ken and get his life back.

JOE:

Here comes the knife man, time to get back in your cage.

Jo-Ken eases his ghostly self back into Joe.

JOE:

Hey, buddy, did you impress our company?

KNIFE WARRIOR:

Them yeller jackets kept me busier than a cat coverin' up crap on a marble floor.

Picked off a few barn flies I hear'd buzzin', and I'll guarantee ya, not one of them pesky mosquitoes escaped with minor injuries neither.

JOE:

laughs Hey! Whatta ya say we give these two lovebirds some time, and you and I head to Seven Mile and start a beer war.

KNIFE WARRIOR:

Got down off my horse! If yer brains were dynamite, you couldn't blow yer nose! You hate Seven Mile, Joe.

JOE:

I've got a few relatives I haven't seen in a while. I'm gonna try trackin' 'em for an old friend of ours. Whatta ya say, old buddy?

KNIFE WARRIOR:

Well, I guess I didn't pack my fancy snakeskin shit-kickers fer nuttin'. Let me glide my daggers across the rock a few times, and we'll git 'er going here dreckly.

CHAPTER FORTY-FOUR

A Night at The Bloody Bucket

Joe and Cross-Eyed Knife Warrior make the trek into Seven Mile to look for Farrah and Joe's brothers. The first place they think to try is a local dive bar called The Bloody Bucket. They arrive to find the parking lot completely full.

KNIFE WARRIOR:

Hey, what's with all the cars, Joe?

Though Knife Warrior can only see shadows, he is skilled enough in his other senses to know these particular shadows are cars.

JOE:

Don't know. I don't hang out in this...HOLY GUACAMOLE!

KNIFE WARRIOR:

What is it, Joe?

JOE:

Look at the marquee!

KNIFE WARRIOR:

There's no way I jist hear'd what I jist hear'd. Sometimes you just make my ass itch, Joe!

JOE:

Sorry, buddy. I'll read it to ya. "Tonight Only! Anthony Reno and the Big Bastard Band - Special Guests: The Russian River Band."

Joe is more into Anthony Reno, but shit-kicking Knife Warrior prefers Country and Western.

KNIFE WARRIOR:

Why in the love of a million-dollar bill is the Russian Rivers playing in this run-down shanty? They must be as confused as a fart in a fan factory, Joe!

JOE:

Not sure. I remember when they performed free at local coffee shops and such. Now look at 'em. They're big stars if they're playing with Anthony Reno and the Big Bastard Band.

KNIFE WARRIOR:

Russian River Band got themselves a number one hit, Joe, "Slow Speed Chase."

Joe is still ducking and weaving, searching for a parking spot.

JOE:

No, sir - don't know such a song.

KNIFE WARRIOR:

Just what in hades you listenin' to these days? Nuttin'?! You better not tell me yer still listenin' to that weird disco crap you always drove me crazy with neither.

JOE:

Hold on ya cross-eyed creep. Just cause I'm not spittin' tobacco doesn't mean I don't tune in to a little Willie now and then. Remember, I got old man living inside of me - Mr. Bennett's more to his liking.

KNIFE WARRIOR:

Hells bells, Joe. I sit in front of my radio just beggin' fer some "Slow Speed Chase." We're in for a treat tonight! Woooooo!

Knife Warrior drums Joe's dashboard with his palms and taps his shit-kickers on Joe's floorboard.

JOE:

Tony Reno's an old buddy of mine. Do you know Tony?

KNIFE WARRIOR:

Personally, I've never met the guy, but I chopped a club owner's hands off with a meat cleaver once, though.

JOE:

What in the heard is wrong with you?

JOE (CONT'D):

Is there any place - any place in the entire world you haven't cut, sliced, diced, stabbed, or killed someone? Besides, what in the hell does chopping a man's hand off have to do with whether you know Tony Reno?

KNIFE WARRIOR:

Well, kiss my go-ta-hell! Thought you'd never ask, nosey!

Tony's manager hired me to collect some funds from a club owner. Hey! It's not my fault that high faluten-er wore diamonds on both hands. I whacked him faster than green grass passes through a goose. I's a'meanin' to leave him with a hand, but I wasn't sure where my cut was a'comin' from.

Joe just shakes his head like always.

JOE:

Do me a favor, try not to stab anyone this evening, okay?

Knife Warrior stretches a grin across his face.

KNIFE WARRIOR:

I'll do my best, puddin'.

342

crowded bar sounds

They finally make it to The Bloody Bucket's entrance, where they are greeted by The Doorman.

THE DOORMAN:

Tickets, please.

A large bouncer wearing a wifebeater stands lurking in The Doorman's shadow with his arms crossed, flexing his bulging muscles for Joe and Knife Warrior to see.

THE DOORMAN:

Tickets, please.

KNIFE WARRIOR:

Tickets?! What tickets?! We ain't ridin' no fancy merry-go-round at a carnival or nuttin'. Who licked the red off yer candy? What in the hell we need a ticket at a bar fer?

THE DOORMAN:

No ticket? No ride. We're way over capacity as it is.

343

KNIFE WARRIOR:

Yer as windy as a sack full of farts. Lord knows ya can't help from being ugly, but ya sure coulda stayed home.

Joe decides to go easy on The Doorman.

JOE:

We don't have tickets. I just need to talk to someone for a minute.

THE DOORMAN:

No tickets? Then you can wait in that long no-ticket line windin' around that building. But trust me, nobody will miss Tony Reno and the Big Bastards. You fellows might want to purchase a ticket next time. I'm sure there are plenty of tickets for the kiddie rides at the carnival in the next town over.

JOE:

Didn't I hear you say you're way over capacity?

THE DOORMAN:

I know I didn't stutter. Stutterin' makes me sound stupid. My mouth's not like your friend's goofy-looking eyes. My mouth works as designed.

Nothin' has changed in the last thirty seconds, however, just in case you forgot your hearin' aids, I will repeat myself. WE'RE. STILL. WAY. OVER. CAPACITY.

JOE:

I'm sure my perfectly designed ears heard this establishment is not adhering to the state's fire code laws. Guess I'll truck on over and see if Freddy the fire marshal's sitting at home with his old hound, Fletcher, this evening.

THE DOORMAN:

Go ahead! I'm sure Fletcher likes company, but if my well-designed memory serves me right, Freddy and his wife cleared themselves a path front and center stage about a half an hour ago.

JOE:

Okay, you got me there. But I'll just bet these underaged split-tails I've witnessed entering this adult, alcohol-driven establishment won't sit well with my upper echelon friends at the old court-house. So now, if you try hard enough, I'm sure you'll find a tiny little corner somewhere in this overcrowded, child-serving, not-to-code palace where a friend and I can hitch a horse or two.

Joe fishes Knife Warrior for a compliment.

JOE:

What do you believe, Mr. Indiana? Do you suppose this well-spoken, non-stuttering gentleman can squeeze two goofy-looking degenerates like us in tonight?

KNIFE WARRIOR:

Here's what I suppose. Mister Doorman could start an argument in an empty house. I'm tired of you two's immature dick-swingin' sword fight! That's what I suppose.

Time for Mister Doorman to roll out the red carpet for us two fine, respectable gentlemen. Watch and learn, Joe.

The doorman crosses his arms.

KNIFE WARRIOR:

I know what yer thinkin'. Does he have one dagger, or does he have two daggers? Tell ya the truth, through all your pun about my goofy eyes - I kinda lost track of myself. So, ask yerself this one question. Do ya feel unlucky, pun'kin? Well, do ya, pun'kin? Am I dirty, or am I hairy, pun'kin?

JOE:

I'm impressed. Now knock it off, movie star, and do something!

The Doorman gets impatient and taps his toe, unknowingly giving Knife Warrior a target.

Knife Warrior delivers two daggers faster than a rattlesnake's strike, clear through the tops of The Doorman's feet, sticking him to the old, condemned, wooden floor.

THE DOORMAN:

Arrgghh! Shit! Damn!

KNIFE WARRIOR:

Lawdy! Looks like I had two daggers, pun'kin. *laughs*

JOE:

laughs Looks more like squash to me.

With a wave and a smile, The Bouncer motions Joe and Knife Warrior through the door as The Doorman continues squealing like a piglet removed from its mother's teat.

THE BOUNCER:

You fine gentleman will not be needing a ticket this evening. Please, enjoy tonight's entertainment - compliments of the house.

Knife Warrior pulls his daggers from The Doorman's feet.

THE DOORMAN:

Ow! Shit!

KNIFE WARRIOR:

Why ya so sad? Chevrolet stop makin' trucks? *laughs*

Knife Warrior politely thanks The Doorman for rolling out his personal display of red carpet. He wipes the blood onto The Doorman's bright, white, shiny coat.

The Bouncer watches The Doorman doing the bunny hop.

THE DOORMAN:

Why in the heck did you let them in?!

THE BOUNCER:

You stupid little weasel did you not know that was Big Joe Turner?!

The Doorman slowly lifts his eyes from his blood-filled shoes.

THE BOUNCER:

Yeah, Big Joe motherfuckin' Turner! I quit! If shit goes bad around here tonight, someone's gonna die, and it ain't gonna be me.

The Bouncer made the wise decision to call the evening done. Unfortunately for him, Anthony Reno's bus driver was pulling through and ran the big intelligent feller over.

CHAPTER FORTY-FIVE

Do The Hustle

The cocktail waitresses barely have room to swing their half-naked, tiny tushies through the packed honky-tonk. Joe's keeping an eye out for his mother and brothers as he and Cross-Eyed Knife Warrior make their way to the backroom to hustle some dart throwers. Joe scribbles their names on the doubles chalkboard and gets it going with a couple of shots and beers.

JOE:

I'll be back. I'm gonna go feed the jukebox. Anything you wanna hear?

KNIFE WARRIOR:

Naught, you go ahead, I trust ye.

Joe drops a few quarters in the flashy jukebox in the corner. He watches the music maker flop a 45 onto its turntable as he searches for another selection. The needle lands softly upon the rotating vinyl, sending sounds of a drummer riding high-hat cymbals and a thumping bass line. The surrounding horny barflies go to showing off their tight physiques, moving and grooving to the disco dance style of music. Joe joins the dancers, snapping his fingers high into the air and bopping his head as he dodges their swinging arms, trying to return to his table.

Knife Warrior doesn't approve of Joe's music selection. He lowers his head, raising his bizarre-looking eyes to Joe, pretending he's making eye contact.

Joe smiles.

JOE:

What?

KNIFE WARRIOR:

Did you bring me here to torture me? I believe yer fuckin' the puckered starfish, ain't ya, Joe?

JOE:

Hold on, tootsie, I believe you started this romance. If you recall, you called me puddin' a bit earlier.

KNIFE WARRIOR:

Love's a beautiful thang, ain't it, Joe?

Their longneck bottles toast their friendship.

Dee-Onie Dartmouth, Seven Mile's champion dart thrower, just finished taking a few bucks from two wannabes from out of town, making him a tad cocky.

DEE-ONIE DARTMOUTH:

Indiana! Turner! You're the next losers! Let's go!

Dee-Onie pulls his custom, solid gold King Cobra darts from the dartboard.

DEE-ONIE DARTMOUTH:

Twenty-five a head if you two bruisers want to throw against this board, fellas. Money on the table.

Knife Warrior pretends to have consumed too much alcohol.

KNIFE WARRIOR:

Twenty-five dollars?! I'm so poor - I can't even afford feed for my pet tumbleweed! I can't see no pool table, let alone throw darts at one. What's a dart look like anyhows, Joe?

DEE-ONIE DARTMOUTH:

Twenty-five each, or you can go suck tap water together in a corner somewhere. Throw it down or get outta town. Time's money, and I'm here to get paid.

Joe can't hold his smirk.

JOE:

I'm a giving kind of guy. Whatta you say we raise ya - uh two-hundred a head?

KNIFE WARRIOR:

No, Joe! I've never thrown a dart in all my born days!

DEE-ONIE DARTMOUTH:

You better listen to your muscle-bound cross-eyed clown. I'm not here to play checkers, boys. I'll take your money.

JOE:

How about one-thousand a head, just so I can shut your braggin' mouth?

KNIFE WARRIOR:

No! Joe?! Come on, I ain't got that kind of money! The rent's due!

Dee-Onie tosses a wad of hundreds on the table.

DEE-ONIE DARTMOUTH:

I won't weep taking money from a disabled, so let's get throwing. I'm all in. Get yer darts, fellers.

Knife Warrior pushes his act.

KNIFE WARRIOR:

Get my darts? What the hell's he talking about, Joe? This guy don't know whether to check his ass or scratch his watch. I ain't got no fuckin' darts. What is he, some kinda pro-fesh-a-nal or sumptin'?

Dee-Onie and his partner bust a gut as they toast one another with their beer mugs.

Joe hands Cross-Eyed Knife Warrior the bent, worn-out house darts.

JOE:

Here, buddy, just use these.

Knife Warrior steps to the foul line with his back to the dartboard. The bystanders laugh and carry on in disbelief, watching the dart charade.

DEE-ONIE DARTMOUTH:

Come the fuck on, I can see your partner's cross-eyed, but I had no idea he's blind. I might as well just take my money now.

Dee-Onie takes the stack of wager money from the holding case. Joe shoots Dee-Onie a look that would scare a lion.

JOE:

Unless you wanna throw those fancy darts with your toes, put the money back before I chop your thieving fingers off. You better pull the reins back on that high horse you're riding and shut your pucker pool before I piss in it.

DEE-ONIE DARTMOUTH:

Have it your way, but you're gonna pay me.

JOE:

You ready, Indiana?

KNIFE WARRIOR:

I'm as lost as last year's Easter egg! I'll do my best, Joe!

JOE:

Let's give old Dee-Onie Donkey Dick a fair chance - no peeking.

Joe grabs a metal spoon from a nearby table and taps the center ring around the bullseye loud enough for Cross-Eyed Knife Warrior to hear.

Knife Warrior fires two darts with his right hand and one dart with his left hand directly over his shoulders at the same time, landing three perfect bullseyes.

Dee-Onie and all who were watching lost control of their lower jaws as their eyes grew to full capacity.

KNIFE WARRIOR:

Did I hit the balloons? Do I git a prize, Joe?

JOE:

Dammit, Indiana, one of them darts just barely made it inside the bullseye. That's okay, buddy. You'll do better next time.

crowd shouts and cheers

DEE-ONIE DARTMOUTH:

You sons-a-bitches snookered us. I refuse to be screwed over by two cross-eyed crooks.

Dee-Onie aggressively takes the wager money from the holding box. Knife Warrior grabs Dee-Onie's expensive darts, firing two perfect strikes, piercing his earlobes at no charge.

DEE-ONIE DARTMOUTH:

Shit! What the fuck was that?!

Dee-Onie gently hands Joe the money and makes his way out of the dart room.

The bystanders pivot, pretending they didn't see anything. They felt this was the wisest and safest thing to do.

CHAPTER FORTY-SIX

Back-Ho Betty

Joe and Cross-Eyed Knife Warrior tuck their winnings away and make their way into the standing-room-only lounge. Miraculously, Joe spots two empty chairs at a table and quickly moves to claim them. What a coincidence - these two empty chairs just happen to be sat at Dee-Onie Dartmouth's private table.

Realizing it's the two suckers from the dart room, Joe prods Knife Warrior to work his magic.

KNIFE WARRIOR:

How's the tap water this evening, friends? Me, and my partner here, we'd like to offer you two dart experts a thousand bucks for those two empty chairs right there.

Dee-Onie, still reeling from his first loss in years, defeatedly raises his head and shoots Joe and Knife Warrior a hateful look - his fancy darts still dangling from his bleeding ears.

KNIFE WARRIOR:

Does this mean we're not friends? Ya know, Mr. Dart-throwa' if I thought we weren't friends, I just don't believe I couldn't bury ya. *laughs*

JOE:

Alright, Holliday. Whaddya say, fellas, we got a deal?

For the first time in Dee-Onie Dartmouth's life, he does not have one word to say. Just like Elvis, Dee-Onie and his buddy left the building, leaving Joe and Knife Warrior with their very own table.

JOE:

Ya know, Gary, for a guy who can't see the TV screen, you sure watch a lot of movies.

KNIFE WARRIOR:

I prolly see more with my eyes closed than you see with yers open. It's better jist to listen. I see what I wanna see that way. It makes yee smarter.

Joe and Knife Warrior shrug and take a seat. The crowd thunders as The Russian River Band takes the stage, returning to the dive bar that once helped put them on the top of the Country and Western charts. Knife Warrior jumps up and down like he did when his parents gave him a Batman and Robin lunch box with matching thermos last week. Not being a Country and Western fan, 'disco' Joe gives a moderate hand clap for the local band that has made it big.

The Russian River Band bangs out a few rockabilly tunes. Knife Warrior can't control the kid inside as he kicks his shit-kickers on the dance floor, knocking everybody he can't see on their caboose. Joe enjoys Knife Warrior's dance performance. He rocks himself back and forth on two legs of his wooden chair, keeping an eye out for Farrah and his brothers.

The steel guitarist glides his slide across the horizontal instrument while the lead guitarist bends his strings in perfect time, kicking off a tear-jerking, romantic love song. The couples in the house cuddle on the dance floor.

Knife Warrior returns to the table, dripping in sweat and sniffing the air like a dog smelling a steak on the grill.

KNIFE WARRIOR:

Whaddya say we stop holdin' our peckers long enough to hogtie us some of this sugar snatch I'm smellin? I like 'em about two biscuits shy of two-hundred pounds myself, Joe.

JOE:

Which two do you want me to lasso, Tex?

KNIFE WARRIOR:

Hell, I can't see 'em anyways. Personally, I like em with their pants so tight if they fart, they blow their boots off. Make sure the shitter on the critter is nice and round, though. Oh hell, jist make sure they smell perty, Joe.

JOE:

laughs I wish it was that easy, buddy. Problem is, for one, you're ugly, and two, having sex in front of my old man makes an erection damn near impossible.

KNIFE WARRIOR:

You think I'm ugly, Joe? My mom says I'm perty.

JOE:

I thought you said your mom and dad are blind?

KNIFE WARRIOR:

Like I said earlier, blind people see really good. Here, look at these pictures my momma took of me when I was growing up.

Knife Warrior removes his wallet and hands it to Joe. The plastic wallet insert full of photos unfolds as Joe takes hold. Joe examines the photos. He sees pictures of the sky, the ground, a bare wall - but no photos that include Knife Warrior.

JOE:

Your mom took these photos of you, huh, buddy?

KNIFE WARRIOR:

Yep! That woman sure knew how to use her camer-y.

Joe feels he is better off sparing his best friend's feelings. He hands the wallet back.

JOE:

Your mom is right. You sure are pretty, my friend.

Catty corner from Joe and Knife Warrior sit two ladies, each sipping a tall, colorful, fruity drink from a long straw, laughing and engaging in friendly conversation.

Joe has always wanted someone to hold and cries himself to sleep every night just imagining it.

JOE:

I'll tell you something. If I wasn't carrying my extra suitcase, I believe I've consumed enough jibber juice to ask the pretty little brunette sitting with the bubble-butt blonde to marry me.

KNIFE WARRIOR:

Well, if that don't light yer fire, then yer wood's wet. Let's shoot another shot of munch-a-muffin and git on with it, Joe!

JOE:

Hold on, Hercules. I'd bout venture to say them pretty little hens have husbands galivanting around here somewhere. You've already stapled one man to the floor and hustled two locals out of a couple grand. Approaching another man's wife just might bring cold steel to the back of our heads. Jerk up the emergency brake, will ya?

KNIFE WARRIOR:

Well, if she's shuckin' someone else's corn, it ain't my fault, Joe.

Meanwhile, the two ladies have had Joe and Knife Warrior on their radar as well. Blondie is in heat and ready to do the nasty.

BLONDIE:

Did you see musclebound, snakeskin gladiator cutting the rug? I'll bet once that cross-eyed clittylicker gets his tongue churnin', I'll really be glad he ate her.

The two girls giggle like teenagers. Brunette Lady crosses her eyes and bites her tongue, making fun of Knife Warrior.

BRUNETTE LADY:

Yeah, he's got the bod, but he might play hell figuring out which hole to stick it in. *laughs*

BLONDIE:

That was a good one. Hell, I can't see what's behind me, anyway, honey. I'd loan silly eyes my backhoe for a couple hours of diggin', that's for sure.

BRUNETTE LADY:

You're still the same old slut I remember you as. Damn, it's so good to see you after all these years.

The guy with your goliath of a man looks awfully familiar, though. Not to mention, I believe he's hot enough I'd do him sunny side up, and I'm only half the whore you are.

BLONDIE:

Half the whore, huh?! Well, that still makes you fifty percent hussy. Besides, at least I'm still a virgin.

BRUNETTE LADY:

You're about as virgin as the little old lady who lived in a shoe. *laughs*

BLONDIE:

No, really. You can ask anyone I've slept with.

BRUNETTE LADY:

Anyone you slept with? That would be everyone we know. *laughs*

BLONDIE:

I really am a virgin - I even got the tattoo to prove it. Noooo body's layin' pipe in this girl's trench until they put a ringer on her finger. I'm not a tractor for fuck's sake! That's why they call me Back-Ho Betty. I got the perfect spot for 'em to dump their load. *chuckles*

BRUNETTE LADY:

You're serious? Your 'gina has never been open for business? Not even once?

BLONDIE:

Yes - and no. Yes, I'm serious as a broken heart, honey. And no, not even once. And I'll bet I've had a whole lot more orgasms than you boring missionary girls.

BRUNETTE LADY:

Well, aren't you just the vestal virgin? My backdoor stays locked. Hell, I need to explore. I haven't gotten off in years.

Brunette Lady spreads her legs and bows her head toward her crotch.

BRUNETTE LADY:

Did ya hear that, ladies? Slide open the deadbolt and send out invitations! There's gonna be a hoedown!

The Russian River Band rocked a few bring-the-house-down country sounds before slowing the tempo for the tune everyone has been waiting for, "Slow Speed Chase." The couples pack the dance floor, leaving the two ladies an open lane to approach their prize eggs.

Blondie puts on her cheesy charm for Knife Warrior.

BLONDIE:

Excuse me. You look lost. Point your arrow towards my back door, and I'll show you the way. *laughs* Come on, sweetie, let's dance.

Knife Warrior's usual keen senses fail him, leaving him clueless to Blondie's advances. Joe gives him a swift kick under the table.

JOE:

Hey! Sugar snatch is knockin', hoss.

Tough guy's legs nervously weaken once he acknowledges Blondie is addressing him. Truth is, Knife Warrior's unfortunate appearance only attracts ladies he pulls his wallet for.

Blondie offers her hand.

BLONDIE/BACK-HO BETTY:

Hi, I'm Betty.

KNIFE WARRIOR:

Gary Indiana, ma'am. Nice to meet ya.

BETTY:

Ain't that where Michael Jackson's from?

JOE:

Janet Jackson too! *laughs*

KNIFE WARRIOR:

I live in a town so small we once had a parade, and there was nobody left to watch.

369

BETTY:

chuckles flirtatiously

Knife Warrior and Betty laugh and head to dance.

Joe sweeps his eyes across the pretty Brunette Lady before him.

JOE:

Your friend has quite a gift. Can you top her line? Please, go ahead, give it a try.

Brunette Lady's heart leaps from her chest.

BRUNETTE LADY:

Damn, it is you!

JOE:

If that's the best ya got, I'll surrender.

BRUNETTE LADY:

I'm not surprised you don't recognize me. Let's not waste my favorite song talking.

Brunette lady offers Joe her hand.

JOE:

I don't dance.

BRUNETTE LADY:

How's come?

JOE:

Don't know how.

BRUNETTE LADY:

I'll teach ya.

She grabs Joe's hand. The two hit the dance floor. Joe places his arms around her shoulders. She gently moves Joe's hands to her waist. Their eyes gleam as if they were saying wedding vows.

JOE:

Was your line for real? Do you know who I am?

BRUNETTE LADY:

Many years ago, I promised you a favor for taking me across the border, Joseph Nathaniel.

The memories of a scared young girl silently pleading with him in his rear-view mirror come flooding back. Joe finally realizes that the pretty little Brunette Lady he is dancing with is the injured stowaway from so long ago.

Cupid empties his bow. They seal their newfound relationship with Joe's very first kiss.

Joe is so smitten by her that he is unaware Farrah and his two brothers are sitting at a table just off the dance floor.

"Slow Speed Chase" ends. Joe and Brunette Lady continue dancing without music.

Farrah is having an enjoyable night out with her sons, Jack and Jerry, and daughter-in-law, Sandy. Farrah spots a somewhat familiar figure on the dance floor.

FARRAH:

Oh, my goodness! Is that Joe?

JERRY:

Where?! I'll kill the son of a bitch right here!

SANDY:

Yep, that's him. Let's go, Jerry. My night's officially ruined. Ain't no way I'm breathin' the same air as that S-O-B.

Sandy detests being in the same room with Joe Turner.

SANDY:

Jerry! I said, let's go!

She and Jerry furiously leave Jack and Farrah sitting at the table.

JACK:

How about you, Mom. Do you want to leave?

FARRAH:

I don't get it. Why the hate towards Joe? He didn't knife Jerry, and he saved your life, Jack. Can I please just take a minute to look at the son I've longed to see, to talk to, to spend time with? Please, Jack?

JACK:

Mom, go talk to Joe if you like, but remember, he's not like us, Mom.

FARRAH:

I know. I don't want to interfere with his evening. I prefer to just look at him if that's okay.

CLETUS MCGEE:

I'm Cletus McGee, and this is The Russian River Band! Good-night y'all!

crowd cheers

Joe, Knife Warrior, and their two lady friends take their seats to enjoy one of Joe's favorite entertainers, Anthony Reno and the Big Bastard Band.

Tony Reno, a native of Seven Mile, makes his triumphant return to the hometown bar where he once honed his craft as a lounge singer. His band lights up the stage wearing bright, colorful tuxedos that sparkle from the Par Can lights.

ANTHONY RENO:

Hit it, Steve. *big band music*

Good evening all my old demon friends from the past. It's been many moons since The Big Bastard Band and I have trod on Seven Mile's unholy ground. So, get your hands in the air this evening. Come on! Come on! Howl at the moon for me one good time, devils. All right! All right! Fasten your coffin lid because here we go.

I got a true story for y'all this evening. I was walkin' down the streets of Seven Mile today, and a cute little demon recognized me. She said, "excuse me, but aren't you the fabulous, famous Anthony Reno?" I said, "well, yes I am." She pulls out her little razor-sharp pin knife and asked, "Mr. Reno, can I have your autograph?" "Anything for a fine-looking fan like you, my lady from the grave." We sliced our fingers and joined our blood. She invited me back to her place. We shared a nice bottle of bubbly and a bit later mixed some of our finest body fluids - if you know what I mean!

Can you feel it?! I mean, lust is in the air. Let's get it goin' here, now. Woooo! So, come on, all you big strappin' studs - put your dicks on. We got us some business to attend to this evening, don't we, ladies?

Then she took those demon filled eyes, and looked me right straight in my heart, and said, "Mister fabulous, famous Anthony Reno, you're gonna die tonight, and there ain't one thing you can do about it."

Then she said with her evil laugh, "I'll see you in Hell!"

CHAPTER FORTY-SEVEN

The Bloody Bucket Gets Bloody

ANTHONY RENO:

We're gonna take a short pause for the cause, 'cause I see a lot of pretty faces I wouldn't mind givin' face to, myself, this evening. Make sure you're tippin' your bartenders and those cute little cocktail waitresses. They're serving my favorite bloody drink specials - the extra bloody "Bloody Fairies," and those knock-your-cocks-off "Serial Killer dark shots," filled with seven different spirits, guaranteed to scare hell into ya. Hey, I'm Tony Reno with the Big Bastard Band this evening. We'll be right back to entertain ya with some more hellacious tunes.

crowd cheers

The band leaves the stage for a short intermission.

Joe remains at the back of the crowded dance floor, away from Tony's sight, careful not to bring attention to himself.

Farrah excuses herself from Jack and fights her way through the crowd to Joe. She stares into Joe's bright eyes for the first time in twenty years.

JOE:

Mom?!

FARRAH:

Yes, Joseph, I'm your mother.

Joe scoops Farrah into his arms, lifting her from her feet. Their reunion brings tears of joy.

JOE:

Mom, this is - this is my girl, Mom.

BRUNETTE LADY/KAMI:

I'm Kami.

FARRAH:

Pleased to meet you. Are you two married?

KAMI:

No, we're acquaintances from years ago.

FARRAH:

So are we.

Tony and the Big Bastards make it back onto the stage to start their next set.

crowd cheers

ANTHONY RENO:

There's a lot of fine lookin' ladies in the house tonight. Can ya feel 'em? Oh, yeah! There's nothin' like a dark-spirited lady to make your night…just right.

Tony puts an eye on Joe and beckons him to the stage. Joe, not wanting to appear rude to his old pal, excuses himself from Farrah and his new love.

Joe hits the stage.

ANTHONY RENO:

Hey, everybody, Big Joe Turner's in the house tonight. He and I go way back. Let's give Joe a big round of applause. Come on, give it up for Big Joe Turner.

The room fills with devilish moans, hisses, and screeches.

Tony recognizes Joe is not one of them.

ANTHONY RENO:

Hey - um, you don't want to keep your beautiful lady waiting, do you, Joe? How's about a kind word before you head back to your seat, Joe?

Jo-Ken comes forth.

JO-KEN:

Welcome to The Bloody Bucket, demons! Soon...and very soon... you're all going to die!

Tables turn at The Bloody Bucket. In an instant, Jo-Ken rips himself from Joe creating a mighty whirlwind. The heavy wind fills the room full of flying debris.

A jagged beer bottle spins violently into Tony Reno's throat, dropping him to his dying knees. His spewing blood covers the dancers on the dance floor.

ANTHONY RENO:

chokes *gasps for air* *dies*

The tormented demons cut themselves and strip naked as they desperately cry to the Evil Devil Cult Leader to remove the good spirits from their presence.

Joe dodges flying objects and directs Kami and Betty to follow him. They fight their way to the kitchen, where Knife Warrior is in the fight of his life. He uses every kitchen utensil available, cutting, slicing, and stabbing any devil he senses.

The demons surround them. Their demonic ear-piercing shrieks and oozing blood alert Joe that he needs to act fast.

Joe grabs Betty's hair spray and lighter from her purse, creating a mini blow torch. Kami grabs a fire extinguisher.

Their quick reactions hold the demons at bay until they all make it to the back door. As a last-ditch effort to escape the demons, Betty turns on the stoves, releasing gas into the air.

The two couples run frantically through the packed parking lot, searching for Joe's truck.

The earth shakes from an enormous explosion. The couples turn to see Jo-Ken thrust through the front doors, splintering them from their hinges. Jo-Ken is carrying Farrah and Jack, but they are tormented by the touch of his clean spirit, so he releases them.

Joe expects Jo-Ken to return to him. Jo-Ken, however, makes good on his promise, deciding once and for all to leave Joe forever. He rises high above The Bloody Bucket and plunges himself into Farrah.

CHAPTER FORTY-EIGHT

Baad Baad Black Sheep

Joe and the crew made it safely to Joe's cabin and called it a night.

Joe awakens bright and early to the smell of sizzling bacon. He moves towards the kitchen, stopping to lovingly admire Kami from afar before carefully approaching her from behind. He rubs her petite shoulders.

JOE:

Are you trying to catch the worm this morning, pretty lady?

Kami lowers the fire and turns to Joe.

KAMI:

No, Joe, I'm giving gratitude to the man who saved my life. I'm not a one-night girl. I swear to you, I've only been with a handful of men my entire life. When Betty invited me to go to the concert, I feared I might run into the creep who beat me years ago. When I found you, I knew I was safe. I swore I'd never set foot back in Seven Mile again. I'm so glad I did. I love you, Joseph Nathaniel.

JOE:

Me too, Kami. I'm glad I didn't wear my usual disguise last night. No one will ever hurt you again. That's a promise.

KAMI:

What now? I delivered the favor I promised. Is this the end? Will you kick me to the curb, Joe?

Joe gently places his hands on the sides of Kami's head, tenderly massaging her tears into her soft cheeks as they fall from her insecure eyes.

JOE:

You're welcome in my life for as long as I live.

Their sensitive moment is interrupted by loud giggles as Knife Warrior and Betty play grab-ass coming down the hall from Joe's spare bedroom.

BETTY:

Stop that, you nasty gladiator man, before we have to go for round six.

KNIFE WARRIOR:

Wooooweeee! Now that was one helluva night, wuttin it? Them devils ain't no joke. I'm still pullin' toothpicks outta my fanny.

BETTY:

He pulled toothpicks from his fanny while sticking timber in mine. *laughs*

Sorry if all that gruntin', moanin', and groanin' kept y'all up last night.

KAMI:

No, you're not! But those loud, "fuck me, gladiator man, fuuuuuuuuck meeee's" sure interrupted my romantic lover. Sounded to me like you're gonna need a new tattoo, hussy!

BETTY:

chuckles

Knife Warrior scratches his butt while sniffing the aroma from the bacon.

KNIFE WARRIOR:

Man! Them vittles sure are making me uh hungry.

Joe notices a long, horribly stitched cut on Knife Warrior's right forearm.

JOE:

That cut looks bad, buddy.

KNIFE WARRIOR:

Betty sewed her up fer me. Looks damn good if yer askin' me.

JOE:

If you say so, friend.

KNIFE WARRIOR:

I'm just as good as new. I'm as happy as ol' Blue lyin' on the porch chewin' on a big ole catfish head.

Betty appreciates Knife Warrior's compliment. However, he might think differently if he saw her stitch job.

They take a seat to share breakfast together. Knife Warrior senses something is not right in Joe's spirit.

KNIFE WARRIOR:

Y'ont talk about it, buddy?

JOE:

Yeah, I guess we'd better. I remembered Austin saying something about a sacrificial lamb. My neighbor buddy, Chester Miller, keeps a field full of sheep. After bacon and eggs, we better visit the old farmer.

The girls clear the breakfast table while Joe and Knife Warrior tie their boots. Before exiting, Joe motions Kami over and gives her a gentle kiss on top of her sweet head.

JOE:

When I leave, look under your bedroom pillow.

Kami squeezes Joe goodbye.

Joe and Knife Warrior drive down Chester's lane, passing the sheep grazing along the fence line.

KNIFE WARRIOR:

I see some shad-ees, Joe. Y'ont me to git cha one?

JOE:

I'm a lot of things, but I'm not a thief. Let's see what my old buddy wants for one first.

KNIFE WARRIOR:

Okay, don't git yer knickers in a knot. Damn, Joe!

Knife Warrior waits in the truck while Joe knocks on the door. Joe gets surprised by a large Rottweiler and a yapping Shih Tzu doing their duties through the thick glass of the old farm's front door. He jumps backwards. There's no reason to knock a second time.

He climbs into the truck, throwing his hands on top of the steering wheel.

JOE:

This is serious, Gary. We're running out of time.

KNIFE WARRIOR:

What we supposed to do with this varmint, anyways?

JOE:

I'm not sure. I just remember Austin saying something about beating it until it's almost dead and nail it on a cross.

KNIFE WARRIOR:

Well, that sounds about as worthless as gum on a boot heel to me. Where we gonna buy a cross that size? The closest church is over a hundred miles away from here, Joe.

JOE:

What do you mean by that?

KNIFE WARRIOR:

Church ain't gonna sell us one. They ass is so tight ya can't drive a needle in it with a sledgehammer. How else we suppose to git us one that big?

JOE:

All I know is we have one day to get the devil out my dad, mom, and brother, or they're gonna die.

KNIFE WARRIOR:

You ever hear'd of uh whack-a-mole, Joe?

JOE:

Can't say I have.

KNIFE WARRIOR:

Well, we gonna whack us a lamb chop.

Joe has no idea what Knife Warrior means. He cruises the lane nice and slow, being careful not to scare the skittish animals.

Knife Warrior's keen senses detect they're nearing a target. Within a split second, he exits the truck, splinters the planks of the wooden fence, grabs a lamb, and hurls it into the back of Joe's truck.

SACRIFICAL LAMB:

baaaa

Knife Warrior slams the camper shell door and is ready to roll faster than he can say, "there's yer goat, Joe."

KNIFE WARRIOR:

There's yer goat, Joe.

JOE:

I'll stop and pay the old farmer for his fence and sheep when we're finished.

KNIFE WARRIOR:

What fence?!

JOE:

Never mind. It sounded like you and Betty had an enjoyable night. Man, that girl sure can howl. What's next for you two noise-makers?

KNIFE WARRIOR:

We tried bein' quiet. Yer hearin's so good you can hear a mouse piss on a cotton ball, can't ya? I ain't no humpy dumpy, Joe.

JOE:

Yeah, what's that mean, buddy?

KNIFE WARRIOR:

I ain't gonna humpy then dumpy. I'm gonna marry that girl someday. Do you know she's a virgin?

JOE:

She's the loudest virgin I've ever heard, my friend. If you humpdy'd her, and please don't try and convince me you didn't, how's she a virgin?

KNIFE WARRIOR:

Well, she likes playin' her little game. When she's hot and juicy, she gits right up on her knees. Then she tells me knock on her buttocks three times - so I did. Then she tells me to come on in, back door's unlocked - so I did it again.

She's even got a tattoo provin' she's a virgin.

JOE:

Did you see this so-called tattoo?

KNIFE WARRIOR:

Joe! Ya keep forgettin' who yer talkin' to.

JOE:

Oops! Sorry, buddy.

KNIFE WARRIOR:

Her pants were so tight I could see her religion, and I can't see a thang - so she described it to me. It's a perty little cherry with the word 'virgin' right underneath it. She said, though her stream flows, it's a place where no one can go.

Joe glances into his rearview mirror. He catches the sheep staring through the camper's pass-through window, directly at him.

JOE:

Well, I'll be a son of a gunslinger!

KNIFE WARRIOR:

What is it, Joe?

JOE:

I know you're cross-eyed, but damn, I had no idea you're color blind too. You grabbed a black sheep.

KNIFE WARRIOR:

Well, shit fire till the barn catches on! Pull that burr outta yer ass, will ya? I don't want Austin's God picturin' we're some kind of racists or sumptin. Shadows, that's what I see! And you know it! That little trotter was the first shad-ee I saw crossin' my path. Dammit, Joe!

Knife Warrior elbows the window, accidentally shattering the glass.

KNIFE WARRIOR:

Next time, nab yer own gosh darn goat. Stupid stump-jumper anyhow, Joe!

JOE:

Aww hell, Gary, I'm sure it won't matter anyway. Sorry, buddy. I'm a little nervous about the whole thing.

Back at the cabin, Kami finishes the dishes and heads to look under her pillow. Somewhere in the night, Joe slipped away to write Kami a poem.

You came through the dark like a thief in the night.

You carved hope in my heart without using a knife.

You stole my innocence. I would have gave.

Kami, I love you. Let's do this the right way.

Will you marry me?

Joe.

Kami hugs the poem tight to her chest. Tears drip onto the page.

KAMI:

BETTY!!! I'M GETTING MARRIED!!!

CHAPTER FORTY-NINE

Tea, Anyone?

marching

The Saints of Seven Mile are in the midst of their sixth day of marching. Joe and Cross-Eyed Knife Warrior enter the outskirts of Seven Mile looking for Austin. They are seeking his spiritual guidance.

As they pass through Joe's old neighborhood, they witness devils on the sidewalk and in their yards, frozen in their tracks.

Joe stops in front of his childhood house. He observes Farrah, frozen, with her house key stuck in the front door lock, and Jack, also frozen, behind her holding a bag of groceries.

Joe finds Austin after the march ends. Joe, oblivious to the sacrifice of Christ, explains his plan to surrender the lamb in hopes Farrah and Jack may repent of their sins.

AUSTIN:

No, Uncle Joe, Jesus was the sacrificial lamb. He suffered and died on a cross for our sins - not a lamb. The scripture is speaking metaphorically because a lamb is innocent and pure as snow, like Jesus.

KNIFE WARRIOR:

Maybe the scripture should speak exactatorially. I just stole a non-racist farmer's goat!

Joe rolls his eyes, pointing to the bed of the truck.

SACRIFICIAL LAMB:

baaaaaa

AUSTIN:

That looks like a sheep to me, Cross-Eyed Knife Warrior.

KNIFE WARRIOR:

Sheep, goat, cow, or hog! They all look the same to me. All I know is I 'bout broke a nail fetchin' that little feller. The only difference to me is that they all taste like frog legs.

UNCLE JOE:

Can you save your grandma and your uncle, Austin?

Austin remembers that Uncle Joe has possibly never seen a Bible, let alone read one.

AUSTIN:

For the wages of sin is death, but by the blood of Jesus, the Christ, all who trust and believe he suffered and died on a cross and on the third day rose from a tomb can call on his name and be set free of all of their unrighteousness - past, present, and future.

Repent and believe and Jesus will come into your heart and save your soul from a burning hell. It's as simple as that, Uncle Joe.

UNCLE JOE:

Austin, after all I've seen and lived through, I'm ready to try anything.

KNIFE WARRIOR:

Me too! And it's obvious I can't see a thang.

AUSTIN:

Then bow your heads and confess and believe this prayer with me.

The three pull into Farrah's drive. Joe and Knife Warrior say the prayer with Austin.

Knife Warrior opens the back hatch to the camper shell to retrieve the sheep.

SACRIFICIAL LAMB:

baaaaaa

AUSTIN:

We won't need the animal. You can leave it, Cross-Eyed Knife Warrior.

Knife Warrior leaves the hatch open and follows Joe and Austin to the front door.

doorbell

Farrah answers the door.

FARRAH:

Well, look what the cat carried in. Jack, It's your brother Joe and nephew Austin. And you are?

KNIFE WARRIOR:

Gary. Gary Indiana, ma'am.

FARRAH:

Ain't Michael Jackson from there?

UNCLE JOE:

Janet Jackson too. *sarcastic laugh*

FARRAH:

Come on in. Jack, come and say hello! Well, my goodness, what a pleasant surprise.

Farrah offers them a seat. The three make themselves comfortable on a long couch along the wall.

Meanwhile, Joe's sacrificial lamb does what sheep do; they wander. The sheep frees itself through the open hatch and grazes the tall, uncut grass in Farrah's front lawn.

Jack shakes hands and re-introduces himself to Cross-Eyed Knife Warrior. He takes the opportunity to finally thank Knife Warrior for rescuing him in Guyana.

During their cheerful conversation, Farrah insists on making hot tea for everyone.

tea kettle whistles

Farrah enters the room wearing the brightest of smiles, carrying a beautiful, silver serving tray loaded with an elegant tea arrangement. She places the tea service in the middle of the long coffee table stationed in front of her three guests.

Jack commits a toast.

JACK:

Here's to our rekindled and eternal happy relationship! Cheers! Tee, tee, tee, tee.

Austin recognizes the devil's snicker and notices a smudge of what appears to be blood on the handle of his teacup.

Joe and Knife Warrior raise their cups. Austin slaps the teacup from Uncle Joe's hand, spilling the hot beverage across the room.

AUSTIN:

Don't drink that! Grandma, pull your hand from behind your back!

She refuses to cooperate.

AUSTIN:

The tea's contaminated with her demon blood!

Knife Warrior drops his teacup to the floor. He panics and spins a shuriken deep into Farrah's forehead.

FARRAH:

demonic growling

Tainted by Farrah's evil spirit, Jo-Ken slings sour words of the devil from Farrah's mouth.

JO-KEN:

Weapons of metal can't harm me, you foolish hoodwink!

Farrah raises her bloody hand from behind her back and removes the shuriken from her forehead, firing it back at Knife Warrior, slicing the top of his ear.

KNIFE WARRIOR:

Owwww!

JO-KEN:

Children of the high God, why have you come to destroy us? I'm happy in my new home. Leave us be! Your presence is no longer welcome here! Flee from us at once!

Knife Warrior pulls a knife. Austin remains calm.

AUSTIN:

Your weapons are harmless. Only the powerful word of God can affect these devils.

Jack is spinning in circles, speaking gibberish, and slapping his face in torment.

JACK:

Go away! Leave us to our master, you whores of good!

Farrah snatches Knife Warrior. Using Jo-Ken's spiritual strength, she throws his gigantic frame through the living room wall into the dining room.

Joe rushes his demon-possessed brother and finds he's no contest for Jack. He sends Joe hurling through the air, landing him violently on top of Knife Warrior.

KNIFE WARRIOR:

Joe! I'm seriously tired of gettin' my ass whipped by a bunch of devils. I feel like I just been 'et by a wolf and shit over a cliff! Bring that frick-frackin' critter in here, now!

Austin calmly rises from the couch, demanding the unclean spirits remove themselves in the name of Jesus. The demon's shriek and tremble at the powerful name of God.

Jo-Ken disconnects from Farrah. He crawls the wall like a crab until his head touches the high ceiling. His eyes bulge. He projectile vomits a vile, toxic sludge, leaving an unbearable stench throughout the room.

Joe takes to his feet. He peers through the doorway into Jack's devil-stricken eyes. Joe charges at Jack, but his large frame is intercepted by Jo-Ken's long evil tongue that wraps around his neck. He drags Joe to the ceiling squeezing him in his clutches.

JO-KEN:

He's not yours, Austin. He belongs to Satan. He belongs to me. He's miiiine!

Austin stays calm, holding to his faith.

AUSTIN:

Ask him, Grandpa. Ask your son who he belongs to.

JO-KEN:

Who lived inside of you for years, Joseph? Your mother and I brought you into this world. Who is your father, Joseph?

UNCLE JOE:

God, the Christ, is my father.

JO-KEN:

demonic growling

Jo-Ken's grip weakens.

UNCLE JOE:

God, the Christ, is my father! God, the Christ, is my father! God, the Christ, is my father! God, the Christ, is my father! God, the Christ, is my father!

JO-KEN:

crying Nooooo! Nooooo! My little Joseph, you're mine.

Knife Warrior enters the room.

KNIFE WARRIOR:

God is my father. God is my father. God is my father.

Tormented by their godly chants, Farrah uses her demonic powers, exploding the front door off its hinges and crashing it violently into a tree.

FARRAH:

Leave us, children of the Christ, before I expire your worthless souls!

SACRIFICIAL LAMB:

baaaa

Joe's sheep roams into Austin's sight. He summons the lamb. The presence of the unblemished animal brings the wicked spirits anguish. They tear at their flesh while Jo-Ken finds comfort lying in a fetal position in the room's corner, shaking and crying like an infant.

AUSTIN:

COME OUT, EVIL SPIRITS! IN THE NAME OF OUR HOLY SAVIOR! COME OUT! I COMMAND YOU!

The evil spirits that have possessed Farrah and Jack for many years are finally forced out of their dwelling place. Farrah and Jack fall into a trance on the floor.

The evil spirits enter the lamb, stealing its innocence. The lamb grows, enlarging to the size of a bull, transforming into a devilish beast with radiant gold eyes and huge nostrils that exhale large red rings of fire. The once innocent sheep sprouts large horns that shoot flames from their tips. The transmuted beast rises and stands firm on its back hooves, pounding its muscular chest.

The beast bellows with a voice from the deepest pit of Hell.

SACRIFICIAL LAMB:

I AM YOUR SACRIFICIAL LAMB!

The beast suffers its sacrifice, expanding like a balloon. The beast explodes. Hooves, hair, and guts splatter the walls and ceilings of the large room.

Miraculously, everyone remains impeccably clean from the animal's debris. It is by their faith that they have been untouched by the blood of the beast.

Farrah and Jack, free from demonic control, become conscious in their right minds. The extraordinary encounter brings the family into one another's arms.

UNCLE JOE:

Mom, where's Dad?

JO-KEN:

weeping

FARRAH:

What's that crying I hear?

UNCLE JOE:

Mom, the crying is your husband. I haven't called him Dad since he lost his fleshly life.

FARRAH:

Ken? Honey!

JO-KEN:

Yes, Farrah.

FARRAH:

I've missed you. Come back to me.

JO-KEN:

Austin, is it ok?

AUSTIN:

Yes, Grandpa. What God has joined together, let no man put asunder.

JO-KEN:

Joseph?

UNCLE JOE:

Yes, Dad?

JO-KEN:

I will stay with your mother where I belong. Thank you for all the glorious years. I love you, son.

UNCLE JOE:

I love you, Dad.

Jo-Ken's spirit illuminates. Farrah opens her arms and receives Jo-Ken into her soul.

CHAPTER FIFTY

Miracle by Faith

Farrah and Jack escort Joe, Austin, and Cross-Eyed Knife Warrior through the massive hole where the front door once stood, trudging through the rancid blood and guts of the demonic beast. They wave goodbye as they inspect the incredible disaster of the home.

Before reaching the truck, Knife Warrior stops Austin.

KNIFE WARRIOR:

Austin, if you think I was to ask the man upstairs fer my eyesight - do ya think?

AUSTIN:

God can do anything if it's his will, Knife Warrior. He's God.

KNIFE WARRIOR:

Please, call me Gary.

Austin looks at Knife Warrior and remembers what happened the last time he called him Gary.

KNIFE WARRIOR:

How do I find out if it's his will or not, Austin?

AUSTIN:

God made you beautifully with your blindness. Do you want healing, Gary?

KNIFE WARRIOR:

More than anything, Austin.

Just as Jesus did, Austin lifts dirt from the edge of the drive and spits on it, making it into clay.

AUSTIN:

Close your eyes, Gary.

Knife Warrior's legs weaken as he falls to his knees. Austin rubs the clay ever so gently, covering the tops of Knife Warrior's tender eyelids. Knife Warrior struggles not to move, but his body sways with the sound of the wind as it gently whispers across his sensitive ears.

AUSTIN:

Gary, ask and believe Jesus to heal your eyes, and I promise, if he doesn't heal your sight now, he will when you enter Heaven.

With a trusting heart, Knife Warrior asks Jesus for his healing hand. He trembles from the presence of the Holy Spirit, the third power of the mighty Godhead, as it moves through his body. His lips quiver with hope as his surrendering hands rise toward Heaven. He pleads with absolute conviction, believing Jesus will restore his faltering sight.

Austin gently wipes the clay from Knife Warrior's tearful eyes. Knife Warrior slowly lifts his fluttering eyelids.

KNIFE WARRIOR:

I can see. I can see! I can see!!

Joe and Austin stand in reverence, witnessing the miracle being performed on Knife Warrior. Tears of joy seep from their welling eyes.

It was Knife Warrior's faith that moved Christ to restore his vision. Knife Warrior looks to the heavens seeking to see the God who graciously healed him. He wants his first vision to be of the one who gave him his transformation.

Standing over him, tall with pride, is the most beautiful oak tree pompously displaying her sturdy branches and glistening leaves. Knife Warrior stares amazed as his mind struggles to comprehend the beauty towering above him. The majestic leaves dance back and forth in the gentle breeze. Knife Warrior has no way of understanding that they have turned to different shades from the new season and at one time were all green.

Knife Warrior delicately rubs his hands across the tops of the tall grass. For the first time, he has a visual of what his bare feet have felt many times. He reminds himself how often he's imagined what the tall blades look like.

Unsteadily, he rises, gazing into the eyes of the man who calls him friend. Slowly and ever so tenderly, he caresses Joe's scarred face.

UNCLE JOE:

sniffling

For the first time, Knife Warrior can clearly see the face of the one who's voice he has so often heard.

414

UNCLE JOE:

Gary, what color is my shirt?

KNIFE WARRIOR:

I've never seen color, so I don't know color, Joe. But I see yer shirt's a different color than Austin's shirt.

UNCLE JOE:

The color of my shirt is blue, and the color of Austin's shirt is also blue.

Knife Warrior doesn't understand the many shades of blue, but he doesn't question Joe.

Joe is overcome by the joy the Lord filled him with. Helplessly, he falls into Knife Warrior's arms, weeping. Love fills every teardrop that wets their cheeks before falling to Earth.

CHAPTER FIFTY-ONE

A Time for Torture

It's time for Joe's sleep aids to go to work. Chandler, Scotty, and Brandon spike their parent's drinks at the exact tick of the clock.

Lucas spikes a shot of vodka for Sam and pours himself a pretend water shot. He meticulously lifts the two drinks, being careful not to partake from the wrong glass.

LUCAS:

hiccup Hey, Dad! That was pretty cool how you played those cops last week. Now that calls for a celebration! **burp** I poured us a double.

Lucas pushes Sam's drink, making it impossible for Sam not to accept it. Like Sam would turn down a drink anyway. They toast their success.

LUCAS:

Cheers, Dad!

Sam hesitates.

SAM:

Yeah, I guess I did. I showed them and you a thing or two, now didn't I, boy!

LUCAS:

Sure did, Pops! You're a motherfuckin' rock and roller for sure! **hiccup**

Lucas raises his glass. His swearing throws Sam's head back.

SAM:

Just when I thought I knew my son. I never imagined I'd ever hear that kind of talk come out of your mouth - let alone you offer me a drink. Well, all right!

Lucas continues shouting, "cheers," but Sam's not shoving it down the hatch.

LUCAS:

Cheers!

He's nervous Sam will spill the poison. He tries butter.

LUCAS:

Here's to the smartest, strongest, greatest football playing dad ever to play for the Jets! Cheers!

SAM:

Let's party!

They shoot their shots. Lucas gazes at Sam with a blank stare.

LUCAS:

It's my turn, you worthless bastard.

Sam noticed Lucas didn't make his usual liquor face.

SAM:

Damn, boy! You're gettin' perty good at this!

LUCAS:

I'm your most valuable player, Dad.

SAM:

Dammit, son. What the fu---- **thud**

Scotty crashes through the door right on time, dressed in black slacks, white shirt, black tie, and red Converse.

SCOTTY:

What's up, my neighbor?

LUCAS:

You, my friend! I didn't think Dad was ever gonna take the bait. How did it go on your end?

SCOTTY:

Pfffft! They were already tanked. Piece of cake.

LUCAS:

What's with the duds, my man, we going to the prom?

SCOTTY:

We're going to a funeral, my friend, I felt the need to dress for the occasion.

It's time for the boys to get down to business. They wrestle Sam's limp, large frame, duct-taping him solidly to the wall in a standing position, securing his hands to his crotch. His forehead's taped firmly with strands looping across his chin, holding his mouth open. To ensure Sam doesn't give any backlash, Lucas jams toothpicks deep into his upper and lower gums, making it excruciatingly painful to speak.

Tippy Toes wags her charming little tail, causing her entire body to shake uncontrollably.

SCOTTY:

Someone's happy!

LUCAS:

That's what I call her "precious prance." That's how she lets me know Dad has not mistreated her when I come home from school, and she hasn't taken a dump on Dad's shoes.

SCOTTY:

giggles

Lucas delightfully watches his adorable canine's joy. He lifts his friend into his arms assuring her things will work out.

He sets Tippy Toes directly in front of Sam.

LUCAS:

Tippy Toes, you sit right here and watch Grandpa, and if he moves, bite him right there.

TIPPY TOES:

Growwwl!

Lucas points at Sam's privates. Tippy Toes gladly assumes her position.

TIPPY TOES:

pants happily

Medical Procedures (Jackie Goes Wacky)

Brainiac Brandon wrote 'Surprise Party,' an imaginative script for Jackie's torturous event. Equipped with creative props, Brandon's eager to assist his sister with her well-deserved opportunity to get even!

Their abusive parents, Brett and Sunny, look as uncomfortable as they deserve to be. They lie flat on their backs, naked, bound to the bed rails so tight with duct tape and zip ties that blood oozes from their wrists. Resting on nightstands are water bottles filled with acid, ready for action. Brandon holds his position on the right side of the bed and Jackie on the left.

The drugged parents show signs of waking. Jackie love taps her father's cheeks. She bends to his face, checking out his dilated pupils.

JACKIE:

Wake-y! Wake-y! Mr. Snake-y. Welcome to your surprise party.

JACKIE AND BRANDON:

Surprise!

BRANDON:

First things first, let's take them blindfolds off.

Brandon pulls a pair of needle-nose pliers from his back pocket, not missing a beat as he violently rips Brett and Sunny's eyelids from their pleading faces.

JACKIE:

Don't want you two devils to miss anything. We're coming right back. Keep those shades open! *laughs maniacally*

The proud siblings grab hands, skipping merrily through the hall, laughing all the way. They enter the kitchen where they've already set the stage with two boiling pans of water that are sending steam signals clear to the ceiling. They remove the scalding pans, which show bright red tints on their bottoms, and return to the bedroom.

Jackie's always fantasized life as a southern belle and now's her chance, she's speaking like a southern belle.

JACKIE:

Oh my, my, me! Just who in this big old world could you've ever satisfied with your teensy-weensy wienie doggie? I'll answer my question in time.

Jackie grips Brett's cave finder, flipping its head back and forth with her index finger, then gives it a hard whack.

JACKIE:

Ding. Ding. Ding… DONG! Brandon, darling!

BRANDON:

Yes, Dr. Michaels?

JACKIE:

You are...drum roll, please.

BRANDON:

tongue-rolling drum roll

JACKIE:

Dr. Brainiac!

BRANDON:

claps and cheers

JACKIE:

Dr. Brainiac and I will perform inside-out-patient surgery on this little guy today.

Jackie delivers Brett's urine spout a hard flick with her index finger.

Brandon prepares for his sister's revenge act. Methodically, he points his puckered lower lip, adding fake sympathy towards his victims. He sneakily uncovers a TV tray equipped with two bouffant surgeon caps, two surgical masks, a pair of large toenail clippers, a yarning needle, and a pair of scissors. Jackie removes her cap and mask from the tray. Brandon repeats her action.

Brett and Sunny begin to struggle. However, that's short lived due to the big surprise party awaiting them. They are unable to lift their heads for Brandon's ingenious torture innovation chokes and slices slivers into their neck. The evil parents' eyes wash away the blood with tears. Looking around, they try to figure out how they became part of such a dastardly arrangement. Brett and Sunny try begging. However, Mr. Duct Tape has sealed their lips tighter than a jar of Grandma's pickled beets.

JACKIE:

Scalpel, please!

Brandon slides the toenail clippers across the bed using his right hand. Confused by Brandon's movement, Brett and Sunny watch as Jackie places the clippers between her thumb and index finger, delicately swaying them precisely in front of Brett's haunting eyes, conducting her symphony of torture.

Jackie gets a firm grip on the head of Brett's penis, pulling it forcefully. Brett groans, clenching his butt cheeks in pain. She clips the circumference of the bottom of his penis skin and without missing a beat, slides the detached skin over his penis head, leaving him raw.

Jackie smiles as she admires her procedure. Brett is not smiling.

JACKIE:

Not too bad for my first surgery, if I say so myself. I guess there's more than one way to skin a cat, or should I say - DOG! *laughs maniacally*

Brett lies quivering in pain. Sunny freaks out. She's vibrating faster than her beloved serial cock-killer pleasure toy with atomic speeds.

BRANDON:

Splendid, Dr. Michaels, simply splendid!

JACKIE:

Can't chance a cold. It's time to stitch Mr. Snake-y! Needle, please.

Brandon skillfully twirls the long yarning needle through his fingers before handing it to Jackie. She raises the needle high above her head to stab Brett with force, lingering, building ginormous anxiety. Jackie quickly thrusts the needle to her side.

JACKIE:

WHAT?! Do you expect I'm some kind of murderer or something? Shame on y'all.

Brandon finds his sister hilarious. She assumed she was pretty wacky herself. Jackie slides the needle ever so smoothly under Brett's nose, as if he were inhaling a fine cigar. She places the needle on the top center of Brett's scrotum, then buries it, penetrating deep into the mattress, pinning him permanently in place. Brett's pain level from one to ten ranges high into the thousands.

JACKIE:

Oooooops, I missed! Maybe more practice will help.

BRETT:

groans

JACKIE:

Aww, come on now, give a good ol' southern girl a break. After all, it's my first surgery and what not.

Brett's tears flood the mattress.

JACKIE:

Oh my! We crying? Well, bless your pea-picking little heart. I'd cry too. That's gonna leave a nasty scar.

The siblings stand with tilted heads and a smile.

JACKIE:

It'll all end not too soon, so dry the crick!

Jackie and Brandon lift the boiling pans. The adult folks in the room witness the steam still rolling.

Jackie enjoys degrading Brett as much as much she enjoys watching him suffer.

JACKIE:

I swear on my soon-to-be mother's grave - for the ever living loving life in me can I see how that teensy-weensy little ding-a-ling Mr. Snake-y's been looking for could create someone as outstanding as my brother and I. But then again it's not gonna matter once I'm finished now is it? But to answer my question from earlier since a duct tape got your tongue - ME, that's who you're gonna satisfy with that tiny little pecker.

Time for cleanup. Chop chop! Can't let the water cool.

Jackie drizzles the scalding water onto Brett's raw, not so private, private parts. He jerks in agony, trying to escape, but the needle, along with the big surprise, keeps him motionless. Jackie finishes her superb cleaning job and puts her skilled bedside manner to use. She softly sits beside Brett, stroking his shiny black hair.

JACKIE:

How's kicks, Mr. Snake-y? I'm under the impression yer gonna suffer like a leech dipped in salt. But what's a little ol' southern girl like me to know?

We wanna give you two the opportunity to remember how my brother and I suffered when you scalded our baby bodies. That's just who we are, huh, brother.

BRANDON:

That's precisely correct. We believe our patients deserve only the worst treatment we can offer. *laughs maniacally*

JACKIE:

That was a brilliant answer, Dr. Brainiac!

You look plum diddly dumb-dumb uncomfortable. That's good! Is your anesthesia wearing off? I guess that would be just downright impossible now wouldn't it? Because we don't use anesthesia. Here at Michaels' Hospital of Torture, we use a numbing process like no other. Each procedure brings more pain than the previous procedure. Which, in time, numbs the previous procedure. So, if you need any help with any of our procedures, just nod! My assistant and I will be more than happy to explain all of our procedures. I used the word procedure a lot, didn't I?

Brandon consults Jackie.

BRANDON:

I believe it's time to proceed with another procedure, Dr. Michaels. *laughs maniacally*

Brandon appreciates Jackie's bedside manner and southern hospitality. But why should she have all the fun?

430

He lays the boiling pot on Sunny's naked belly. It burns hotter than a bright red coal in a potbelly stove on a cold winter's day in the mountains of Montana. Potbelly to potbelly you might say.

The more suffering their victims display, the cheerier the assailants become.

JACKIE:

Doctor Brainiac will perform the first ever nipple and tuck procedure on Mrs. Pretty Scarf today. Oh damn, I spoke that procedure word again, now didn't I. *laughs*

Though participation wasn't part of Brandon's plan, he rolls with the punches.

Jackie delivers the scissors and follows Brandon's lead. He whistles a merry tune, mostly to entertain and calm himself for his next move. He grasps Sunny's well-kept, silver-dollar nipple tightly between his index finger and thumb. Brandon stretches her nip like he's pulling a weed, and with no hesitation, scissors Sunny's pride spot as if he were pruning a perfect rose.

SUNNY:

screams in horror

Sunny's pride hurts worse than her pain. However, Brandon has a job to do. So off with her twin sister.

431

Without missing a beat, he removes his glasses and tilts his head back, arranging Sunny's beauties over his eyes. He places his glasses over top of the bloody trinkets and consults his surgical assistant.

BRANDON:

Now from where I'm standing, sweetheart, I must confirm this surgery looks like a tremendous success. But it's hard to see with these eye patches. How do you like my pepperonis, Dr. Michaels?

Brandon pushes his interesting looking eyes towards Jackie. She needs a moment to collect herself from Brandon's titillating performance.

JACKIE:

I can see how you can see your surgery was a great success, Dr. Brainiac.

Brandon high fives himself above his head.

JACKIE:

Now my neck knows all too well how you two tied-up toads enjoy a pleasant surprise, and my genius brother knows all there is to know about the a-c-i-d business. Don't you, water boy?

BRANDON:

Mama said - Ma - Ma - Mama said I should learn all there is to know about the a-c-i-d business so I can burn her face off with it.

JACKIE:

Well, I morally respect your mother's high ethical standards of yer fetchin' ups. What an honorable whore your mother must be. She only wants what's best for her water boy. Enough chitter chatter about her. Time's a wastin', Dr. Brainiac. You're now, Acid Maaaaan!

BRANDON:

Yayyyy! Acid Man is the man! Woooooo!

Jackie and Brandon grab the acid bottles - ironically, the same acid Brett burned Jackie with before the football games. They aim for the open wounds. All the pain in the world couldn't appease the siblings for the torture they've endured from these two devils. They're living for the moment.

Brandon raises his arms and performs a quick tap dance.

BRANDON:

This is fun. Let's pour some in their eyes. Yeah, a surprise in their eyes!

JACKIE:

Now, Acid Man, we've no time for poetry. There's plenty of work we must finish before the big surprise.

Brandon can't resist.

BRANDON:

Roaaaaaaaar! I'M THE ACID MAN! Ha! Ha! Ha! Ho! Ho! I'm the Acid Maaan, so here I go!

JACKIE:

What a witty poet that mother of yours hatched from between her disgusting loins.

JACKIE AND BRANDON:

Hardy-har-har-har.

Jackie gives Sunny a squirt between the legs. She squirms from the immediate burn.

Jackie's memories of acid trigger her anger.

JACKIE:

Time for my devil fucking mother to lather her smoking hot twat. Soon, you'll be sucking your child molester's fiery cock in Hell, and Daddy Tube-socks will be right there watching, getting his rocks off while he chokes the shit out of you with your whore scarf. You fucking slut!

Jackie widens Sunny's scrumptious mounds using the tip of the water bottle. She buries it, blasting her full of the flesh-eating liquid with her angry double-handed power squeeze. Sunny wails in agony as the acid eats her insides.

Brett frees the tape from his mouth.

BRETT:

Please stop. Jackie, we're sorry! Please, Brandon, stop her!

Jackie pulls, tears, and sticks tape in its respective spot, showing her parents the exact mercy they've shown her.

JACKIE:

Don't you die on me now, 'cause Acid Man and I have saved the biggest surprise for last. Welcome to the no-sympathy ward surprise party!

The siblings share 'T' handles with their worried-sick parents. Only this time, they're tied to something much more sinister - piano wire.

Brandon takes the stage.

BRANDON:

Look familiar?

Brett and Sunny find it hard to see but their ears work fine.

BRANDON:

Huddle up! Here's the play, assholes! It's a for sure game winner. We call it the 'T'-handle-piano-wire-surprise. Oh yeah.

Brandon holds the 'T' in his right hand and calls the play.

BRANDON:

Piano-wire surprise on three! Break! *clap* Down! Ready set! Hut one! Hut two! Hut three!

Jackie and Brandon pull the 'T' handles, playing tug of war, until the wire cuts Brett and Sunny's heads clean off.

BRANDON:

Yay! Bravo! Bravo! Mr. and Mrs. Michaels, you're discharged. Free as a bird to go STRAIGHT TO HELL!

Brandon and Jackie bow to one another.

BRANDON:

Let's get Fondue and get out of here.

Brandon and Jackie race to the outbuilding where Fondue's been hiding, only to find her gone. They find a note placed on top of her sleeping bag.

FONDUE:

Dear Brandon and Jackie,

Nothing will stop my grandfather from coming here. He will appear and he will make us his. It's complicated. I hold a dark secret inside of me. I pray to share it with the two people I care about the most. He must die, or we will. I hope to meet you on the bridge.

Love, Fondue.

BRANDON:

What the hell? We have to find her!

JACKIE:

There's no time, we've got to trust Austin's plan. We've got to march.

CHAPTER FIFTY-THREE

Waltz of the Puppets

Across the river, Scotty and Lucas have reconvened at Scotty's house after leaving Sam duct taped to the wall.

Scotty leads Lucas to his parents' bedroom where he has prepped his victims for a wonderous night of torture. He has dressed Frank and Mary Jo with matching barbed wire mummy-suit pants that wrap evenly from their ankles to their bulging beer bellies. In addition, they wear razor wire necklaces and bracelets, offering a slice of flair to their most fashionable arrangement. Scotty has meticulously picked out gleaming ball gags for his victims - a blinding pink one for his homophobe father, Frank, and a glowing chartreuse for his mother, Mary Jo. These accoutrements promise Scotty and Lucas unequitable assurance that their chosen models will endure glorious agony.

Every good sadist knows that a wonderous night of torture needs a little entertainment. For that reason, Scotty and Lucas have handpicked two roughly two-pound catfish for their upcoming puppet show.

Their 'puppets' enjoy a cool swim in the Thomas's bathtub while waiting to take the stage. Puppet Master Scotty plays puppet Sting, while Puppet Master Lucas is Ray.

drum roll

Sting and Ray slowly rise over the foot of Frank and Mary Jo's bed. Sting opens the show.

STING:

Well, look who it is. If it ain't Fuck and Fucker!

Sting and Ray stand on their tails and glide slowly across Frank and Mary Jo's bodies as if they're walking.

Sting stops, looking for someone.

STING:

Hollyyyy! Scottyyyy! I know you're here. Get your asses over here. Give me a five.

Sting and Ray high five with their pectoral fins. Their tails give Frank and Mary Jo a tickle, making them twitch.

The two victims quickly recognize that any movement causes painful pricks from the barbed wire mummy pants.

Ray is eager to get in on the action.

RAY:

There's nothing I'd rather do, and I mean nothing, than fillet me some Blue Cats right now.

Ray comes face to face with Frank.

RAY:

Well, here we are, bitch! Looks to me like we're the only ones gonna slice and dice around here. *laughs maniacally* Hey, let's go humaning, yeah? Let's catch us some dumbasses. I brought poles.

STING:

I've always wanted to go humaning with a friend like you. If we're lucky, maybe we'll catch us a big mouth bastard - or - or a cocksucker. *giggles*

Scotty and Lucas place Sting and Ray back into their icy bathtub, keeping the stars of the show fresh. They grab two fishing poles that Scotty stashed beforehand. Treble hooks made for snagging are tied on the end of each line. They dangle the razor-sharp hooks above Frank and Mary Jo's eyes.

SCOTTY:

Here fishy fish fish! Here fishy fish fish!

LUCAS:

Let's try snagging one, Scot-tayyy.

SCOTTY:

Okay, Luc-ay.

The boys sway the hooks around their victims' faces.

Scotty snares the inside of Frank's nostril.

FRANK:

groans in pain

442

SCOTTY:

Well, I think I got one!

Lucas snags Mary Jo's jaw and yells like a ten-year-old catching his first fish.

MARY JO:

squeals in pain

LUCAS:

I too!

The boys pull hard on their poles, setting the hooks deep into their victims' flesh. Frank quickly discovers that any movement of his head results in painful slices to his neck from the razor-wire necklace.

Turning the handles aggressively, the boys fight to land their catch. The reels zing as they continue cranking. They viciously jerk the poles until the hooks swing free, tearing flesh from their human prey.

SCOTTY:

Aww. Mine got away, Lukie.

LUCAS:

Mine too, Scot-tay.

Scotty takes hold of the bloody treble hook, examining the flesh that remains on the nifty torture device.

LUCAS:

Let's cast back out. This time let's go deep, real deep.

The two buddies hold their poles outward, waiting for a bite.

LUCAS:

What are we fishing for, ol' chap?

SCOTTY:

Unholy mackerels! I've heard this lake's full of devil fish.

Scotty runs his hook through the head of Frank's penis as if it were a nightcrawler.

FRANK:

muffled screams

SCOTTY:

I believe I've hooked a Prince Albert fish! Ha! Ha! Ha! I made a humorous.

Frank's pain sends a jolt into Lucas's groin, causing him to grab his own privates. He glances at Mary Jo's disgustingly unkempt vagina and hesitates, not wanting to touch it. Begrudgingly, he threads the hook through Mary Jo's hood.

MARY JO:

painful moaning

LUCAS:

Fish on! I'm sure it's a clitopatra!

Scotty and Lucas jerk their poles hard until the hooks tear through their victims' genitals.

FRANK AND MARY JO:

horrifying muffled screams

The boys continue hooking Frank and Mary Jo until they tire, leaving them dozens of agonizingly painful lacerations.

drum roll

Sting and Ray stroll into Frank and Mary Jo's view. They are toting sharpened fillet knives in their fins. Mockingly, they wiggle the sharp objects in Frank and Mary Jo's tormented faces.

RAY:

Never filleted me a dumbass before.

With a hard grunt, Sting stabs Frank's leg while Ray plunges his blade deep into Mary Jo's shoulder. Mary Jo attempts an escape, but the razor wire slices her, squirting tiny spurts of blood onto Frank's face and body.

Sting and Ray do a chest bump and mock their victims.

STING:

Blah! Blah! Come on, Frank, I'm sick. Let's go. Blah! Blah! I think I've had too much to drink!

RAY:

Fuck all you summer beaches! Fucking traitors!

Hey! Before we kill these sorry specimens, ya wanna dance?

STING:

But of course!

drum roll

RAY:

Wellllllllllllll! Ya put your right fin in. Ya take your right fin out!

STING:

Ya put your left fin in. Then you stab them till they shout. That's what it's all about.

The fish take a bow.

Scotty shines his smiling face over Frank, reminding him of his missing front tooth.

SCOTTY:

Difficult to sing without my tooth. You try it.

Scotty pulls out a ball-peen hammer and painstakingly beats Frank's teeth out. Frank gums his pretty pink ball.

Scotty is pleased with his dental work and flips the hammer to the floor, dusting his hands for a job well done.

SCOTTY:

We better get moving now. We've got bigger humans to fry.

Scotty is done playing.

SCOTTY:

You killed my sister, you sick fucks!

Viciously and repeatedly, Scotty and Lucas stab Frank and Mary Jo with the fishes' pectoral fins.

And if you've never been stung by a catfish, you should know their poisonous fins are often compared to the sting of a scorpion.

Frank and Mary Jo beg for death. Scotty and Lucas make one last stab with the fish, leaving their fins buried deep into Frank and Mary Jo's chests. Scotty and Lucas make the joint, unemotional decision to allow the poison to pass through their victims' systems, torturing them with maximum effect.

Scotty makes his way to the phonograph sitting on an old oak dresser. He motions for Lucas to join him. The dresser's mirror reflects the bloodstains covering Scotty's once dazzling white shirt. The two make eye contact in the dirty mirror.

Scotty lifts an old seventy-eight from the record player's turntable to his lips. He turns and blows the thick film of dust from the collectible towards his suffering, evil parents. He proudly announces the record's title for all to hear.

SCOTTY:

Waltz of the Puppets. Hmm... perfect.

The needle lands carefully onto the scratched disc.

SCOTTY:

May I have this dance, darling?

LUCAS:

I'm sincerely honored and delighted, my forever precious mate.

Scotty offers his bloody hand. Lucas gently takes hold.

They softly grasp and stretch forth their arms as they properly place their free hands on one another's waists. They dance gleefully, gliding softly to the incredible sound of an orchestra as though no one else were present in the room.

Scotty and Lucas have lived only a few homes apart their entire lives, and although they go to the same school and are captains and stars for the Seven Mile River Rats football team, they have only recently begun exploring their feelings for each other.

Scotty knows that Frank, being a homophobe, is devastated watching his son dance with another boy.

Frank once caught Scotty peering at Lucas through a slightly cracked curtain, and Scotty sees this as a way to get revenge for all the homophobic badgering he's had to endure because of it.

For a fleeting moment, Mary Jo is proud of her son's enchanting encounter.

Scotty and Lucas bond and come to appreciate that they are made for more than murder. They find they are made for one another.

After their extraordinary dance performance, Scotty and Lucas tenderly embrace before concluding with their last scene.

Scotty gracefully whisks himself from Lucas. He places the fillet knife's handle to his mouth, pretending it's a microphone and speaks to his suffering parents as if they are part of a large crowd and he is the announcer.

SCOTTY:

Ladies and gentlemen, it's time for the push of the puppet show, the pinnacle of climaxes, a performance of perfect preparation. Ladies and gentlemen, we are your infectious disease. We proudly present to you the filleting of my devil parents!

Scotty and Lucas sink the knives to their handles, penetrating Frank and Mary Jo's abdomens. They slice back and forth to the ribcage.

FRANK AND MARY JO:

screaming

Blood floods the bedframe as "Fuck" and "Fucker" enter shock.

The boys stare at the death they've committed, showing no regrets as they watch the blood regurgitate from their victims' mouths. They dip their hands inside the carved carcasses, bathing their arms in the guts of the egomaniacal demons.

The boys' insanity intensifies as they bask in the odors steaming from the mutilated bodies. They remove the innards of their despised abusers and place them onto their chests.

451

Scotty and Lucas stare contently at their gross accomplishment before returning to their senses. It's time for Lucas to check on Sam.

LUCAS:

I need to go. Dad's probably awake enough for what he has coming.

SCOTTY:

Thank you for your help. I might make an excellent assistant host if you desire.

LUCAS:

Taping my old man to the paneling was good enough, my friend. Tippy Toes and I have fantasized about killing that puddle of scum for our entire lives. Thanks anyhow. I'll meet you at the march.

Lucas makes an advance, kissing Scotty on the lips. Scotty approves with an embrace, making the kiss linger.

Scotty lifts Lucas's scarred hand, softly massaging it before gently touching it to his lips.

SCOTTY:

Never again, my friend.

Lucas holds Scotty one last time and heads home to deal with his next victim. He shamelessly leaves his hands and body covered with dried blood, enjoying the pleasant reminder of his and Scotty's newfound love.

CHAPTER FIFTY-FOUR

Sam's Sticky Lips

Lucas enters his front door to find Tippy Toes glaring at Sam as if she were observing a bird through a sliding glass door. Sam squirms at the sight of Lucas.

Lucas turns his attention to Tippy Toes as if Sam's not stuck to a wall right in front of his face.

LUCAS:

How's my pretty girl?

Tippy Toes wags her tail, then proceeds giving her master happy kisses.

Because of the toothpicks, Sam moans from his sore gums. Lucas remains unfazed by Sam's noisy pain. He removes an oak glass case from the wall in which Sam so proudly displayed his New York Jets jersey inside of. He slaps Sam's prized possession on his back, mainly for the sole purpose Lucas was frequently reminded he'd never become man enough to wear that particular jersey.

Lucas reluctantly puts Sam's L.A. Rams hat on his head as if it was giving him cooties.

The correlation between the Jets and the Rams? "Broadway" Joe Namath, Sam's obsession. The only thing Joe and Sam have in common is they both like to drink.

Lucas discovered through the grapevine that Sam was a decent quarterback, but no Joe Namath for sure.

Lucas stands toe to toe with Sam, ever so slightly shaking his head, staring disappointedly into Sam's eyes as if to say, "it could have been different, Dad." He mocks Sam within inches of his face, using the same soothing voice Sam used to trick him into taking the trip to the river. Lucas wants to remind Sam of his previous drunken, abusive conversations that will scar him for life.

LUCAS:

Good morning, Dad. Nah, I'm not mad. After all, it's only a game, right?

Lucas kicks Sam in the balls, causing him to flinch, driving the toothpicks further into his aching gums, knocking the air from his lungs. Lucas slowly marches back and forth, not taking his gaze from Sam's tracing eyes.

LUCAS:

I imagined you and I spending a little time together blowing you the fuck up today. That sound good? Boy?!

SAM:

muffled Fuck you! Fuck you!

LUCAS:

Tippy Toes, fetch the stick, girl.

Tippy Toes runs to her toy box and fetches a stick she brought in from the backyard.

LUCAS:

The other stick, Tippy Toes.

She drops the stick and fetches Lucas a stick of dynamite.

LUCAS:

Good girl.

Sam's worried his son's about to get even. He shows concern but hangs on to his "I'm daddy" tough guy persona.

SAM:

muffled You don't have the guts, pussy!

Lucas ignores his comment and continues reminding him of his verbal abuse.

LUCAS:

You're right, Daaaad! I have learned more from a fool than I could ever learn from a clever man, and as you can see, I appreciate the lesson. But you disrespected me, Daaaad! Every time I mentioned my mother, you skated the question with a drunken, "shut the fuck up!" You got off reminding me I'm nothing but a whiskey baby.

Well, Sam, I believe you believed I would remain a child, and this day would never come. Guess what? Your baby's all grown now.

Lucas delivers another swift kick to Sam's groin.

LUCAS:

And ya embarrassed me, Saaam!

He kicks him again.

LUCAS:

I don't believe you gave it your all, Sam! You never saw one play with the New York Jets because ya never played for the New York Jets! Now that's embarrassing! Guess you're gonna have to learn a little lesson, that's all, Saaam!

Sam tries to spit on Lucas through his sore, taped-open mouth. His revolting saliva drips from his chin. Lucas eyes the dripping drool. He must remain in control and conjure an idea to put Sam in his corner.

Lucas springs a combat boner. Sliding down his pants, he wipes Sam's slobber onto his penis and masturbates vigorously.

Without a care, Lucas catches his ejaculate and wipes the sticky on Sam's lips, wetting Sam's eyelids with the remains. Sam freezes in disgust from his son's odd, bold behavior. But knowing tough guy Sam, he tries spitting on Lucas again.

Lucas retrieves the pocketknife Sam used to threaten his puppies. He unfolds the razor-sharp blade and, with one swift motion, slices Sam's ear off.

LUCAS:

Damn! That was easy!

SAM:

muffled moaning

Lucas chews his father's flesh and spits it in his face.

LUCAS:

Never! Spit! On! Me! Again! Got it, Saaam?!

Lucas pours two shots of whiskey. He bangs the glasses together.

LUCAS:

Cheers!

Lucas splashes the first shot in Sam's face, degrading him, then dashes the second shot onto his bleeding ear, punching and kicking him.

LUCAS:

Fumble fingers! Fumble fingers! Fumble fingers! FUMBLE
FINGERS! FUMBLE FINGERS!

*He continues by pouring the entire bottle of booze on Sam's head.
Sam fights for every dribble of the liquor, slurping at the runoff,
trying to catch the slightest drop, desperate to help ease his pain.*

LUCAS:

Wow! That was disgusting! You must have forgotten where I
just wiped my cannon juice.

Here's the deal, Daaaad! I will give you two choices. One, get
blown to smithereens. That would leave you with no head on
your shoulders. Two, get burned alive, then blown to smithereens. That would leave you with no head on your shoulders
also, wouldn't it? Just a tad more painful, perhaps. I'll make an
administrative decision. One and two, that way the fire and the
smithereens can share in their happiness.

*Lucas takes the stick of dynamite and tapes it tightly to Sam's
bound hand, then reminds him of his own brutal mutilation.*

LUCAS:

It's the Fourth of July. Here, hold this, Daaaad! It won't hurt you.

DEVIL'S BACKBONE: THE INVISIBLE WALLS OF SEVEN MILE

Sam goes into a full panic as Lucas heads to the table. Just like a pit bull, precious Tippy Toes follows Lucas's every step right under his feet, back and forth.

Sam watches Lucas grab a can of lighter fluid and a box of stick matches. Lucas pulls the tip of the lighter fluid, squirting Sam's mouth and throat full of the flammable liquid. Sam gags, doing his best not to swallow the poison. He begs Lucas to spare his life through his mumbling.

SAM:

muffled Son, I'm sorry. Please, son, I'm sorry!

Tippy Toes sits pretty, watching her master even the score.

LUCAS:

I believe Grandpa just asked me for a favor. Should we give the old man a little sympathy?

Tippy Toes turns her head one way, then the other, trying to figure out what Lucas just asked.

LUCAS:

That was a plain no if you ask me. It's unanimous. Okay then, say goodbye to Grandpa.

TIPPY TOES:

Grrr, grrr, growwwl.

Tippy Toes hates the word "Grandpa."

LUCAS:

Now, Tippy Toes, Grandpa's not worth raising a hair over. But before that stick of dynamite splatters him to splinters. We must first impose the vilest torture possible to a Seven Mile River Rat. Okay, Tippy Toes?

All Tippy Toes understands is Tippy Toes.

Lucas dials Austin's number. He stretches the phone receiver close to Sam's ear so he can hear the conversation.

AUSTIN:

Hello? Austin Turner speaking.

LUCAS:

How's my favorite Seven Mile Blue Cat?

AUSTIN:

I'm probably a lot better than your dad is right about now. Are we ready to go, my favorite Seven Mile River Rat?

Sam overhears Austin's words. His eyes explode with anger.

LUCAS:

I just need to finish a few things around the house for my dad.

Lucas smiles grimly. Austin ends with a rhyme.

AUSTIN:

The town is wired and ready to expire.

LUCAS:

That's good news, my friend. I'll see you on the bridge.

Lucas unhooks the receiver from the cord and bashes Sam in the side of the head.

LUCAS:

That's from our praying neighbor across the river. He sends his love.

SAM:

muffled Fuck you! You fuckin' traitor!

Lucas stares into Sam's supplicant eyes. He strikes a match, landing it at Sam's feet. The match lies burning, but the fluid does not ignite. Continuing in their stare, he shakes the lighter fluid in Sam's face.

Lucas removes his dad's jersey. He wipes his behind with it, sharing the faint stain by rubbing it on dear old Dad's smeller.

Lucas places the jersey and hat in a pile on Sam's feet. He douses the clothing with the accelerant and strikes another match, only this time the fire takes hold, climbing Sam's perpendicular frame.

SAM:

muffled Lucas! Lucas! Your mother's still alive.

LUCAS:

Then I will find her.

He accelerates the already growing flame, then whistles for Tippy Toes. Sam knows that whistle all too well; it means it's time to go. Sam painfully begs Lucas through the toothpicks.

SAM:

muffled Lucas! Lucas, I'm your father! **weeps**

LUCAS:

You're not going all pussy on me, are ya? Now are ya? Pussy!

SAM:

muffled Lucas, I'm sorry! Son! Son!

Lucas and Tippy Toes exit the front door. The two hit the sidewalk with not a clue or a care where they're heading. They hear the loud KABOOM, blowing Sam to bits.

Lucas stops and pets Tippy Toes' loveable head.

LUCAS:

We're free, Tippy Toes. We're free.

CHAPTER FIFTY-FIVE

Rocket Man

Chandler Fowler will never forget the disgusting abuse he has endured his entire childhood at the hands of his abusive father, Greg. Divulging his innermost secrets at the bonfire has brought freedom for young Chandler. He is ready to murder with the worst intentions imaginable.

Out of respect to his deceased Grandma Fowler, whom he called Mammie Yammie, Chandler has painted himself in traditional red and black Shawnee war paint. Red to symbolize war and strength, and black to symbolize power and victory. He has painted a lightning bolt on his chest, believing the symbol will give him the power in his spirit that he needs to vanquish his wretched enemy.

Most kids have games and toys to keep themselves occupied, but Chandler had nothing like that. Deer hunting and Mammie Yammie's yearly visits from East Bernstadt, Kentucky, were the only thing Chandler had to look forward to growing up. Chandler loved his Mammie Yammie's butter-baked cinnamon yams, and she delighted in baking them for her favorite grandson almost as much as he enjoyed devouring them. They would eat pans and pans of her magical yams while she was visiting. Chandler was always a great listener when Mammie Yammie would talk about the Native American myths and legends, well, at least until he dozed off from all the yams he ate.

Greg, still unconscious from Joe's sleep aids, is sat in his favorite un-reclined, worn leather recliner. The broken low-back is not fit for charity but is still too good for this evil, abusive demon. From his neck to the bottom of his waist, Greg is wrapped in a highly conductive twenty-gauge, copper wire sweater binding his naked body to the chair.

Chandler has created a copper headdress with three copper "feathers" and has secured it tightly around Greg's head. Hanging from the ceiling, roughly six inches behind the copper feathers, is the Bug Annihilator 9000, the most powerful bug zapper sold west of the Rocky Mountains. Chandler borrowed it from the back porch and has it all plugged in and ready to zap the stink bug that sits before it. Chandler refers to the bug zapper as his Fry Daddy.

Greg's situation only gets more dire. Chandler has permanently superglued an enormous and girthy double-ended dildo inside Greg's mouth. He has expertly whittled out the center of the double-sided marital aid and equipped it with a quarter stick of dynamite and a twelve-inch wick that hangs from its soft silicone pee hole. Chandler has guaranteed that this rubber schlong will give Greg the best bang of his life.

Chandler's plan also includes the hottest and most outrageous enema ever constructed. Running deep inside Greggie's oil well is a four-foot-long, one-inch diameter rubber tube, ribbed for long-lasting staying power. So, long story short, there's a four-foot-long tube up Greg's ass, and it ain't coming out.

Greg is finally waking from his drug-induced sweet dream and is about to enter his awakened nightmare.

Chandler pours a half can of beer on Greg's head. Being the professional alcoholic he is, the aroma of the beer lifts Greg's spirits.

Chandler wants to wake Greg up fully, so he decides to energize him by giving the free-floating bug zapper a light bump with a broomstick. The apparatus swings through the air, scraping the copper feathers of Greg's headband, sending painful bolts of electricity across the copper sweater and into his body. Greg tries to scream, but obviously, he's cock blocked.

CHANDLER:

Hey, Rocket Man! You've been sitting in that chair like that for hours.

Greg, though groggy, tries to figure out if Chandler just called him Rocket Man or if he's dreaming.

Chandler wrote a script and included all the things he has ever wanted to say to his abusive dad. He considers himself a master at creating clever contraptions, however, he's not the most ar-

ticulate, so he spent hours and hours rehearsing it in front of the bathroom mirror.

Chandler grabs his notebook and sets his eyes to his poorly written script.

CHANDLER:

What?! Did you backtalk me, boy?

His nerves quickly take control. The pages shake from his rocky grip as he fumbles through, looking for his next line.

CHANDLER:

Awwww!

Frustrated, Chandler grinds his teeth, bends his body, and violently rips the script pages from the notebook.

Chandler pours the other half of the beer onto the page, wadding it into a large spitball. He fires the soaked paper and hits Greg square in the chest.

CHANDLER:

There, Rocket Man!

Greg flinches. He tried protecting himself with his knees, but no dice. His smelly pigs have been drenched in superglue and stuck permanently to the hardwood floor.

Chandler turns from Greg to gain composure. He lifts a coach's whistle, blowing it deafeningly into Greg's face. He screams and mocks in his best pissed-off coach voice.

CHANDLER:

What?! Did you backtalk me, boy? You talking back to me, boy? I'm gonna wash your mouth out with a dildo and dynamite!

He slaps Greg in the face, reminding him of the slap he received from his coach.

CHANDLER:

Answer me, Rocket Man! Oh, you can't - you got too much dick in your mouth.

Greg is dumbfounded. He had no idea Chandler had this much anger inside.

CHANDLER:

Better to remain silent and be thought a fool than to speak and remove all doubt. Abraham Washington learned it to me in the schoolroom. He also chopped down the gum tree. He invented rubber teeth.

Chandler might not be the sharpest hatchet ever ground. After all, Greg was always too stoned to care about Chandler's education. He didn't even start first grade until he was nine.

CHANDLER:

How does my doggie taste? Those grits floating around in the back of your throat's some of Crack Pot's finest feces.

Chandler's dog hears his name and comes running.

CHANDLER:

Ain't it, Crack Pot? I rolled that pecker in yer mouth around in Crack Pot's sweltering shit mighty good. Don't want ya to go hungry, chief!

Greg throws up in his mouth.

CHANDLER:

I remember you once telling me to eat shit and die. I'm the literal
one around here. Bank's open, Rocket Man, you can deposit
them words - you will eat shit and die!

I've never eaten a turd before, guess ya missed that one, chief
sitting bully shit! I heard dog poo probably makes ya thirsty,
though. I also heard lemon water will warsh it right on down.

*Chandler pisses a stream straight into Greg's face. Greg shakes his
head, dodging Chandler's relief.*

*Unfortunately for Chandler, he didn't think this one through.
Greg's copper feathers kiss Fry Daddy and set off a chain reaction,
sending Chandler a nasty jolt to his privates, literally knocking
the piss out of him.*

*He slowly lifts himself from the floor and cautiously pokes Fry
Daddy.*

*Chandler wants to show off his war paint. He lifts his right leg high
into the air, then slowly lowers it. He repeats the motion with his
left leg. He tilts his head back and spreads his arms wide open,
then freezes and stares at the ceiling. He drops his head forward
and leads into a full-blown Shawnee war dance.*

*Chandler's body rocks back and forth. He lifts his knees high into
his chest and skips around Greg, beating his fingers and palms
to his open mouth.*

CHANDLER:

Wooo wooo wooo wooo! Wooo wooo wooo wooo! Wooo wooo wooo wooo! Wooo wooo wooo wooo!

Chandler comes to an abrupt halt. He lights a cigarette and blows smoke rings at the ceiling. He takes another drag and whips his head dramatically at Greg. Greg stares in disbelief that his son smokes. He and Chandler's mother despise smoking ever since Greg quit as a young man, and Chandler is well aware of this. He blows the smoke directly into his dad's face.

CHANDLER:

Smoke signals, chief! Chief?! Pfffft! More like Pocahontas. I'm a freaking kicker, Rocket Man. Not like a few short breaths will keep the ball out of the upright. That's a proven fact that has been proven.

Greg continues staring at Chandler, disturbed by how unintelligent he really is.

Chandler grabs the fuse hanging from the fake penis and connects it to his cigarette.

The fuse ignites.

Greg whips his head around in panic as he tries to extinguish the sparking fuse. The flying sparks remind Chandler of swirling sparklers with Mammie Yammie when he was a kid.

473

Greg's panic-stricken rampage continues as he tries to escape his imminent demise.

The fuse stops fizzing. Greg can't believe he still has a head attached to his shoulders.

CHANDLER:

Oooooops! Looks like someone forgot to pack the stick. Unholy smoke, Rocket Man! I sure wish you saw the look on your dildo face - you looked like a horny rhino was having his way with yer nasty ass.

Chandler takes another drag from his cigarette and blows the smoke into Greg's frightened face. He puts the cigarette out on the top of Greg's foot.

CHANDLER:

I will show you the look on your face as soon as I knock all these pesky cockroaches from the mirror. I once watched your stoned ass light a cockroach instead of your dope roach. Its little feet tickled yer ugly lips, or you'd never know the diff. I'll show you the ignorant bully you are.

Chandler shoves a hand mirror in Greg's face.

CHANDLER:

I want you to see what a low-life pedophile looks like!

Greg is not about to allow himself even a tiny glimpse of his own reflection. He closes his eyes and turns his head.

CHANDLER:

Look at your dreadful self, Rocket Man. Look at you. You can't even look at the man you are in your own home.

Greg weeps. For the first time in his life, Greg begins to feel shame for the things he has done.

CHANDLER:

Mammie Yammie told me some filth ya can't even warsh off with lying soap, and Jesus knows a man named Karma. He's listed in the Webster, Karma, K-A-R-M-A! It's your lucky day, Rocket Man, cause I'm gonna introduce him to ya for free.

Chandler plugs in Greg's powerful, industrial shop vac and sings an old Christian hymn that Mammie Yammie used to sing when she visited.

CHANDLER:

Was blind, but now I see. Was blind, but now I see.

Chandler flips the switch. The vacuum roars to life, accompanying his singing with its obnoxious noise.

CHANDLER:

Could see, but now you're blind. Could see, but now you're blind.

This is gonna suck!

Chandler plunges the hard-sucking vac quickly to Greg's eyeball. The vacuum squeals from the suction.

Greg cannot shake the one-armed octopus. Chandler flips the switch, listening to the noise dissipate as the plastic hose falls to the floor, leaving Greg's eye pulled from its socket.

CHANDLER:

Damn, Rocket Man, I can see plum inside your head. You're not the man I thought you were at all.

Chandler remembers one of Mammie Yammie's old southern phrases, "if you had a brain, it would rattle," so he moves Greg's head from side to side, checking to see if he hears a rattle.

476

CHANDLER:

Chief, you're long overdue for a vacation. What do you say you take a trip - to Mars! I think it's been a long, long time. Mars ain't no place to raise a kid, so I'll just stay home. It's cold as hell, which in fact is where you're going. Aww, maybe not. Hell's way too good for you.

Chandler fills the plastic hose that he inserted into Greg's rectum with lighter fluid. He connects the shop vac hose to the blower side of the vacuum and makes a seal between the two hoses with his hand. Chandler hits the switch - and bingo, Rocket Man's innards become full of the cheap rocket fuel.

CHANDLER:

Change of plans, Rocket Man. Mammie Yammie told me if I don't tell Jesus I'm sorry for all the bad things I've done, then I will burn in Hell forever. Obviously, you didn't listen to your mother, chief. Being the nice guy you made me and all, I'll give you a minute to tell Jesus all the bad things you've done.

Greg's head falls forward.

CHANDLER:

Tick-tock. Tick-tock. Tick-tock! Time's run out, not even Jesus has enough time to hear your wrongdoings, and he's gonna live forever.

Greg raises his head - one eye in and one eye out.

CHANDLER:

If you see Jesus, tell him I appreciate his invention of fire. Oh yeah, tell Mammie Yammie I'll see her someday.

I don't understand all the science, but you're full of fuel and ready for blastoff. Now ya know why I named you Rocket Man. Oh hell, I almost forgot. It's lonely out in space. Stay right here. I got somethin' I want you to see.

Chandler drags his mother from the back room by her feet, leaving a trail of blood from her head - probably because of the arrow sticking through it. Greg is devastated. He finally accepts that there is no escape.

Chandler smiles and tosses his dead mother onto Greg's lap.

CHANDLER:

Kindlin'! Don't want you two child molesters catchin' cold - the grave will handle that.

478

Chandler ignites the hose protruding from Greg's insides and delights in hearing the flames rush through the tube.

Greg burns from the inside out.

Chandler soaks his dead mother and the floor under the chair with the remaining lighter fluid. He lights a smoke, takes a puff, flips the burning stick to the floor, and walks out the door with Crack Pot.

The flames climb Greg's old worn recliner, slowly vanquishing Chandler's wretched enemies.

CHAPTER FIFTY-SIX

On the Seventh Day

The Saints of Seven Mile are approaching the Seven Mile Bridge, ending their seventh and final journey around the perimeter of Seven Mile, on what is the seventh and final day of the march.

Just as the Israelites brought down the walls of Jericho, so too shall the Saints of Seven Mile command their voice to shout down the spiritual barrier that separates the two towns.

THE SAINTS OF SEVEN MILE:

Hey! Hey! Hey! We shout hey! Hey! Hey! We shout hey! Hey! Hey! Hey! Hey! Hey! We shout hey! Hey! Hey! We shout hey! Hey! Hey!

You think your walls can keep us out?

We're coming in to burn it down.

We'll raze the city to the ground, and there's nothing you can
do to stop us.

Go and hang your scarlet rope.

Do as we say or abandon hope.

If you're against us then be prepared, there will be no life
spared.

Walk the perimeter! Walk the perimeter! Walk the perimeter!
Walk the perimeter! Walk the perimeter! Walk the perimeter!
Walk the perimeter!

And the seventh time. On the seventh day.

And the seventh time. On the seventh day.

We shout hey!

Your walls are crumbling down, storming the evil unholy
town.

Today is a glorious day, the righteous are going to get their
way.

*The triumphant Saints of Seven Mile stand on their respective sides
of the Seven Mile bridge with their hands outstretched toward
their counterparts from across the river. Austin, Brandon, and
Jackie lead the charge on the Blue Cats side, escorting the faithful
to the center of the bridge. Lucas, Scotty, Chandler, Tippy Toes,
and Crack Pot do the same for the River Rats.*

Anyone and everyone who wasn't frozen by the spirit of the march has made their way to the Seven Mile Bridge, beginning the long-awaited reunification of Seven Mile.

Austin climbs to the top of a concrete ledge in the center of the bridge. He gazes out over the river and raises his hands towards Heaven.

Like the Israelites' great leader, Joshua, Austin commands his army of followers.

AUSTIN:

I, Austin Gabriel Turner, before the God of Heaven, the God of Earth, and master of my soul, declare the Russian River is now the Seven Mile River!

THE SAINTS OF SEVEN MILE:

cheer

AUSTIN:

We, the good people of Seven Mile, stand together to unite our town. And we declare war against any evil who comes before us!

THE SAINTS OF SEVEN MILE:

cheer

CHAPTER FIFTY-SEVEN

Saving Grace

THE SAINTS OF SEVEN MILE:

Pull the trigger! Pull the trigger! Pull the trigger! Pull the trigger! Pull the trigger!

Austin raises Uncle Joe's flare gun, aiming it against the current of the Seven Mile River towards Ukiah. The Saints of Seven Mile are aware that once Austin pulls the trigger, vengeance will rain down upon the wicked.

Austin checks his timepiece.

AUSTIN:

It's your turn, Uncle Joe.

Austin pulls the trigger. The flare burns brightly, illuminating the afternoon sky as it soars north against the river's current.

Uncle Joe and his ragtag militia have received their signal. Operation Saving Grace is in full effect.

Explosion after explosion rocks the town of Seven Mile, as house after house is leveled by the dynamite that the Saints have rigged as part of Austin's plan. Like dominoes, one building after another crumbles to the ground, creating a cacophony of destruction.

The explosions rip through the flesh of the evil ones, dismembering them and ravaging their bodies - leaving what's left of them completely unrecognizable. Those who were fortunate enough to escape their exploding homes take to the streets where they are unaware the city's sewer system and gas lines have been booby trapped. Each time their wicked feet tread over a steel manhole cover, the devils are ripped to pieces by an explosion and those around them are mangled and mutilated by shrapnel.

The resulting mass panic and hysteria brings forth devilish cries from the Demons of Seven Mile as they wail and plead for their leader to return and guide them to safety.

The Saints remain on the bridge, mesmerized by the embers of the raging flames that are floating in the gentle breeze. The tiny ashes dance before their eyes until they disappear in the cool current of the river.

The smoke floats high. Like a warm, soothing fire burning in the most beautiful fireplace, it tantalizes the Saints' nostrils. They breathe in deeply. The smoky aroma of victory delights them and assures them that, at last, they are free from the evil that haunts them.

CHAPTER FIFTY-EIGHT

Frenemies

explosions *car alarms*

Joe, Cross-Eyed Knife Warrior, Chester Miller, and the boys who traveled to Guyana with Joe on Operation Watercolors hunt the town for any devils who survived the explosions. Their militia is decked out in full combat gear and armed to the hilt.

Operation Saving Grace gives the order to Joe and his army that anyone on the streets and not on the bridge is a threat and must be destroyed immediately and with extreme prejudice. Their demonic power must end.

Joe and his army wait for the explosions to cease and begin sweeping both sides of the river, killing anyone who moves and torching the homes that the dynamite missed.

Joe notices Knife Warrior hasn't struck a single target.

JOE:

You okay? The barn's broad - you're missing your targets, Gary! Why?

KNIFE WARRIOR:

I don't know. I'm looking right at 'em!

Joe realizes Knife Warrior's expert combat skills come from his sense of hearing and not by the sight God has blessed him with.

JOE:

Here! Wear my bandana.

Knife Warrior places Joe's bandana over his eyes, blinding himself. Within seconds, three attackers charge at Joe. Cross-Eyed Knife Warrior drops all three assailants before Joe can fire a single shot.

KNIFE WARRIOR:

How'd I do, Joe?

JOE:

You're back, brother, you're back. Stay close.

Knife Warrior and Joe stand back-to-back, mowing down devils in every direction. It's a massacre.

Out of the rubble, a bald subject walks toward them, surrendering, with both hands in the air.

JOE:

Stand down, Gary. It looks like a little girl.

You lower those arms one inch, and I'll lower you into your grave! State your name and business.

RITA:

I'm Fondue Gamble, sort of.

Knife Warrior draws a blade, but Joe stops him, remembering Austin mentioned Fondue's name. Knife Warrior reluctantly slides his bowie knife into its sheath.

JOE:

Go on.

RITA:

Your army's killing the flesh of many, but what about their souls, Joseph Turner?

JOE:

Why aren't you on the bridge with Austin?

RITA:

I don't belong there.

Joe raises his gun. Fondue doesn't flinch.

JOE:

I refuse to follow or listen to you then.

RITA:

Always getting your way can have severe consequences, Joseph.

JOE:

How do you know my name, and what do you want from me?

RITA:

I want your souls. You both owe them to me. I mean, after all, you stole mine.

I'm Rita, your trophy Joseph. When I was just a child, I bathed my insides with the poison you prepared for me in Guyana. I choked to death on my vomit right before your sorrowful eyes. I'm sure you can remember murdering me now.

Joe's convictions have never allowed him to forget Rita.

RITA:

My father's a prophet of Satan. He prophesied you would come to destroy him and his kingdom. He made me his angel because I trust and believe in him. I pleasured when he raped me. It gave me power.

JOE:

Go on.

RITA:

I entered your brother Jack and flew back to the states with you and your cronies.

JOE:

You're a liar!

RITA:

And the father of. I jumped from Jack to Austin while searching for Fondue. Austin became such a do-gooder Jesus freak. I still shriek from his hypocrisy. Satan later led me himself to Fondue Gamble while she slept.

Go ahead, Fondue, say hello to Joseph.

Rita allows Fondue to speak for herself.

FONDUE:

Help me, Joseph!

JOE:

I can't take this anymore!

RITA:

Sound familiar, Joseph? How's old Ken doing anyhow?

Joe realizes Fondue is possessed by Rita's evil spirit and like Jo-Ken, can take control of Fondue whenever she pleases.

RITA:

Satan named me Demon Flea Bug, which is an anagram of the name, Fondue Gamble.

JOE:

Why Demon Flea Bug?

RITA:

Why not? It's better than Fag De Men U Blo.

KNIFE WARRIOR:

Fag what?

RITA:

Because I jump from soul to soul like a flea, he chose me to help fulfill his prophecy.

I'm a grown woman now, can't you hear it in my voice?

Joe takes aim.

RITA:

Go ahead, kill Fondue. Her and I don't get along anyway. Kind of like you and Ken, Joseph.

JOE:

Stop it! Please! Just stop it!

RITA:

I'm just a troll. A troll in control of you, Joseph. If you pull that trigger, in less than one minute, I'll swim the river to your tiny cabin and pay a visit to little miss Kami. You can never get rid of me, Joseph. You belong to me now.

JOE:

I belong to Jesus, the Christ.

Knife Warrior spins a blade deep into Fondue's forearm. Rita slowly removes the knife and licks the wound, instantly sealing the slash with her wicked tongue.

RITA:

Don't force my hand, Gary. Violence has no answer. I could destroy your flesh where you stand, but what might that contribute master Jimmy?

KNIFE WARRIOR:

Who?

RITA:

How do you not remember the name of the one whom you removed his head from his body, Mr. Indiana? Gary Indiana - oh, just such a peculiar name.

KNIFE WARRIOR:

I swan. She's meaner than a wet panther. Don't call me that again!

RITA:

Do you prefer I call you Gary Indiana Michael Jackson Jones? I guess I should feel privileged to meet G. I. and Joe, the unshakeable duo.

Knife Warrior pulls his trench knife.

KNIFE WARRIOR:

Keep it up! Just keep it up! I'm just about ready to cancel yer birth certificate.

RITA:

His name is Jimmy, Jimmy the great and powerful. Your repentance of what we call pleasure and what you call sin - your God's grace has made you useless to us. Killing you or Joe sends you to Heaven. Oh, how boring that must be, singing Kumbaya, floating on a cloud while all your friends enjoy a life of the finest. Personally, I don't suppose that lifestyle fits either of you. You look so strong - only the weak go to Heaven.

KNIFE WARRIOR:

Then I reckon yer going to Heaven then, wimpy.

RITA:

Sticks and stones can't break my bones. And words? Well, they can possibly hurt me. Anyway! My father offered your father a grand deal many years ago when he led him into the wilderness. Your father balked at turning a stone to bread. My father led him to the top of a mountain, offering him his entire kingdom if he only follows him. Ha! Let's just say your so-called savior doesn't know a good deal when he sees one.

KNIFE WARRIOR:

Our God gave me my eyesight, and I can see that yer so ugly,
I'll bet yer momma used to borrow a baby to take to church
on Sunday.

RITA:

You're a fool. You don't know a blessing when you see one.
Excuse my unpassionate pun, Mr. Gary Indiana Jones.

If my father had not taken your sight at birth, you would have
vanished long ago. You were bred to kill, to send unsaved souls
to Hell by murdering them before their time. You haven't hit a
single target since receiving your sight until Rambone loaned
you his bandana. Where's your pride, Gary?

Allow me the opportunity to offer you both the deal of a lifetime.

*In a blink, the three find themselves standing on the bank of Devil's
Backbone Cove. Joe and Knife Warrior adjust their eyes, unable
to fathom the transformation.*

*Rita has left Fondue's body behind and finally unveiled her true
form to Joe and Knife Warrior.*

*Her skin is many shades of green as a result of the poison she in-
gested in Guyana, and her eyes have become yellow from the evil
coursing through her veins. She wears a revolting cape made of
thousands of wiggling worms and proudly displays a black heart
tattoo on her chest, branded by Satan himself.*

Topping everything off is her well-kempt mane of witchy salt and pepper hair and a pentagram medallion necklace.

RITA:

Welcome to Jimmy's headquarters. He named this cove Devil's Backbone the day Joseph's dad threatened his brain with a bullet.

JOE:

What the hell?

RITA:

That's a reasonable assumption, Joseph. Allow me to share what your fleshly eyes cannot see.

Rita plucks out Joe and Knife Warrior's fleshly eyes, allowing them to see from the depths of their souls. They're paralyzed by the overwhelming sights surrounding them.

The sand sparkles with tiny granules of solid gold. The bark on the trees is made of glistening and exquisite brown tourmaline and their radiant leaves are a beautiful jadeite with glowing hints of red and yellow and mixtures of green. The skies constantly change with the most spectacular streaks of blue, highlighted by streams of fuchsia.

Blinding white clouds absorb the reddish sunbeams, creating stunning rays of gold. Raindrops falling gently on the horizon appear as tiny crystals, gleaming tones of brilliant color, generating elegant rainbows. The water in the cove is a breathtaking, bright fluorescent blue. Its calm waves lightly lap against the golden shores.

The sound of a piano resonates in the air as a symphony floats leisurely through the sky, playing an exceptionally soothing composition.

The cove is filled with beautiful lost souls who politely invite Joe and Knife Warrior to join them as they swim near the righteous pair. Joe and Knife Warrior recognize Sam, Frank, Mary Jo, Brett, and Sunny as they float across the tranquil water. They all appear so happy, smiling and embracing one another with love and compassion.

Joe and Knife Warrior are overcome by the unbelievable beauty and kindness displayed before them.

RITA:

Impressive - I'm sure you agree.

Thou shall not kill, sound familiar? You can now see what the two of you have accomplished for Jimmy's kingdom. You and Austin's murderous friends can destroy the flesh, but only God of Heaven and Earth holds power to destroy a soul. Not even Satan himself can destroy a soul. He can only own them.

We're born of free will to choose the god we serve. You've killed many nonbelievers of Christ, setting them free from a world of strife, poverty, anger, and hatred brought on by a rebellious woman who lived in a garden.

God knew it was impossible for her to restrain from eating a forbidden fruit from a forbidden tree. God named that tree the Tree of Life, but in reality, it was the tree of death.

Eve, he named his little Guinea pig. The form of her name is Extraterrestrial Vulnerability Experiment. That was exactly what she was, a dangerous experiment gone wrong, derived from a rib of a man.

He created us for deception. He deceived us all. So please try to see. He designed flesh to self-destruct from the beginning, Joseph.

JOE:

What do you want from us Demon Flea Bug?

RITA:

I already told you, I want your souls, gentlemen, a mere collection for my trophy case. Can't you see the elation our friends enjoy? And soon your brother will join us. Deny your maker, and he will know you not. He will have no part of you. Join our family for true serenity, gentlemen.

JOE:

What do you mean my brother will join you?

RITA:

Before the day ends, you will kill your brother Jerry if you return to the fleshly world. You don't want that! Join us, be our guests of honor.

CHAPTER FIFTY-NINE

Sin-timidation

A magnificent centauress strolls peacefully along the boardwalk that neighbors the cove's golden shore. Her firm, milky breasts peek from under her flowing copper hair. A crown of lustrous diamonds glistens atop her perfect locks as she brandishes a bright, flirtatious, naughty smile. She walks on jewel-encrusted hooves as her golden palomino coat reflects the translucent rays of sunshine. Riding on the back of the glowing goddess is a headless man, wearing fine threads and clutching his severed head with an outstretched hand.

The centauress approaches Joe and Knife Warrior. With his free hand, the rider removes his dark sunglasses from his disconnected head. Joe and Knife Warrior recognize it's the Evil Devil Cult Leader.

He raises his disembodied head to address his distinguished guests.

EVIL DEVIL CULT LEADER:

A lot of time has come between us since our last unpleasant clash. I mustn't share my lemons - perhaps a spoon of sugar?

JOE:

We're not sophisticated. Layman terms only, please.

EVIL DEVIL CULT LEADER:

Thank you for bringing my father and I face to face. If the opportunity presents itself, perchance I will introduce him to you personally. We appreciate the remarkable citizens you so generously provided to our magnificent kingdom, and for that, we must bestow upon you many rewards.

KNIFE WARRIOR:

What rewards?

JOE:

Don't listen to him, Gary. Stick to the mission.

EVIL DEVIL CULT LEADER:

Land sakes! Someone woke the south up in your mouth. Allow the man to speak. After all, he placed me here, and I must say, I'm doing reasonably well. Do you concur?

The Evil Devil Cult leader waves his hand about, showcasing his fascinating kingdom and offers a handshake. Knife Warrior declines.

JOE:

I'm not intimidated by your modest act or impressed with your shithole.

EVIL DEVIL CULT LEADER:

Shithole?! Hmm... sounds as if you're coming on to me, Joseph.

JOE:

Don't flatter yourself! You killed my dad. You deserved to have your head twisted off.

EVIL DEVIL CULT LEADER:

Quite the contrary, my friend.

The Evil Devil Cult Leader pauses and twists his head back onto his shoulders with three turns.

EVIL DEVIL CULT LEADER:

There! Much better.

I swear - and believe me, I do swear. When my head's unattached, my body often has a hard time finding itself. Now, where were we?

JOE:

You killed my Dad!

EVIL DEVIL CULT LEADER:

Oh yes! Again! Quite the contrary, my friend. It was not I who murdered your parent. That was the man who carried a hatchet. Shame on you, blamer!

Now, if I haven't lost my mind, and I'm notorious for misplacing that sucker...

Sometimes, I search for my head everywhere for days only to find it attached to my body. Ha, ha, ha! Idiotic me! Pffft! Forgive me, I'm rambling, aren't I?

Anyway! You savage! You can't blame me for that one, but I will throw a nasty stone to remind you of the Matos you planted this past season. Say hello, fellows!

The three Matos brothers swim to the shore, greeting Joe with a sneer.

Cherry Matos flaps her ribbed wings as she floats quietly by, smiling.

EVIL DEVIL CULT LEADER:

Ya see fellows, I'm a follower of your God also. For without his permission, I have no power. He created me, and for that, I must respect. Have you ever heard the saying, why do bad things happen to good people?

JOE:

Yes, I suppose I have.

EVIL DEVIL CULT LEADER:

Before my father can allow one of his children to bring harm or death, we must first seek to receive permission from the high God. So why not cast the blame to whom it belongs? I mean, give a child a cookie, and they will savor the crumbs. Have you not heard the story of Job?

KNIFE WARRIOR:

No thank ya. I already have a Job.

The Evil Devil Cult Leader extends his hand. Within seconds Joe and Knife Warrior both can recite the entire book of Job from the Old Testament.

EVIL DEVIL CULT LEADER:

Now you see - not possible for Job to suffer as he did without permission from an all-knowing God. Job could've cursed God, and his heart may never have beat another beat. Our Father, *clears throat* as in the God of all creation, will only test his children. He will never tempt. This he promised. That's where we come in. Our duty as "bad people" is to bring strife, sickness, confusion, and my favorite, lust of the heart. Lust weakens, but also produces truth to discover who's his sincere servant.

Why did God grow a tree no one's allowed to partake of? I ask you, test or a temptation? Well, It's the same if you ask me. Satan, my father, took blame for the weakness of God's servant. He knew damn well flesh had no chance. He instilled persuasion to bring sin into a perfect world because sin brings forth death.

So, riddle me this, who do you believe deceived who? My father, once a beautiful angel who was cast out of Heaven along with a third of his followers to do the dirty work of an all-mighty God? Someone had to step to the plate.

Ask, and you shall receive. I ask you... won't you join my friends and I in our celebration?

The Evil Devil Cult Leader holds out the palms of his hands, inviting Joe and Knife Warrior to join him.

JOE:

What's there to celebrate?

EVIL DEVIL CULT LEADER:

The magnificent, tortured souls we just collected. The ones your army and Austin's friends just set free from bondage. Celebrate the blood I see dripping from your killing hands - if I may, the blood your God so willingly permitted.

Your rewards in Heaven will vanish. You will throw your crowns at his feet, just as David, a man talked about in the Bible as having a heart after God's own heart. Yet he was a warrior, a murderer, just as you. Responsible for sending many souls to my captivating kingdom. God rest his wretched soul.

Here your rewards will never fade, and believe me when I say, you've earned many. What good's a reward without a celebration? Choose this day whom you will serve, gentlemen. Let's toast to keeping the curse of Seven Mile.

JOE:

My partner and I choose everlasting life with Jesus, the Christ.

EVIL DEVIL CULT LEADER:

Are you sure, Joseph? Strong never-ending relationships come from good communication. Do you agree, sir?

JOE:

I'm finished here. Send us back.

EVIL DEVIL CULT LEADER:

Not so fast. I'm just a speck curious to how you make a perpetual ruling without first consulting your fiancée.

Joe turns around and is surprised to see his beautiful Kami standing before him.

KAMI:

Yes, Joseph! I'm honored to take a wonderful man like you to have, to hold, and never ever part.

This is my home. Please, come live with me here in this paradise, forever.

Knife Warrior sees Kami is not covered and steps behind her and turns his back.

JOE:

I'm the one who's honored, Kami. I can't live without you. Last night will remain in my heart for eternity. What must I do?

KAMI:

Kiss me like you did last night, my love. You are my hero. Never let me go.

Kami and Joe kiss the longest and sweetest never-let-go kiss.

Knife Warrior turns to check on Joe.

KNIFE WARRIOR:

Joe, are you seriously kissin' a horse?

Blinded by love, Joe doesn't realize that the centauress is a shape-shifter and has transformed into Kami. She unloads both barrels kicking Knife Warrior square in his chest, sending him deep into the cove.

CENTAURESS:

Tee, tee, tee, tee.

JOE:

You're not my love! You're not Kami!

The façade is cracking. Joe and Knife Warrior have resisted the temptation of evil and now see Hell for what it really is. The cove's water has turned into a bloody slime. The stench is more than anyone can bear. Ear-shattering squalls arise straight from the pits of Hell.

The centauress shapeshifts into a colossal, black praying mantis with fangs and fiery eyes, ready to consume Joe.

KNIFE WARRIOR:

Help me, Joe! I'm uh, drownin! Help me! Help me, Joe!

Joe remembers Knife Warrior can't swim. He dives into the devil-infested cesspool, risking it all to save his friend. The demons scream unintelligible, satanic profanities as they scratch and tear at Joe. Joe swims with all of his power, holding Knife Warrior across his neck.

Joe and Knife Warrior's only escape from the bloody slime is the polluted, unholy shore where the evil praying mantis is awaiting her prey. Vile and disgusting drool oozes from her mandibles as she craves the scrumptious delight heading her way.

Joe and Knife Warrior are covered in giant, bloodthirsty leeches which are draining their blood and what is left of their energy. They both try to stand, but are unable - so exhausted they can only crawl on their hands and knees.

The praying mantis closes in. Joe and Knife Warrior can't go on. They close their eyes and surrender to the evil spirit they know will chew their heads from their shoulders.

The praying mantis stretches forth her spiky front legs, reaching for her victims.

Joe and Knife Warrior feel a strong tugging on their skin. They open their eyes only to find the evil praying mantis plucking the large demonic leeches from their bodies, devouring them like a hungry dog.

Quickly she gobbles, for in the distance comes an army of giant praying mantes, racing to take their share of the bloodsuckers.

Joe recognizes it's the righteous blood they thirst for.

JOE:

Gary, these devils are trying to escape Hell. It's our blood they're after! Our hearts pump the blood of Christ.

The devilish organisms shrivel at the precious name of Christ, releasing themselves from the flesh they're attached to. Professing the powerful blood of Jesus sends all of Hell into a demonic frenzy.

The demons on shore run panickily into one another, the giant praying mantes devour one another's heads, and the helpless souls swimming through the slimy cove cry for redemption from their pain and suffering.

Amidst the chaos, Joe and Knife Warrior lay upon the shore, battered and beaten, barely clinging to life. Suddenly, they both feel peace in their hearts as a righteous spirit fills their souls.

An ethereal choir echoes in their ears as a beam of light shines down upon their faces. The choir sings the powerful name of God, and in a flash, Joe and Knife Warrior are whisked away from the Evil Devil Cult Leader's kingdom.

CHAPTER SIXTY

Free Fondue

Joe and Knife Warrior find themselves back on the streets of Seven Mile. They have no time to try and comprehend the events that just took place, for they have been thrust immediately back into battle.

MILITIAMAN 1:

walkie talkie Ay pendejos, donde estas ahora? Where are you guys?

MILITIAMAN 2:

walkie talkie ¡Ven aquí! Imbéciles hijo de puta. Que te den por culo. Mierda!

Joe notices Fondue passed out on the sidewalk and runs over to her, praying that it is actually her this time. Her unconscious body jerks and contorts as Rita re-enters her.

RITA:

Almost fooled you, didn't I? *laughs menacingly* You're both boring imbeciles!

KNIFE WARRIOR:

I oughta jerk you bald-headed! I'll show you not hittin' a thang since I received my sight, bitch.

Knife Warrior hurls a dagger, missing her by five feet from only ten feet away.

JOE:

Hold on, Knife Warrior, let's not rush this. If we kill this vessel of flesh, we will send Fondue to Hell, and Rita - or Demon Flea Bug - or Fag De Men U Blo - whoever in the hell she is to find another human to possess. It's not Fondue we're talking to. It's the devil, not the child.

Fondue fights Rita for control of her body.

514

FONDUE:

Saaaaaave meeeeee. Please help me, children of God. Help meeee!

RITA:

You stop your lips from moving. Stuff a cock in it! They're but babes in Christ sucking their mommy's saggy titties. They can't help you, Fondue!

JOE:

Don't listen to her, Fondue.

FONDUE:

Killlllllll her!

RITA:

Your daddy sucks cheesy pussy in heavenly places! Zip it, ya female dog!

Joe and Knife Warrior remember that Christ living in their hearts is their strength against evil.

JOE:

Jesus is Lord. Jesus is Lord. Jesus is Lord.

RITA:

Go suck your mommy's titties and stop wasting my time, little dick. Your dog is uglier than you are.

JOE AND KNIFE WARRIOR:

Jesus is Lord. Jesus is Lord. Jesus is Lord.

Rita's power over Fondue begins to weaken.

FONDUE:

Please, take me to the bridge, children of God.

RITA:

Swallow the yellow prick road, you deep-throating twat!

KNIFE WARRIOR:

Jesus is king!

Rita hisses and squeals like an angry cat. Her wicked spirit can't withstand the power of the all-mighty God.

KNIFE WARRIOR:

I'll take you to the bridge, Fondue. Jump on!

The closer Knife Warrior approaches, the more violent Rita becomes.

RITA:

Turn from me, lovers of God! Your daddy steals food stamps in Haiti! Hit - cunt - tatty - tally-whack, bastard fucks!

Fondue throws herself to the ground and gnaws on her feet, biting off her big toe. Her eyes roll to the back of her head. She convulses violently, thrashing around like a fish out of water.

She slowly sits up, spewing blood, and spits out her toe.

KNIFE WARRIOR:

Jesus is Lord. Jesus is Lord. Jesus is Lord.

RITA:

demonic growling

JOE:

Jesus is Lord.

Rita will not relent control of Fondue's body but is weakening from the chants of Jesus' holy name. Knife Warrior walks backward, offering Fondue a piggyback ride.

KNIFE WARRIOR:

Get on, Fondue! Get on!

Fondue leaps onto Knife Warrior's back. He takes off in a gallop, coaching Fondue to hold on tight.

KNIFE WARRIOR:

Hold on, Fondue! Hold on! Hold on!

Joe runs alongside, gunning down the devils that enter their path.

Fondue forces a death grip around Knife Warrior's neck. She strangles him until he collapses face-first on the sidewalk.

RITA:

Die, child of God! Die!

Joe watches his friend turn blue.

Freeing Fondue's demon possessed death grip is impossible. Joe pulls Knife Warrior's machete and hacks Fondue's arm off at her shoulder.

RITA:

AHHHHH! What have you done to my princess?! Leave us good spirits, or we will perish! She's my home!

Fondue passes out.

Knife Warrior lays coughing from his near-death experience. He recovers quickly and gathers Fondue's severed arm, placing it into his mouth. He lifts Fondue's torn, bloody body and runs toward the bridge.

Joe, Knife Warrior, and Fondue make it to the bridge where the Saints of Seven Mile are still gathered. Rita cannot withstand the power of the Holy Spirit. She is forcefully driven out of Fondue's body, angry and defeated.

Knife Warrior lays Fondue at the foot of the bridge. Joe removes Fondue's bloody arm from Knife Warrior's strong bite and places it next to her bleeding body. The nearby Saints stretch forth their hands toward the battered Fondue as they pray.

KNIFE WARRIOR:

In the name of Jesus, heal this child. Heal this child.

Knife Warrior and Joe watch as the Saints cry out to God.

Miraculously, Fondue's wounds on her feet are healed. Her fingers crawl along the asphalt, dragging her amputated arm into position as God reconnects Fondue's arm to her shoulder. She awakens, realizing that she has been set free from the demon that has possessed her for so long. She clings to Knife Warrior, thanking God for saving her.

KNIFE WARRIOR:

Go. Hold on to yer friends. Joe and I got a job to do.

Fondue runs across the bridge, looking for Brandon and Jackie.

Brandon and Fondue's eyes find one another. They fall together, holding each other tight. Fondue opens her tearful eyes to see her once severed arm wrapped tightly around Brandon. She slowly releases from Brandon and looks into his joy-filled eyes.

FONDUE:

Hey, watch what I can do!

Fondue takes two steps back and performs a perfect cartwheel.

BRANDON:

Yay! Woo hoo!

Brandon does not understand the reason for the performance, but he applauds her happily.

CHAPTER SIXTY-ONE

The Invisible Walls of Seven Mile

The ravaging ends.

Confident the Lord brought them through the raging battle, Austin gives thanks to God. He climbs from the bridge's cement platform, leaping to the asphalt. He straightens himself and finds Uncle Joe waiting for him. Uncle Joe warmly embraces Austin, proud of what he has accomplished.

The Saints cry out, overwhelmed by the glorious reunification of Seven Mile. Their tears fall to the asphalt. The once lonely Seven Mile Bridge soaks up their passion. The bridge is strong again, and enthusiastically accepts the responsibility for why it stands - to be crossed.

Lucas and Scotty exercise their newfound freedom and decide to explore the Cats side they've often fantasized about. They're popular on the bridge for being two of the heroes that united the town. They fight through the cheering Saints as if they're rock stars.

They make it to the foot of the bridge, smiling and waving to their grateful fans, but for some unseen reason, they can't move forward. Some invisible force won't allow their exit. They push and kick, but the forcefield won't budge. The Saints watch as Lucas and Scotty struggle. Panickily, they attack the forcefield as well, but the unseen force holds them captive, trapping them all on the bridge.

The earth begins to quake beneath the Saints' feet. They cling to the bridge's balustrade, holding on for dear life as the bridge sways violently back and forth.

The brightly shining sun begins to diminish, quickly casting darkness down upon Seven Mile.

The Saints' faith begins withering as the blackness envelops them. Fear grips their hearts.

The absence of light draws out the evil spirits that have terrorized Seven Mile from their resting place deep below the murky depths of the Russian River. Quickly, demonized worms of war with the head of a Sinister Wasp, the body of a centipede, and the tail of a scorpion come forth. Shoulder to shoulder, they climb the invisible walls, making traction with their octopus-like suction cup feet.

The rancid Waspicedes drip with slime and spew putrid sludge while cursing the Saints with threatening, demonic shouts. Encased within the mammoth monsters are the spirits of the Evil Devil Cult Leader's demonic followers. They're ready for war against the Saints of Seven Mile.

Unbeknownst to the Waspicedes and the evil spirits, resting high in the sky are great and powerful angelic warriors, arrayed in pure white, calmly awaiting the spiritual battle set before them. The warriors ride bareback upon enormous, white, winged horses that slowly hover above the forthcoming battlefield. Branded proudly across the stallions' broad muscular chests, is the word, "JUDGMENT."

The great angels of war are armed with two arrows, the Arrow of No Mercy and the Arrow of Death. They pull the Arrow of No Mercy from their quivers, raising the tips to the heavens in perfect rhythm, watching as they become inflamed by the immense power of God.

The holy warriors take aim at the monstrosity growing below. They release their burning arrows which blaze through the opened skies like a meteor headed for destruction. The evil Waspicedes catch the great balls of fire in their wicked mouths, chewing and swallowing the flame as if it were candy. The evil souls inside the demonic beast giggle with delight.

The Waspicedes advance slowly, mocking the angelic warriors with evil laughter. The demon souls wallow in the wombs of the Waspicedes, confident of their victory.

The weary Saints bow their heads in defeat, shuddering in fear. Their hearts wax cold. They, being young in their faith, show little wisdom, for it's not emotion that pleases God, but unwavering faith. Their emotions will bring no sympathy from their father in Heaven.

Austin, strong in his faith, knows their fearful emotions will never suffice. He rallies the Saints.

AUSTIN:

Oh, ye of little faith! Faith is the substance of things hoped for - the evidence of things not seen. This battle doesn't belong to you. It belongs to the Lord! Raise your voice to Heaven!

The emotional Saints hesitantly release soft words of song from their quivering lips.

ethereal singing

AUSTIN:

Yes! From the heart, children of God! Sing praises from your heart!

The Saints build their voices. Fear loosens its grip.

The demons living within the repulsive worms scratch their ears vigorously, abhorred by the sound of the Saints' Godly vibrations. The Arrow of No Mercy was delivered to bring wrath and torture to the wicked. Abruptly, The Flame of No Mercy reignites, glowing like a firefly in the bellies of the mammoth fiends.

The Saints watch as the riverbanks reflect the red tint that swelters through the Waspicedes' expanding stomachs. The slimy creatures dry heave and cough and choke but are incapable of discharging the burning Flame of No Mercy that is trapped inside them.

The wretched souls discover there is no escape from the vile, burning bellies of the Waspicedes. Darkness cannot prevail. God's Flame of No Mercy shines brightly, delivering unquenchable pain.

Tiny angels of faith revel in the righteous sound of the Saints' praises. The beautiful cherubs flap their teeny wings, joyfully collecting each note that is released by the Saints' choir. The tiny cherubim carry each precious tone through the atmosphere, delivering their cries of song directly to God's angelic warriors who, once again, wait patiently in the sky.

One by one, the mighty warriors illuminate dimly, like a star resting far from Earth, but bright enough to give the Saints a glimmer of hope. As the Saints sing louder and with greater confidence, the warriors shine brighter, illuminating the sky.

Reveille rings out from the heavens, reawakening the angelic warriors' spirit of war.

Spiritual warfare fills the atmosphere.

They have received their command and arm their bows with the Arrow of Death. The Arrow of Death brings everlasting torture, and no evil can escape its affliction, for the arrows are made of love, purity, and honesty, the ingredients of righteousness.

In perfect harmony, the winged horses take a nosedive and pull back their pointed wings, gaining momentum. They swoop beneath the Seven Mile Bridge, flying parallel to the Waspicedes that cling helplessly to the invisible walls. The sweltering flames inside the grotesque creatures become an easy target.

The angels loose the Arrows of Death, striking the red-hot bellies of evil, dealing the final, fatal blow.

Slowly, the Waspicedes slide powerlessly from the invisible walls.

The evil spirits wail, crying out for the Evil Devil Cult Leader as their wretchedness is dragged deep into the river below.

The winged horses carry the victorious angelic warriors back into the heavenly skies.

The people of Seven Mile, the Cats and the Rats, are united at last.

CHAPTER SIXTY-TWO

Blessings In Disguise

The squelches from the Waspicedes return. The wicked walls refuse to surrender, keeping the Saints of Seven Mile trapped helplessly on the bridge.

Horrified, the Saints watch as the Waspicedes wretch an army of wicked souls from their burning gut. Evil has found new life and continues on its journey of destruction. The Saints' fear expands into full-blown pandemonium as the evil Waspicedes once again climb the invisible walls.

Suddenly, from the depths of the river rises a boulder-sized head with slicked-back hair and dark-lensed designer sunglasses. The Saints pin themselves to the invisible wall on the far side of the bridge, trying to escape the evil face that many of them recognize.

EVIL DEVIL CULT LEADER:

Good has no place here! This is my cove, my kingdom from Hell! I will destroy you! There will be no escape! Tee, tee, teeeee!

The terrified Saints cover their mouths in fear. That voice, that hideous laugh, haunts their souls.

Austin's faith begins to falter.

AUSTIN:

My God! My God! Why hast thou forsaken me?! Have you caged us together like meek helpless rabbits for the wicked wolves to devour us? Why, my Lord? Whyyyy?!!

Slithering along the river comes a behemoth demon electric eel, flashing a mouth full of sharp teeth and spitting lightning bolts high into the heavens. Controlling the reins and riding double on the monstrous beast is the headless body of the Evil Devil Cult Leader. Rita holds him tight, shooting fire from her fingertips.

The monster eel halts in front of the bridge, rearing and firing bolts of lightning at the Saints. The frightened Saints squint their eyes as the lightning bolts ricochet off the invisible walls. The deafening noise sends streams of chill bumps down their spine.

Fondue recognizes Rita, the demon who dwelled inside of her, and lets out a terrifying scream. Brandon clings to her tightly, comforting her.

Rita dismounts from her evil eel and creeps across the water with her shoulders hunched high. She stops abruptly in the middle of the river, directly in the Saints' view, and makes certain that her captive audience is giving her their full attention.

For her next spectacle, she shoves her long arm down her throat and retches violently, regurgitating an enormous skeleton key. She points the slimy object toward the nervous Saints while laughing her devilish laugh. To impress three-time championship drum major Fondue, Rita catapults the giant key high into the air like a baton while twirling her body like a majorette. After catching the key, Rita, pleased with her performance, takes a bow and points the key directly at the freaked-out Fondue.

The evil eel fires a lightning bolt that strikes the key's tip, electrifying it. The enormous key shoots sparks as if it were a rocket lifting off for space. Rita lifts the sparking key above her head and plunges it into the river, where not even the cool water can snuff out the evil sparks. She carefully guides the key to a hidden lock beneath the river's surface.

JOE AND KNIFE WARRIOR:

No! Nooooo! Nooooooo!

Joe and Knife Warrior pound their fists violently onto the invisible walls - they know what evil lies beneath the devilish cove.

The Saints realize that Joe and Knife Warrior know something and pound the walls around them, wailing in despair for the key not to turn.

Rita can't resist the opportunity to wickedly pester the righteous Saints. She slowly turns the key, teasing the lock's tumblers. Shockwaves vibrate the invisible walls with each click.

Below the riverbed, the demons hear the ruckus and know that someone is toying with Hell's door. They scrunch against the gate, ready to infect the fleshly world.

Rita removes the key from the lock and slides its tip slowly across her forked tongue, snuffing out the evil sparks.

Rita opened the gates.

The river turns to blood as the demons slither through Hell's door. They rise from the water blaspheming the Christ and screeching at the Saints. Once again, evil is free to roam the mighty Russian River.

The Saints begin to realize that they recognize the figures in the water. For the first time, they come face to face with the consequences of their murderous plan.

Sam floats slowly before Lucas. He brandishes an enormous knife which he uses to slice his other ear off. Gallons of blood spew onto the invisible wall right before Lucas' eyes.

Frank and Mary Jo drift in front of Scotty, waving with one hand and dangling fishing poles in the other.

Brandon and Jackie can't bear to look as Brett and Sunny hover over. They are sawing a flaming wire back and forth and sliding their index fingers across their scarred throats.

Through all the panic, Austin hears Grandma Farrah. He runs toward her voice to find her on her knees, crying out to God. Austin cringes with great pain for his lack of faith.

He bends to Farrah and prays.

AUSTIN:

Dear Lord! Dear Lord! You teach us where two or three gather in your name you're among them. The wicked will destroy us! Where are you, Lord?!

GOD:

I chose you for this day, to be audacious, to lead. I have already saved you from the wicked. Your heart tells me you believe I've forsaken you. I will never leave or forsake you. I gave you your heart, not to reserve for yourself, but to return to me. Why do you not trust me? Give to me all of your heart, Austin.

God's voice is so bright in Austin's spirit he becomes frightened. He looks around to see if anyone else heard the calm, powerful voice he heard.

GOD:

It is I, your Father, speaking to you, Austin. Why do you not trust my walls surrounding you? Place your hands against them.

Austin outstretches his trembling hand. A demon lunges at him and roars.

GOD:

Be not afraid. Touch them, Austin.

Austin gently places both hands on the invisible walls. The demons viciously attack, pouncing the walls. Austin falls on his behind.

GOD:

laughs Like the wind, you feel but cannot see. You feel the walls, but you cannot see the walls. I made them for your protection. Like air, without the walls, you perish. Austin, be still and know I am God.

Austin raises his head in faith.

GOD:

There is nothing like a praying grandmother.

God raises Farrah to her feet. Entranced, she spreads her arms wide toward Heaven.

Unexpectedly, the sweetest of odors, a scent escaped from Heaven, seeps through the enclosed walls and surrounds the bridge. The Saints are calmed by the pleasant odor that caresses their lungs.

A gentle wind whispers as Farrah stands, faithfully absorbing the holy breeze as it passes through her body.

Traces of light and expressions of love euphorically fill the air. The spiritual sight drowns out the disturbance outside the walls.

The traces gather above the bridge, forming a being of pure light. It's Jo-Ken. He blows Farrah a tender kiss.

Jo-Ken enlarges as he spins faster and faster until he becomes a full-blown tornado. The demons lunge at the vast whirlwind. The roaring wind repels the evil souls, splattering them against the invisible walls.

Jo-Ken's face ascends above the cyclone. He gazes at Farrah. She stands with her hands pressed against the wall, crying tears of pride for her hero.

Jo-Ken's mighty twister forms a whirlpool spreading from bank to bank, creating a gaping bottomless pit in the bloody river.

The Evil Devil Cult Leader must put an end to the raging tempest that is threatening to destroy his kingdom. Rita saddles up behind him as he kicks the giant eel's flanks, guiding the monster into the eye of Jo-Ken's tornado. Waiting for the couple inside the storm is the Christ.

The Evil Devil Cult Leader pulls back the reins, backing and steadying his eel.

EVIL DEVIL CULT LEADER:

I've not erred in my destruction. Why do you come to destroy my kingdom and I, Lamb of God?

RITA:

Your Saints' protest cannot prevail against our darkness.

GOD:

I form the light. I create darkness. I make peace and create evil. I, the Lord, do all things in my time.

EVIL DEVIL CULT LEADER:

But it is not my time, great creator. I need more time to discover the diamond.

GOD:

You err in your words, evil one. For this day, your power will be no more. Your final hour has arrived.

The evil eel attacks the Christ with violent strikes of lightning, but like the three Hebrew children, not a single hair on the head of Christ is singed.

GOD:

I will chain you one-thousand years underneath your kingdom, which will stand no more. It is your time.

535

An angel of time appears and shackles the Evil Devil Cult Leader, who now understands his season is at hand, for God is God, and God cannot be defeated.

The Lord commands the mighty whirlpool to swallow and devour the Evil Devil Cult Leader, Rita, and the monstrous eel. The churning current carries them deep below the river's rock bed, where the angel of time will guard the Evil Devil Cult Leader for the next one-thousand years.

The wretched, demon parents can't accept defeat. They gently slap their open hands to the walls, staring their worn, beaten children in their wishful eyes and asking for forgiveness. The children can only look away, for they've chosen the straight and narrow path.

Evil has lost its power. Without their Evil Devil Cult Leader, the demons no longer possess the strength to survive in the world of the living. The screeching spirits lift their hands, screaming in horror as the invisible walls crumble down, returning the light to Seven Mile and scorching their wicked souls.

The unjust succumb to the strong current of the Lord's whirlpool. They cry with loud voices, but their cries return void. They have met their demise.

The giant whirlpool diminishes, and the river flows once again.

The bloody waters become so crystal clear that the Saints standing on the bridge can view the river's rocky bottom.

The tiny cherubs return and remove small slivers of the fallen invisible walls, gently placing each fragment into the feeble hands of the Saints. Each sliver becomes satin cloth and is embroidered in elegant pure gold with the words: love, serve, give, honesty, and respect - the ingredients of how God's people will one day live a life of peace on Earth.

CHAPTER SIXTY-THREE

Narrator Nate

It's been a few short years since the Saints of Seven Mile have rid the evil spirits who haunted their little town. Sin is no longer welcome, and there's no room for such a thing called evil. Only good spirits live here.

Speaking of a friendly spirit, Narrator Nate is on his old raft, floating up the Seven Mile River.

NATE:

When pride comes, then cometh shame, but for the lowly, it's wisdom. Where evil abounds, truth abounds more. Wickedness is but a season prohibited to go unpunished. Can seed from evil deliver righteousness?

We are all born of sin. Sometimes you got to kill a few devils to make room for a lot of angels. Live by the sword, die by the sword. Truth always prevails.

A lot has changed for the united, righteous town. The Seven Mile River flows so crystal clear you can cup a soothing drink with your hands.

They renamed the old Seven Mile River Bridge the Holly Thomas Bridge of Life. Hundreds of vehicles make their way across Holly's bridge in both directions every day.

church bells ring

NATE:

Austin received his dream. The townspeople built a beautiful church on the river's edge. Every Sunday morning, the friendly folks come to hear him talk about his friend, Jesus.

There's no more football. No one's interested. The old football fields overflow with rows of beautiful, tasty wild berries. Both sides of the river are lined with fields flowing with daisies and sunflowers standing strong in the never-fading sunlight.

On the town's glistening streets sit fancy expensive homes. However, not one of these mansions' doors wears a lock. There's no need. It's a safe place.

There's no sickness, no suffering. The Saints wear permanent smiles. These remarkable people share love. They spread love toward all mankind.

NATE (CONT'D):

People gather from miles to enjoy the wonderful festivities of the famous Seven Mile Catfish Festival. There's never a fee. Like always, the people furnish the feast from love.

The sparkling lazy current drifts Nate up the river. He steers his raft towards a beautiful mansion - his mansion. The beautifully landscaped side yards are lined with Saints who are smiling and waving at Nate as he approaches his dock. Much to Nate's surprise, these fine people have planned a surprise reunion.

Nate docks his raft and makes his way onto the solid gold stairs that lead to the back patio of his home. His closest friends gather with him, and even Tippy Toes and Crack Pot happily greet him with wagging tails.

NATE:

And who might these three eye-catching canines be? None other than the three pit bulls from the riverbank, all grown. Meet Tilly Girl.

TILLY GIRL:

ruff

NATE:

Kaiser Blue.

KAISER BLUE:

woof woof

NATE:

And Lazy Bones.

LAZY BONES:

snores

NATE:

See why he's named Lazy Bones?

Nate enters through the back door and views his lovely guests, all dressed to the nines, wearing fine jewelry and such.

clapping *cheering* *For He's a Jolly Good Fellow*

Nate is beside himself from the warm welcome. Standing before him is Austin, Lucas, who has his arm around Kami, Scotty, Jackie, Brandon, Fondue, and Chandler.

Brandon waves with his right hand high in the air. Wait! Isn't his right arm paralyzed?

NATE:

So how did Brandon help his best friend, Preacher, move the dynamite Uncle Joe dropped at the cove? The story tells us just what makes Brandon Michaels so special.

flashback

Brandon holds the 'T' in his right hand and calls the play.

BRANDON:

Piano wire surprise on three! Break! **clap**

flashback

JACKIE:

Scalpel, please!

Brandon slides the toenail clippers across the bed using his right hand. Confused by Brandon's movement, Brett and Sunny watch as Jackie places the clippers between her thumb and index finger, delicately swaying them precisely in front of Brett's haunting eyes, conducting her symphony of torture.

flashback

Uncle Joe glances at Brandon's arm.

UNCLE JOE:

How's Brandon gonna help you load with an arm like that?

NATE:

What was so special about Brandon Michaels? He refused to cooperate in the town's debacle. He was never paralyzed.

Brett and Sunny's stunning looks and incredible physiques was who they were. They longed to be desired in every facet of their egotistical life. Brandon and Jackie cared nothing for their phony pathetic lifestyle. They longed to bring them to shame and embarrassment for their devilish secret deeds.

NATE (CONT'D):

Loading a little dynamite was the least a friend would do for his closed-mouth best buddy, Austin. Besides, Brandon needed both arms to carry his new bride across the threshold after Austin joined Brandon and Fondue along with Gary and Betty in a double matrimony ceremony.

I guess Brandon was our only hero who figured a way to rip the pride from the hearts of his abusive, vicarious parents. That's why we call him Brainiac.

KNIFE WARRIOR AND KAMI:

laughing

NATE:

Kami introduced herself when she got caught hiding in Joe's big rig sleeper. But who else is sweet Kami?

flashback

THE INTRUDER:

My drunken boyfriend beat me. He tossed me over his deck. I laid waiting for him to kill me. Lucky for me, he passed out. I kissed our two-week-old baby boy goodbye. I'm so sorry I've left him.

544

flashback

Lucas is not fond of his abusive, obnoxious dad. He knows in his heart Sam's responsible for the absence of his mother. Sam's indicated his mom died when he was a baby. He doesn't believe Sam, but it's a subject he dares not touch.

NATE:

Not only did Joe Turner make Kami his bride, it appears Lucas finally found his precious mother.

SCOTTY:

What's up, Lukie? *kiss* Someone's happy! *laughs*

NATE:

They never came out of the closet because they were never in one. All the students felt Lucas and Scotty were different back in the day, but no one had the nerve to call out the two star football players.

NATE (CONT'D):

Besides, they're sweet to everyone, always willing to help at the drop of a hat, encouraging those around them to love and respect, never making life about themselves or their sexual preference, but who they are from the heart.

In walks Holly to join the gang. Wait a minute. Isn't she dead?

NATE:

Nope! And neither is he. Rusty joins her. Hello Rusty, it's been a while. Devil's Backbone reader people imagined you and Holly were goners.

What about your spirits Preacher saw on the riverbank?

flashback

Rusty and Holly's spirits slowly rise from the water, walking towards the bank.

RUSTY:

Preeeeeeacher.

HOLLY:

Auuuuustin.

RUSTY:

Preeeeeeacher. Preeeeeeacher.

AUSTIN:

Rusty?! Holly?! This can't be happening. I haven't touched that bottle. I haven't had one drink of that stuff.

flashback

The spirits walk into the river and slowly dissolve. Austin's shuddering body opens his eyes.

NATE:

It is hard to see with your eyes closed.

NATE (CONT'D):

Okay, that was easy. Austin was dreaming or having an out-of-body experience - however you want to view it. Sometimes things just aren't what they seem. But how did Rusty and Holly survive?

flashback

Sam sets the puppies free. He turns, conjuring a way to dispose of Rusty's dead body. Freaked out, Lucas stares at Rusty's lifeless, bloody face. For a second, he swears Rusty winked at him.

They place Rusty's upper body in the burlap bag with the river rock, hoping the rock will sink Rusty to the bottom of the river. Together, they roll Rusty's corpse into the water.

flashback

Holly finds Rusty's cap. She brings it to her face, sniffing the fragrance of Rusty she so vividly remembers. She places it on her head, then wraps her feet and hands with the duct tape in hopes of drowning once she plunges herself into the river.

Looking out over the water, she prepares to end her life in the rushing current...

RUSTY:

Help me!

HOLLY:

Hello? Who is it? Who's there?

RUSTY:

Somebody, please help me!

HOLLY:

Uhhh!

RUSTY:

My head hurts.

HOLLY:

Rusty?! You're alive! Rusty!

RUSTY:

When you're ready, I'll go with you. I'm soaked.

HOLLY:

You crazy nut. I love you. Let's dance.

Sam and Lucas return home. Sam pours a full glass of whiskey, believing a strong drink might not be a bad idea right about now. Lucas can't decide whether or not he actually saw Rusty wink.

LUCAS:

Hey Dad, I'm gonna go take a float down the river. Maybe the cold water will clear my head.

Don't worry, Dad. I'm not telling anybody about Miller.

Rusty makes it to his feet, cupping his bloody head. He notices Holly is wrapped in tape. He lifts the noose, putting two and two together.

RUSTY:

Holly, what were you going to do?

HOLLY:

I didn't want to live without you. I was coming to join you.

Rusty drops the noose and rushes to Holly.

RUSTY:

I love you, Holly.

Before their lips meet, Lucas appears with two tractor inner tubes and a towel.

LUCAS:

I was hoping to find you alive. You okay, friend?

RUSTY:

My head hurts, but I'll be fine. Thanks for coming back, friend.

HOLLY:

His head's cut bad.

LUCAS:

I can see. I brought a towel. My dad sucks! I'm so sorry, buddy.

RUSTY:

It's ok. Things happen for a reason, and I'm looking at one right now.

We got to get out of here. We all do before we die. I got a plan. Do you trust me, Holly?

HOLLY:

With all my heart, Rusty.

RUSTY:

Preacher said his uncle, Joe, lives seven miles down the river. He's a friend of my dad. Maybe he'll help us out till we figure something out. We gotta get there.

The three go to work bandaging Rusty's head with the towel and Holly's duct tape. They collect whatever logs they find and use Holly's rope to tie them together with the inner tubes creating a makeshift raft.

Rusty hands Lucas Holly's suicide note.

puppies barking

Holly scoops up the three puppies. Rusty, Holly, and the puppies set sail, waving to their new lifelong friend, Lucas.

Narrator Nate makes himself comfortable in his easy chair on the back porch while the rest of the gang mingles with their old friends.

So, how did the poor little town of Seven Mile become so prosperous in just a few short years?

NATE:

Well, it seemed Uncle Joe and Austin's plan included all the wonderful Saints of Seven Mile. Uncle Joe assumed Austin would need financial help to rebuild the mess they created.

With a little pressure, Banker Bob became close friends to Uncle Joe.

explosions

Banker Bob convinced himself to work late hours the night Seven Mile burned to the ground when his buddy Joe Turner stopped by, expectedly.

Joe knew all the loud booms and commotion would keep the dated fire department and local police busy. Besides, what's one more explosion?

NATE (CONT'D):

Now, these banks might be small entities, however, they're loaded. Instead of Swiss banks for the Golden State demon rich to hide and launder their monies and jewels, these tiny dwellings were almost their best-kept secret, hiding treasures four floors underneath the bank's earthly surface - protected by devils.

Joe's well-planned heist gifted the Saints four floors of safe-deposit boxes crammed full of - hmmm... Hollywood's nuggets.

Bob took his cut and headed towards a lifelong road trip south of the border.

Right on time, Chester Miller arrived, driving a long stake-body truck with eight good buddies from Mexico along with Gary Indiana. Them fellers already hit the bank on the Rats side, and now it was time to assist Joe with the Cats side. Uncle Joe didn't see any reason to leave a trace of evidence. The only visible part of the bank left was an empty vault, the concrete foundation, and an elevator shaft of four stories deep.

They're all loaded, but before they drive off, Uncle Joe made Austin a promise he had to make good. Ironically, Austin's parents live right around the corner from the bank.

Joe connects the wires. Jerry and Sandy didn't make it to the front door. Joe made good on his promise, killing them both and burning their home to the ground to rid Austin of any memories.

Rusty and Holly are as much of the plan as everyone else. Payback for Joe taking them in for a time.

Joe's two new friends floated Joe's big boat into the cove, eager to help receive the goods. Looks like the old raft stayed intact with Rusty, Holly, and the dogs for at least a good seven miles down the river. Can you imagine the special surprise on Chester's face finding Rusty still alive?

Joe made good on his promise to the cartels - I mean the fine gentleman from Mexico. They took the truck with their cut and headed home - wherever that is.

Joe always keeps his word, no matter to who or what.

Nate rises from his easy chair and removes his fake beard and long-haired wig. As he makes his way to join the others inside, everyone recognizes him as the scar-faced man they all know well.

As a matter of fact, we know him well ourselves. This is his story.

UNCLE JOE:

Or rather, this is my story. It's none other than your good friend, Narrator Nate, or, better known to you as Uncle Joseph Nathaniel Turner.

This fine team pulled off the largest bank heist robbery ever to be committed in the United States of America.

Looks like the nice guys always sin. So, we need to stop acting like we don't. The good book is correct, especially where it says there is none righteous, no, not one.

UNCLE JOE (CONT'D):

Y'all come visit Redwood Valley and Ukiah, California, for some of the country's finest wines and cheese platters - complemented by appreciative hard-working folks always ready to accommodate and prove their powerful side. Great hospitality.

Join the good folks of Seven Mile for the amazing Seven Mile Catfish Festival. When fresh cats dipped in the finest recipe of beer batter are cooking, you can smell the yum from seven miles away - all while Kami and I sit on my back porch watching the river flow.

Don't forget Grandma Farrah's hushpuppies or cast-iron skillet golden cornbread smothered in honey butter with a smidgen of cinnamon. She's just liable to swat ya one if ya do.

For dessert, stop by Holly's Ice Cream Parlor and say hello to Rusty and Holly for some of the absolute best handmade ice creams smothered with handpicked wild berries mixed with Holly's secret berry sauce.

Seven Mile's a town made in Heaven, sent to Earth. That's why you can drink the clear river's flow, and my homemade raft can travel up stream.

There're no locks, and all the townspeople wear a smile. They saw the writing on the invisible walls.

So, please, smile. Give. Bring kindness to all mankind, and remember, we never know what someone's going through.

THE END

Characters and Cast

Joe Turner/Nate	DARRELL CALK JR.
Cross-Eyed Knife Warrior	JAMES PRESLEY
Rita/Demon Flea Bug	LEI ANAND
Evil Deril Cult Leader	GEORGE CAUDILL
Jo-Ken	BRANDON LEITH
Back-Ho Betty	LANI FRANKS
Kami	LEI ANAND
Detective Nolan	ANDY ANAND
Sterie Snitchie Snatchie	LISA CAUDILL
Slayer Coo-Coo	JARED LEITH
The Matos Mob	BRANDON LEITH
Dee-Onie Dartmouth	ANDY ANAND
Ken Turner	J.C. TREGARTHEN II
Bucket & Tarred	BRANDON & JARED LEITH
The Doorman	MASON WRIGHT
The Bouncer	BRYAN CAUDILL

SEVEN MILE BLUE CATS

Austin Turner	BRANDON LEITH
Brandon Michaels	TYLER BURGESS
Jackie Michaels	ALYSSA JANEWAY
Rusty Miller	LOGAN THAYER
Chester Miller	BRYAN CAUDILL
Jerry Turner	ROGER POTTS
Farrah Turner	ALYSSA JANEWAY
Sandy Turner	LEI ANAND
Jack Turner	JAMES BARTRUFF
Brett Michaels	LOGAN THAYER
Sunny Shade Michaels	LANI FRANKS
Coach Holland	BRYAN CAUDILL

SEVEN MILE RIVER RATS

Holly Thomas	Alyssa Janeway
Scotty Thomas	Jared Leith
Lucas Spicer	Jeremy Beckner
Fondue Gamble	Lei Anand
Chandler Fowler	Tyler Burgess
Lucky Lackey	Brandon Leith
Sam Spicer	David Kilpatrick
Greg Fowler	Jerry Lee Burgess
Frank Thomas	Bob Cole
Mary Jo Thomas	Christy Hartranft
Tippy Toes	Kaiser
Crack Pot	Tilly

Devil's Backbone

The Invisible Walls of Seven Mile

WRITTEN BY:
GEORGE CAUDILL

RECORDED AND ENGINEERED FOR AUDIO BY:
BRANDON LEITH

NARRATED BY:
LISA CAUDILL

Special Thanks

TO

BLVCKBOX STUDIOS

LAS VEGAS, NV

FOR

EQUIPMENT, EXPERTISE, & FINANCIAL SUPPORT

TO

ALL OF OUR EARLY SUPPORTERS

FOR

BELIEVING IN US AND IN DEVIL'S BACKBONE

About the Author

George Caudill is from the small town of Camden, Ohio, and has resided in Las Vegas for the last 20 years.

He was born to entertain and has overcome his struggles with dyslexia to become an emotional and endearing author. George uses his immense imagination to bring his writing to life and fictionalizes the things and people around him to bring an unmatched sense of realism and humanity to the worlds he creates. He spares no emotion in his writing, swinging for the fence with every line and gripping the hearts of his listeners and readers.

Made in the USA
Las Vegas, NV
30 August 2022

54350692R00340